THE DUKE OF RUIN

❧ *The Untouchables* 3 ❧

DARCY BURKE

The Duke of Ruin
Copyright © 2018 Darcy Burke
All rights reserved.

ISBN: 1986650758
ISBN-13: 9781986650755

Book design: © Darcy Burke.
Book Cover Design © Carrie Divine/Seductive Designs
Photo copyright: © Period Images
Photo copyright: © BackgroundStor/Depositphotos
Photo copyright: © romankosolapov/Depositphotos
Editing: Linda Ingmanson.

For my sister in insanity and frantic plotting phone calls, Julie Kenner.

Thank you for introducing me to Amy's Mexican vanilla ice cream!

Chapter One

HE REALLY HOPED he wouldn't have to kidnap her.

Simon Hastings, twelfth Duke of Romsey, rode his horse along Curzon Street until he found the house in which Miss Diana Kingman resided. Spotting it, he rode past—he had no intention of calling—and formulated a plan. With many, many contingencies, one of which would be kidnaping, but he dearly prayed it wouldn't come to that. He didn't know Miss Kingman well, but from what he did know, she possessed a sound mind and more reason than most women her age.

Her lips were also incredibly soft.

He ought not know that, of course, but as a result of some silly games they'd played at a house party several weeks before, he was well acquainted with her mouth and the way she smelled—like honeysuckle buzzing with bees eager to taste its sweetness.

Was he a bee?

Simon shook his head. He couldn't be a bee to Miss Kingman's flower. Or anyone else with a "miss" in front of her name. Hell, he'd be lucky to find a woman who could bear to look at him without flinching. And if he did, he might just have to marry her on the spot.

He nearly laughed at the thought. It was more than likely he wouldn't marry again, not after the tragedy of his first union.

Shaking the maudlin thoughts away, as he did every day, he focused on his plan as it came together in his mind. He made his way back to his town house in Berkeley Square and scratched off a missive, which was immediately delivered to Miss Kingman. Then he went back out and walked to Green Park to wait.

The day was gray and cold, and Simon was quite chilled by the time Miss Kingman strolled into the park nearly an hour later, a maid trailing her by several paces. She paused, scanning the area and moving right past him. She continued onto the path, her head moving as she looked for Nick— that is, the Duke of Kilve and Simon's closest friend. And also Miss Kingman's fiancé. Or *former* fiancé.

Simon stood from the bench on which he'd been lounging and made his way toward her. As he neared, recognition flickered across her face, and she stopped.

She offered a curtsey. "Your Grace."

"Good afternoon, Miss Kingman. How lovely to see you here. Might we ask your maid to sit on the bench while we take a turn?" He didn't want the retainer overhearing anything he said.

Miss Kingman was a lovely young woman, with an emphasis on the word young. She couldn't be much past twenty. Petite of stature, she possessed dark, nearly black hair and vivid blue eyes. "I'm supposed to meet His Grace, the Duke of Kilve."

His note had invited her to meet Nick. "I know. He asked me to come in his stead."

Her eyes widened. "Is he all right?"

Damn. She cared for him. This was going to be painful. "He's, ah, fine. Shall we walk?"

She turned and walked to her maid. After speaking with her for a moment, the retainer went to the bench, where she perched on the edge. Miss Kingman returned to Simon's side.

He offered her his arm, and she stared at it a moment before taking it. "See, that wasn't so bad, was it?"

"I wasn't reluctant to take your arm," she said coolly. "I'm merely trying to puzzle why you're here and not Kilve. Furthermore, I'm trying to determine why Kilve wanted to meet me here."

"It's a rather delicate matter." Simon walked with her along the path and tried to choose his words carefully. "You recall Lady Pendleton? From the house party."

That was where Simon had met Miss Kingman. And Lady Pendleton.

"Of course. Is something amiss with her?"

"There was—she had an accident—but she's all right now, I believe. That isn't the issue, however." He grimaced. "There just isn't a good way to say this, I'm afraid. Nick and Violet—Lady Pendleton—were acquainted in the past. *Well* acquainted." He gave Miss Kingman a pointed look. "They were in love."

Miss Kingman slowed but didn't stop. "I see."

"They are still in love. It's quite a romantic tale. Er, except for the part where Nick can't marry you."

She was quiet a moment, but Simon felt the tension in her as her hand briefly tightened around his arm. "If he's in love with her, why did he agree to marry me?"

"That is, ah, where things grow complicated. We men sometimes behave poorly when love is involved. I know it makes no sense, but because he was overwhelmed with love for Violet, he felt as though he had to leave her. He was afraid. And foolish."

"And I'm going to pay the price for that, apparently," she said with considerable aversion. "He sent you to tell me this?"

"No. I offered to take care of the matter. Because of Lady Pendleton's accident, it's vital that he travel to Bath at the earliest possibility. I suspect he's already on his way out of London." Simon hoped so, anyway.

Her silence was longer this time, but Simon didn't feel any tension. He peered down at her, a bit alarmed at her reaction. But what had he expected? A dramatic outburst? A fainting spell? He hadn't brought any hartshorn.

"How could he do this?" she whispered. She turned her head, and her gaze pitched down.

Oh dear. Was her heart broken? He'd had the impression from Nick that this was to be a marriage of convenience. But maybe she'd just *told* him that to get him to agree.

"I'm terribly sorry," he said, feeling rather inadequate. "Nick is an ass. He never should have contracted to marry you."

"No, he shouldn't have." She still didn't look at him.

Simon sought to soothe her, if he could. "Miss Kingman, this needn't be the end of the world."

Now, her gaze snapped to his. "Of course not, but it's quite a disaster. My family will be a laughingstock. My father will be furious."

Simon couldn't argue with either of those things. "You're likely right. But, if you cry off, it will be much better, don't you agree?"

She was silent a moment, her blue gaze boring into his. "Better than being abandoned? I suppose so, but isn't that rather like comparing breaking one's arm to breaking one's leg? They're both highly undesirable."

Damn, this was worse than hysterics. How could he combat logic?

With logic, he supposed.

He edged closer to her, keeping his voice soft. "Nick is incontrovertibly in love with Violet, and she is with him. There can be no marriage between you and him."

She looked away again, her lips clamping together. She stared toward the reservoir for a long moment before saying, "I wouldn't want to come between two people who love each other. However, my father will not agree with this sentiment. The banns have been read. He will cause a problem for their wedding." She turned her head toward Simon. "I assume they plan to wed."

"I'm sure they do." Simon and Nick hadn't discussed that, but since he and Violet had been pining for each other for nigh on a decade, Simon couldn't imagine another outcome. He only hoped he'd be there to witness it. "This is why I invited you here today—not Nick, *me*. I insisted he leave to care for Violet and promised to help you mitigate a potential social disaster. The best I can see is you need to cry off. That's the only way to keep the scandalmongers somewhat at bay and to satisfy your father."

She finally stopped and turned toward him, withdrawing her arm. Her eyes were wide beneath the brim of her exceedingly fashionable hat, and she stared at him a moment before a laugh exploded from her soft, pink lips. "If you think that will satisfy my father, you're mad."

While Simon hadn't known what to expect, *this* hadn't been anywhere in his imagination. "Tell him you've changed your mind, that you no longer wish to marry Nick. Surely he'll understand."

"*You* don't understand. My wishes don't signify. They never have. Unless you're prepared to cart me off against my will, my father will ensure this marriage happens as planned."

Hell and damnation.

"Carting off is certainly an option," he said drily. "Or I could escort you somewhere while your father calms down and comes to terms with things."

"Unlikely," she muttered darkly, averting her gaze once more.

"Do you have any other ideas? I will fully support anything you want to do."

She gave him an arch look. "What does that mean exactly?"

"It means I am at your disposal. I will take you anywhere you wish, and I will cover any expense."

This seemed to have an impact. Her eyes widened briefly, and her lips parted. She really was a beautiful young woman, despite the tiny lines of stress that marred the space between her eyes most of the time. Right now, however, they were gone, and he glimpsed what she might look like if she didn't have the weight of expectation on her.

For that was what it was, Simon decided. It was clear her father expected her to marry well, which she'd been on the verge of accomplishing. Simon would do whatever necessary to ensure she didn't bear the brunt of her father's rage. "Perhaps we should tell your father that Nick has broken the engagement, and then the public story can be that you cried off. Would that satisfy him?"

"I told you—nothing will satisfy him that doesn't involve me becoming a duchess."

"You could marry me, I suppose. I'm a duke." As if she didn't know.

"My father doesn't want me to marry you. Believe me, my mother suggested you at the house party—you were far more affable than Kilve. He really is the Duke of Ice."

"Try not to judge him too harshly," Simon said. "He's suffered a great many losses to become that giant block of ice. Violet is thawing him, however." And Simon couldn't be happier. As much as he hated how this situation affected Miss Kingman, he would do whatever necessary to ensure Nick found happiness. They'd been friends far too long, had suffered together through far too much. And dammit, one of them ought to be happy.

"Wonderful. While he gets his heart's desire, I get to decide how to survive a scandal—privately or publicly."

"You'd want this to be public?"

She speared him with a stark stare. "Honestly, I don't care. I'd be quite happy leaving London altogether. I'd be delighted to teach at a school for young ladies. Or work at an orphanage to help abandoned children. Hell, I-I'd even move to the country to tend sheep."

Her casual use of a curse surprised and amused him. There seemed to be much more to Miss Kingman than met the eye.

"Then why don't we make one of those things happen? I said I would take you anywhere you wish." An outlandish idea struck him. "I know—we'll change your name and set you up somewhere else in whatever capacity you like. You could be a widow in a cottage outside Bath." He winced, recalling that Violet lived in Bath and that was where Nick was currently headed. "No, not Bath. How about York? Or you could go to Wales or even Scotland."

"You're going to pay for my cottage? *That* wouldn't cause a scandal." She rolled her eyes.

Simon grinned, glad that she was finding a bit of humor. "No one would know. My name wouldn't be involved."

She cocked her head to the side and studied him. "Why do you want to help me?"

He opened his mouth, then promptly closed it again. Why *did* he want to help her? Because he was helping Nick. Only it was more than that. He was offering her his protection—in as non-scandalous a way as possible—as well as his support. And he did want to ensure she wasn't ruined. He nearly laughed aloud. The Duke of Ruin sought to protect a young woman from ruin. This had to be the single most ironic moment of his existence.

"I always try to help people," he said. "They seldom allow me to do so, but I always try."

"Because of…" She didn't say it, but they both knew the words she'd left unspoken.

Because he'd killed his wife. Generally, he was anathema. And that didn't leave much room for altruism. Was she going to shun him like most other

people did? She'd been pleasant at the house party, but then all the
younger set had, particularly that afternoon when they'd joined together in
the ballroom to play games. When he'd kissed her. Did she think of that as
often as he did?

Probably not. It entered his mind far too frequently, but he supposed
that was bound to happen given how long it had been since he'd kissed
someone. In fact, if he thought about it too much, he grew uncomfortable.
He hadn't ever planned on kissing anyone else, let alone enjoying it.

"Will you let me help you?"

She looked up at him. "I don't think I have any other choice."

It wasn't a ringing endorsement, but this wasn't about him. He was just
relieved that she would let him. "Good. Where are we going?"

She turned from him and started to walk. Quickly. He hurried to catch
up. "I need to think," she said without slowing.

Simon kept up with her, and they strode along the path in silence. He
glanced back at her maid, whose head was turned watching them.

"We should probably turn back," he said. "Will your maid tell anyone
whom you met?"

Miss Kingman stopped abruptly and spun to face him. "B-blast it all!"
She continued turning and started back along the path, her already rapid
pace increasing.

"Tell her I'm a friend's brother."

"Which friend?"

He shrugged. "Any friend."

She made a soft sound of disgust. "You didn't think this through very
well."

"Pardon me for not planning every detail. Rest assured that your escape
will be expertly plotted. I just need to know where you want to go."

"I'm still thinking."

"We need to leave tonight, Miss Kingman. Nick is already gone. It's only
a matter of time—and not much of it—before the betrothal must be
broken."

She stopped again and faced him. "Forgive me for not being able to
decide my entire future in the span of a few minutes." The fire in her eyes
diminished a bit. "I'm not sure what to do. The temptation to leave is
great, but it means an end to the life I currently lead."

"Or you tell your father you don't want to marry Nick. There will be a
small scandal, but you'll weather it."

"I don't care about the scandal."

He saw the flicker of fear in her eyes, and since it wasn't due to a
potential scandal, it had to be her father. "You should go. Anywhere. I'll

be waiting for you at midnight at the intersection of Curzon Street and Bolton Street." He touched her hand. "I'll wait all night long."

She jerked back, her gaze flicking to the maid, who was still watching them. "I have to go."

He took a step back. "I hope to see you later."

She turned and hurried to her maid, said a few words, and then they left the park.

Simon exhaled, realizing he'd held his breath while he'd watched her depart. What if she didn't meet him? Would he simply return home in the morning and go about his business?

He couldn't. Not knowing what she would be going through if she decided to stay and tell her father that she didn't want to marry Nick.

Goddammit, Nick had made an utter disaster of things. Simon wanted to punch him, and yet he wanted to hug him at the same time. He understood the depths of the despair that had propelled him to agree to marry Miss Kingman. Simon knew what it felt like to suffer unimaginable loss. But for him, it was even worse because, for all he knew, he'd caused that loss.

Miriam's face, framed by her thick, honey-blonde hair, rose in his mind. He saw her lips curve into a smile and heard the musical lilt of her laugh. The hole within him was still deep, but at least it had stopped expanding. He could think of her without doubling over, without an overwhelming rush of grief. He'd reclaimed his life, such as it was.

The guilt, however, was still there. And it always would be. She'd been carrying his child when she'd fallen down the stairs to her death, and Simon was certainly to blame.

However did one recover from that?

⬦⬦⬦

THE BUTLER HELPED remove Diana's cloak after she entered the house. She was grateful to be rid of the heavy woolen garment. Though the day was cold, she was quite heated from her walk. And from agitation. Her meeting with the Duke of Romsey had been thoroughly vexing.

Diana told her maid that she'd been talking to her friend Abigail's brother Theodore because he was worried about Abigail, who'd developed a tendre for an inappropriate gentleman. Diana said she'd promised to dissuade Abigail from pursuing a courtship.

Relatively confident the maid had accepted her story, Diana felt slightly better. But only slightly. Her entire life was in a shambles. Because of love.

What a useless, irritating emotion. It supposedly brought people joy, but Diana didn't see it. In her experience, misery was far more likely. Even with the case of her fiancé—former fiancé—he and Violet had apparently suffered years apart.

Though she'd no desire to pursue love for herself, Diana wouldn't begrudge others if they wanted to expose themselves to such vulnerability. She hoped they would be happy together. They'd better be after all this trouble.

Crossing the entry hall, Diana pulled her gloves off and reached for the ribbon of her bonnet. Her mother came in from the drawing room. "How was your walk, dear? Come and sit with me so we can discuss the wedding."

Even when the wedding was going to happen, Diana hadn't been enthusiastic about it. She'd asked him to marry her so that she could get out from under her father's roof. The Duke of Kilve had seemed as though he was looking for a solution to something too, so she'd proposed that they wed. Now it appeared he'd been running away from Violet. But why? That was a question she'd likely never have answered. His business was none of hers any longer.

Diana forced a smile. "Can we talk later? The cold air gave me a touch of a headache, and I'd like to lie down."

"Pathetic." The dark, bitter word darted around the entry hall like a weapon, which, of course, it was. Everything her father said was intended to hurt or manipulate or destroy. "When your mother asks you to do something, particularly to do with this wedding, you'll do it." He came from behind Diana, likely from his office, which was in that corner of the town house. He could overhear just about anything that occurred in the hall.

"It's all right," her mother said feebly. "We can talk later."

Diana knew her father wouldn't accept that, but before she could acquiesce and save both herself and her mother grief, he said, "She'll do it now. The demands of a duchess will be constant. She needs to learn that her own needs don't come first."

Diana bit back a hollow laugh. She'd never been allowed her own needs.

"If she can't be bothered to plan her own wedding—or be enthusiastic about it—perhaps she has no business being a duchess." He glowered down at her from his nearly six feet, his dark brown eyes raging.

She turned her head away from him. "Then maybe I shouldn't be a duchess," she muttered, especially since she wasn't going to be.

He grabbed her arm, his fingers pressing ruthlessly into her flesh through the sleeve of her gown. "What did you say, chit? Perhaps a visit to a nice dark closet would help your headache improve."

"N—" She bit her tongue until it bled. "No. Thank you. I find I'm eager to discuss the wedding plans." She turned to her mother. "In fact, I had a few thoughts about the flowers."

Her father released her arm and straightened his coat. "Excellent. I'll leave you two to manage things." The fire was gone from his gaze, and it was moments like these that made Diana wonder if she were mad, if the man who'd threatened her actually existed. Especially given what he did next. He smiled at her, warmth lighting his eyes. "You *will* be an excellent duchess. We've worked so hard. You'll make us all proud."

After he returned to his office, Diana heard her mother's exhalation. "That was unwise, Diana," she whispered.

Diana knew it, but sometimes the words just tumbled from her mouth. Weariness pulled at her frame. "What did you wish to discuss, Mother?"

"Just the breakfast menu. It won't take but a moment." She turned and went into the drawing room and didn't stop until she'd reached the desk in the corner, where she picked up a sheaf of paper, then retraced her steps.

Diana pulled her bonnet from her head and met her mother in the middle of the room.

"I'm not sure if we should have duck or pheasant. What do you think?" *That none of this matters.*

She nearly told her mother the truth right then. But fear of her father's wrath—so quickly after one of his outbursts—held her tongue. "Duck. What else?"

Her mother looked at her a moment, her gaze softening. "You really shouldn't provoke him. You know better than to do that."

Yes, she did. But sometimes, particularly after a long period of calm, which they'd enjoyed since she'd become engaged, she forgot herself. Or, more accurately, she forgot *him*.

"And why would you joke about such a thing?" Her mother scoffed and then ended up laughing. "Don't you want to be away from here as soon as possible?"

They rarely spoke of his anger or the ways in which he tortured them both, which, despite the way he'd just grabbed her, was almost entirely nonphysical. He'd pushed her mother a few times, but once in a while, Diana wondered if it had ever gone further between them. She'd always been too afraid to ask.

She looked into her mother's soft blue eyes. "Don't you?"

Her mother flinched. "Of course not. I'm quite content. In spite of things." She summoned a smile that Diana didn't completely believe. "You mustn't worry about me. I love your father, and he loves me—never doubt that."

Strangely, Diana didn't. But it forgave nothing.

The headache Diana had professed to have earlier bloomed behind her left ear. "What else do you need me to look over?"

"That's it for now. Go and rest. I can tell you don't feel quite right."

"Thank you, Mother." Diana leaned over and kissed her cheek, then departed the drawing room.

Upstairs, her maid attended her immediately, helping her to undress so she could lie down before dinner. "Are my parents staying in tonight?" Diana asked. She'd won a reprieve from social events this week because her fiancé had asked for one. Whereas her father would've dragged her out anyway, now that she was engaged—or supposedly so—he'd decided to allow her the freedom of remaining home.

"I believe they are attending a ball. Do you wish to join them?"

Diana shook her head. "No. It will be nice to be alone. In fact, please have my dinner brought here. Then I shall retire early." That would give her plenty of time to pack.

Wait, had she decided to leave? Where would she go?

The maid finished up and left.

Diana sat on the edge of her bed and stared at her armoire. Inside was a wardrobe any young miss would crave. But she'd walk away from it all if it meant true freedom. Not just one night in which she didn't have to parade around the town with her parents, but a lifetime of deciding what she wore, whom she talked to, and whom she married. *If* she married.

A bead of excitement bubbled inside her.

But, again, where would she go? And what would she do?

The only way she could avoid her father would be to marry someone. The Duke of Romsey *had* offered.

She shivered.

He was the Duke of Ruin—or so everyone called him. He'd been a terrible rake before marrying, and then his wife had died under very mysterious circumstances. It was widely accepted that he pushed her down the stairs in a drunken rage. Apparently, he never disputed that, which only lent credence to the rumor.

She couldn't spend her life with someone prone to rages. Never mind that he'd never demonstrated such behavior. It wasn't just that she'd never seen it—their acquaintance had been rather brief after all. She'd asked and been told that he was always affable and kind. He was also witty and charming.

And he kissed divinely. Not that she had anything at all to compare him to.

She abruptly stood and paced around her bed, clasping and unclasping her hands.

If she stayed, her father would be furious, and there was no telling how he might punish her, especially if her reputation suffered. He might even try to enforce the marriage with the Duke of Kilve, but Diana suspected that wouldn't end well.

She could absolutely rely on him arranging a marriage with someone else as soon as possible, and this time, she doubted he'd take her preferences into account. He'd suggested a few other men whom she'd judged too old or too unpleasant—they'd all made her uncomfortable, and she was too afraid to see what a marriage to them would mean. It was better to stay with the devil she knew than one she didn't.

It certainly looked as if she had to go. But really, it would only postpone the inevitable doom.

Unless she was able to disappear entirely. She sat on the bed and lay back against the pillows, indulging her fantasy. She'd live at the edge of a charming village where she'd run a small home for orphaned girls. She'd teach them and help them find their way—independently—in the world.

She dozed off, but not before she decided what she had to do.

Chapter Two

❧·❦·❧

ANOTHER COLD BREEZE whipped past Simon, making him burrow deeper into the wool of his cloak. Perhaps saying he would stand outside all night in December hadn't been his best plan. It had only been fifteen minutes, and he was ready to find a fire.

He'd expected her to come, but with each minute that passed, he feared he was wrong.

It was a huge decision, and it would change her whole life. Probably. Did she want that?

Her father sounded like an ass. For her sake, Simon hoped she came.

He began to walk—the length of two town houses and then back again—hoping the movement would warm him a bit. When he turned for another circuit, he squinted down the street, as if he could conjure her appearance. Her house was at the other end of Curzon Street, near Chesterfield House.

Four more circuits. He wasn't much warmer, but it kept his mind off the cold. He was glad there was a warming block in the coach. He checked his watch. Half past. Damn. He'd really thought she would come.

He turned at the corner and started back along the street, then froze. Was that a figure coming his way? He increased his pace, taking long strides. It was her.

"You came."

She carried a small valise, and he promptly took it from her. "Is this all you have?" he asked.

"It's all I could carry."

He nodded. "It's enough. We can obtain anything else you might need along the way." He curved his arm along her lower back and guided her quickly back the way he'd come. "My coach is up here around the corner."

"I'm sorry to have kept you waiting. It's nearly freezing."

He appreciated her concern. "It wasn't long. I'm fine."

They turned the corner, and his coachman jumped down from the box to open the door.

"Thank you, Tinley." Simon handed the valise to the coachman to stow behind his seat.

Simon paused before helping her into the coach. "Where are we headed?"

"Lancashire."

"Excellent." Simon assisted her into the vehicle before turning to the coachman. "You have our direction."

"Just so, Your Grace." He bowed, then waited for Simon to climb inside before closing the door behind him.

Simon sat beside Miss Kingman on the forward-facing seat.

"Aren't you going to sit over there?" she asked.

"I'd prefer if we share the seat and the foot warmer." He reached for the woolen blanket sitting atop the opposite bench and drew it over their lower halves so that the heat from the foot warmer was trapped against them.

Her brow furrowed slightly, and her body seemed a bit rigid, but she didn't say anything. She'd get used to it, Simon thought. She'd better, because they were going to be together for quite some time. It would take them a week to get to Lancashire. He hoped they'd be able to make thirty miles a day, but it would depend entirely on the weather and road conditions, both of which were bound to be trouble in December. Suddenly he wondered at the wisdom of undertaking this journey— heading north at this time of year.

"What's in Lancashire?" he asked as they started moving.

"My cousin." She was still quite tense, both vocally and physically. Perhaps she was cold. Or just nervous. Of course she was nervous. This wasn't at all what she'd planned to do when she'd awakened that morning.

"And why did you choose to go there?"

She cast him a quick glance, and in the dim light from the single lantern hanging inside the coach, he confirmed from the concern in her eyes that she was agitated. "Honestly, I couldn't think of where else to go. I left a note saying I didn't wish to marry the duke and that I'd gone home to King's Grange. That's our family home in Norfolk."

He admired her courage. "That couldn't have been easy. What will happen when the note is found tomorrow morning?"

"My father will rage and likely leave immediately for Norfolk. It will take him three and a half days to get there or perhaps less because he'll wish to overtake me. He won't, of course, and so he'll go all the way before finding I'm not there."

"You've thought this through."

The look she gave him then would have shriveled the staunchest of knights. "I had no choice."

No, she did not, and for that, he would feel eternally regretful.

She exhaled, and finally, a bit of tension seeped from her frame. "I don't blame you. I'm angry and frustrated, but it isn't your fault. You're doing your best to help me."

"You blame Nick."

"I should, but you're right—I wouldn't want to be married to someone who was in love with someone else. I'm glad for him and Violet. Or I will be when I'm finished being angry."

Simon smiled in the near darkness. "I like you, in spite of your youth."

Her gaze took on a glint of circumspection. "My youth?"

Damn, he hadn't meant to sound insulting. He'd never had much interest in young debutantes, which was precisely what Miss Kingman was. She couldn't be a day over twenty-one and maybe wasn't even that old. "My apologies. In my experience, the younger set is typically lacking—and I include myself in that description when I was your age." At thirty-one, he felt positively ancient beside her. "How old are you anyway?" He winced inwardly, wishing he hadn't asked.

"Nearly twenty-one. But as to whether I'm lacking… You scarcely know me." Her tone carried a hint of scolding, which he heartily deserved.

"That will be rectified in the coming days, and I can already tell you are quite… What's the opposite of lacking?" he asked.

She blinked at him. "Profuse? Or perhaps sufficient."

Sufficient was not a word he'd use to describe her. That seemed to indicate a bare minimum and there was nothing bare or minimal about Miss Kingman. "You are delightful, and I'm a beast. Will that description suffice?"

She nodded primly. "For now, yes."

A chuckle escaped his throat. Yes, he liked her. And perhaps in time, she'd grow to like him in return during the course of their journey. On that topic, he wanted her to know what to expect. "We will enjoy close quarters as we travel, both in the coach and where we stay. I will purposely choose smaller lodgings, and we will pose as Mr. and Mrs. Phineas Byrd."

She stared at him. "Phineas Byrd? That's the name you chose?"

"It's a bit dashing with a dose of humor. Don't you agree?"

"Do I have a name?"

"I thought you should choose, though I will endeavor to refer to you only as Mrs. Byrd. I do admit I thought Kitty might be amusing."

"Kitty Byrd?" There was a beat of silence followed by her lyrical laughter filling the coach. She laughed loud and long before finally putting her hand over her mouth. "I'm sorry," she managed at last. "That's preposterous. I love it."

Damn. He more than liked her. He enjoyed her company. The trip would be long and perhaps challenging, but Simon suspected he would enjoy it more than any other journey he'd undertaken during the past two years. And he'd undertaken quite a few. That was what one did when one didn't want to be at home to face the horrid memories there.

She took a deep breath and burrowed her gloved hands beneath the blanket. "I hadn't thought about us posing as a married couple, but I suppose that makes the most sense. Don't I need a wedding ring?"

Hell, he hadn't thought that far ahead.

"Never mind. If anyone inquires, I will say I lost it," she said. "But we'll, ah, have to share a room?"

He sensed her unease and wanted to reassure her. "Undoubtedly, but your virtue is entirely safe with me." The tension around her mouth and eyes seemed to loosen a bit. "Masking our identities will also offer protection, and, as I said, we'll be staying in smaller lodgings away from the main road so it's less likely that people passing through would recognize us. Discretion will be key to our success."

"I do appreciate the thought you've put into this, Mr. Byrd."

"My pleasure, Mrs. Byrd."

"Are we going to travel all night?" She sounded skeptical.

"No. We'll get to the outskirts of London and find a small inn where we can sleep for a few hours. It will take us a little while, so if you'd like to rest now, please do so."

"I'm not sure I could sleep if I tried."

He wasn't sure he could either.

And yet a scant quarter hour later, her body had completely relaxed and her head nodded against his shoulder. She really was quite petite, her body pressing into his so slightly that she could be nothing more than a large woolen blanket propped against his side.

He shifted slightly, angling himself toward her and lifting his arm so she could settle against his chest, which likely made a better pillow than his shoulder. She sighed in her sleep, nuzzling into him and making his breath catch.

He hadn't been this close to a woman in over two years. Now *his* body tensed.

How in the hell had he maneuvered himself into this situation? It wasn't a question that needed answering. What he should strive to remember is that it was a temporary arrangement. He would help her get to Lancashire.

And then what? It didn't sound as if she had a plan beyond going to her cousin's. But maybe she did. He'd ask her for more details tomorrow. If she didn't have a plan, they'd have plenty of time to come up with one.

He sent another prayer heavenward that they would be met with fine weather and fast roads. Then he remembered that his prayers usually went unanswered and always when they pertained to him. He clarified his request: *Do this for her. Keep her safe. Preserve her future. Guide her to happiness.*

And what of his happiness? He didn't pretend to believe he would find any, nor did he deserve it. He'd long ago decided his only saving grace would be helping others, which was why he gave most of his income to the workhouse in his district and several orphanages in London. He certainly didn't need to save it for his heirs. The title would die with him, and that was just as well, since he'd tainted it for all time.

The Duke of Ruin indeed.

❦

THE COACH HIT a particularly deep rut, causing Diana to drop the book she'd been holding for the third time. Romsey—which was how she'd taken to thinking of him—folded at the waist and plucked it from the floor.

"Perhaps I should find a way to secure it to your lap," he offered.

"I'm not sure how. I do appreciate you having the forethought to bring books."

"Don't forget the cards, though that's trickier in a moving coach."

"I'm afraid I don't play cards." Her parents hadn't ever allowed it, deeming it an unnecessary and uncouth activity for a debutante.

His brows climbed with brief surprise. "I see. Well, I can certainly teach you at the inn later if we aren't too tired."

Just thinking of being closeted with him in a room again made her body temperature spike. She blamed it on embarrassment at having to share such close quarters with a near stranger, but she feared it was maybe something else. Something she'd prefer to ignore, so she did.

Surprisingly, she'd fallen asleep on the way to their stop last night. Even more surprisingly, she'd awakened in his arms upon their arrival. For a brief moment, she'd felt his warmth and the steady beat of his heart, and she'd felt something she never had before: safe. It had unnerved her completely. She'd practically fallen to the floor in her efforts to get away from him.

Then they'd gone upstairs to their tiny room at the coaching inn. The bed was barely large enough for two people, particularly when they'd placed a rolled blanket in the middle. They'd both slept completely clothed, and Diana woke in the very same position in which she'd fallen asleep. Clearly, she hadn't dared move.

They hadn't changed into nightclothes since their stop was only a few hours long. But tonight would be different. Tonight, they would be there all night, and truthfully, Diana couldn't bear to sleep in her corset and petticoat again.

If only her parents could see her now. Her mother would faint in horror, and her father would rage in fury. Indeed, they were likely doing that today anyway.

She'd thought of them often throughout the journey, wondering if Father was already on his way to King's Grange. Had Mother gone with him? Had he taken his anger out on her? Diana hoped not, and in fact, she'd written to that effect in her note, saying it was her decision not to marry Kilve and to retreat to King's Grange. She'd also said she was looking forward to spending the holidays at home instead of in London. That part, at least, was true. Or it would have been if she'd actually gone home.

Home. Where was that now? Nowhere, she realized.

"You're not reading."

Romsey's voice intruded into her thoughts. She held the book in her hands but hadn't opened it since he'd returned it to her.

Grateful to push aside the worry in her mind, she opened the book.

"What were you thinking about?" He closed the book he was reading, his finger keeping his place.

"The future." It wasn't a complete fabrication. She had been about to contemplate that.

"Ah. That can be a delicate endeavor. What are your plans once we reach your cousin's?"

"I don't know." She turned her head to find him watching her intently. He was very handsome—a fact they'd all agreed upon at the house party. The Duke of Kilve was the more sought after, but only because he wasn't saddled with the horrid reputation of the man in front of her. They were very close friends, the two dukes, but their demeanors had been quite different. Kilve had been cool and aloof—a façade he'd erected to protect himself. Romsey, on the other hand, laughed easily and worked his charm with anyone who would pay attention. And Diana and her friends had paid attention, as much as their parents had allowed.

Diana's father had made it very clear that he wouldn't tolerate a match between her and the *Duke of Ruin*, the abominable nickname attached to him because of his past sins. Or alleged sins. Diana wasn't his judge.

Yes, he was very attractive, with dark hair and dark eyes. And yet both were touched with gold. In his hair, there were lighter strands woven here and there with the dark, and in his eyes, sparkling flecks near the center that gave him an air of mischief. But there were also fine lines around his eyes and a few around his mouth that revealed a private agony perhaps. And given what she knew of his wife's death, she didn't doubt that he'd suffered. She longed to ask him the truth but hadn't gathered the courage.

They had days and days together. She might find the audacity yet.

For now, she would tread carefully—and try very hard not to fall under the spell cast by his enchanting gaze. He always looked at her with such care and honesty. It was nearly impossible to think of him as a murderer. But she reminded herself, as she always did, that appearances could be deceiving. She had no further to look than her father.

"Well, you have several days to decide what to do," he said bringing her attention back to the conversation. "How can I help?"

"You're already helping, thank you."

"I won't feel right just depositing you in Lancashire without a plan. In fact, I'm still not entirely certain of our final destination."

That, at least, was something she knew. "Blackburn."

His brows climbed to an alarming height. "As in the Duke Who Disappeared?" It wasn't the same sort of duke nickname that Romsey and Kilve were saddled with, but it served its purpose, she supposed. It told you precisely who the Duke of Blackburn was with the utmost notoriety.

"Precisely. My cousin is the Duchess of Blackburn."

Romsey blew out a breath between his lips. "I remember when he went missing. What a tragedy. How many years ago was that now?"

"More than six. Long enough that his absence doesn't trouble Verity." As if it ever had. She'd immediately regretted marrying him, so much so that she'd felt guilty at her relief when he'd disappeared without a trace. "I look forward to seeing her—it's been nearly two years since we were together."

"It sounds as if you and she are close. Once you arrive, perhaps she can help you decide what to do. Unless you have your mind set already."

Her thoughts went immediately to the fantasies she'd indulged the day before—an independent life with a home of her own, teaching young girls…

"It looks like you might," he said softly, stealing into her thoughts once more.

She'd averted her gaze to the window beyond him in the door of the coach. Now she adjusted it back to his. Those gold flecks seemed to dance with anticipation.

Suddenly, she thought of his lips against hers at the house party. She'd been so shocked that she hadn't reacted. His mouth had lingered on hers just long enough for her to feel as if she were melting. And then he'd gone, leaving her cold and strangely bereft.

She blinked. "It's nothing." She bent her head to her book once more.

"It can't be nothing. I detected the very beginning of a faint smile.

Nothing doesn't spark smiles."

"What a ridiculous sentence," she said, allowing the smile to come.

"Indeed it is, but you gather my meaning. Tell me your heart's desire."

He used the phrase she had yesterday when referring to Kilve. 'Heart's desire' typically meant love, didn't it? But only the luckiest people fell in love, and Diana had never felt particularly lucky.

When she still didn't respond, he leaned closer. "You can tell me. I'm good at keeping secrets."

She swung her gaze to his and, for some reason, decided to tell him. "What you suggested yesterday… It might be nice to have my own cottage. Somewhere I could teach. Maybe." She shrugged as heat rose up her neck.

"That's lovely." His response was gentle, almost reverent. "There's a workhouse in my district that recently opened a small school as part of its program. I gave them much of my library—well, what they would want, anyway. I'm afraid there are many volumes that would be absolute drudgery to get through."

"You gave your library away?"

"I found a place where it would get far more use." He cocked his head to the side. "What would your family say about marrying me?"

And just like that, the magic of the moment was lost as reality invaded. "Nothing good. I wouldn't be allowed to do such a thing. Which is where the other part of your suggestion comes in. I'd have to disappear—change my name and leave Diana Kingman behind."

"You can certainly do that, but you really would leave this life behind you. That includes everyone you know, even this cousin you're going to visit. Are you close?"

She hadn't thought about that. "Yes. She'd keep my secret."

"Could you ask her to?"

She could, but he had a point. While she and Verity had grown up together, Diana couldn't expect her to lie to their fathers. They were brothers and very alike, especially in temperament.

"I probably shouldn't." She worked to keep the defeat from her tone.

"You don't have to decide anything right now," he said with warm encouragement. "I'm here, and I'll help you in whatever way I can. You're not alone."

She might not be alone, but she certainly felt that way. It was impossible not to, given the way she'd been forced to live. She wondered whether the independence she craved would mean a lifetime of loneliness. Could she accept one to gain the other?

It was almost laughable, thinking she had a choice. But maybe, just maybe, she did. Thanks to this disaster Kilve had left her in. And Romsey seemed intent on rescuing her from.

"Thank you," she murmured, lifting her book and trying to focus on the page. She was all too aware of his body next to hers, not quite touching, but close enough to feel his heat. Which was the point of their proximity since it was rather cold.

Reason told her it was foolish to plan her life with or depend upon this near stranger. Yet he'd shown her more kindness than just about anyone she'd ever known. She could only hope this was his true self. Time would tell—hopefully within the next week.

A few minutes later, the coach slowed. Romsey leaned toward the window to look outside.

"We're here," he announced.

Once the vehicle stopped, Romsey opened the door. He waited for the coachman to lower the step, then hopped out and helped Diana descend.

Her legs protested after the last several hours in the coach, but it was good to feel her blood circulating again. The inn was a bit larger than last night's, boasting a charming gabled roof.

The duke escorted her across the yard. The ground was hard, and she marveled at their luck in avoiding any rain. Perhaps her fortunes had changed.

"Where are we?" she asked.

"Just outside Luton, I believe."

"Are you familiar with this road?"

"Somewhat," he said, opening the door to the inn and ushering her inside.

Before she could ask him what had brought him this way, a plump woman with bright blue eyes and extraordinary dimples greeted them. "Well, if it isn't Mr. Byrd!"

The name jarred Diana, but then she shouldn't have been surprised—that was their disguise. Except why would this woman know that? She couldn't have been expecting their arrival. Unless Romsey had plotted this course all along. What if they weren't on their way to Lancashire? She realized he could have kidnapped her, spiriting her away wherever he wanted. He *was* an alleged murderer after all…

She looked at him warily as he spoke to the woman, who was quite pleased to see him.

I'm being ridiculous! Diana admonished herself. Why would he kidnap her? What purpose could he possibly have? Did he mean to take her to Gretna Green and force her to marry him?

"My love," he said, startling Diana and reaching for her hand. The endearment drove every other thought from her mind. "Kitty, come and meet Mrs. Watt, the innkeeper's wife. Allow me to present my *wife*, Mrs. Byrd." He drew Diana against his side.

She connected with his warmth, and her body thrilled to the contact, despite the distressing turn her mind had taken. Forcing a smile, she nodded at Mrs. Watt. "Pleased to meet you."

Mrs. Watt clapped her hands together as her eyes danced with glee. "My goodness, felicitations are in order! We just saw you this past summer, and you were unwed. This sounds like a grand love story. I look forward to hearing it over dinner." She winked at Romsey, then asked, "Would you like the same room?"

"That would be more than acceptable, thank you."

"Come along, then." She led them through the small common room and up a narrow flight of stairs.

Diana's mind churned with what they could possibly say at dinner. And why had he been here last summer as Mr. Byrd?

They reached the landing, and there were just two rooms, matching the gables Diana had seen. Mrs. Watt led them to the one on the right side of the landing. "Here we are. Dinner will be in just a little while. Do you want me to send a boy up to start your fire?"

"No, I'll take care of it. And my coachman will bring our cases. Thank you kindly, Mrs. Watt."

"My pleasure, Mr. Byrd. See you at dinner!"

After the woman left, Diana faced the duke. "How does she know you? You couldn't have arranged this in advance."

He went to the mantel and picked up the tinderbox. "Of course not. You didn't tell me where we were going until we set out. As it happens, I've been here before. I didn't remember at first."

That eased her concern somewhat, but it didn't entirely make sense. "As Mr. Byrd?"

He knelt at the hearth to start the fire, which was already laid. He didn't turn his head when he answered. "Er, yes."

She wanted to make sure she understood. "You've been here before as Mr. Byrd?"

Once he had the fire going, he stood. "Yes."

She tipped her head to the side, waiting for him to elaborate. When he didn't, she set her hands on her hips. He was being decidedly circumspect. "Why did you come here under an alias?"

"I like to travel." He shrugged and still didn't meet her eyes, which didn't help his cause. "I prefer to remain anonymous."

"Except you weren't. You used a specific name. A name we're now using on this...trip." She wasn't sure what to call it. Escape?

He finally looked at her. "You needn't worry. No one knows who I really am. And they'll only know you as Mrs. Byrd. Kitty Byrd." He sniggered, and she rolled her eyes at his finding humor in this situation.

"Yes, they'll know me as your wife, with apparently some fantastical tale about how we fell in love."

"Fantastical?" He stroked his chin. "I'd thought we could simply say we were introduced by a common friend and decided to wed, but I suppose we could concoct a more amusing story." His eyes lit. "I know—you left your fiancé at the altar and ran off with his best friend." He laughed.

She stared at him, uncertain of whether to laugh or cry. She managed to say, "That's a bit too close for my comfort."

He sobered immediately. "Yes, I'm sorry. I shouldn't have said that. Later, perhaps, you'll laugh about it."

Laugh at being thrown over by a duke because he loved someone else? She could laugh, but she wasn't sure it came from being amused. More like feeling powerless. How she hated that sensation after enduring it about every aspect of her life for as long as she could remember. She lifted her chin. "You've loved me for years and finally persuaded me to marry you."

He took a step toward her, his gaze sharpening on hers. "I could believe that might be true."

What was he doing, flirting with her? "But it isn't."

"It'll be fun pretending it is." He gave her a devilish smile that made her insides pitch like the time she'd ridden in a high-perch phaeton.

Fun? Pretending to be married? To him?

If things had gone as planned, she would be well on her way to being married. Granted, to someone else, but surely she could pretend for one evening.

Of course she could. She'd mastered the art of living a lie, of feigning interest when there was none, of displaying joy that didn't exist. Tonight would be no different.

Chapter Three
❧3❧

EXCUSING HIMSELF FROM their room so Miss Kingman could perform a toilette in private, Simon made his way downstairs to the dining room where Mrs. Watt had laid out a rather impressive table setting for such a small inn.

Once she'd reminded him that he'd been there before, he vaguely remembered visiting last summer on his travels. He remembered Mrs. Watt's enthusiasm and a particularly succulent pheasant.

The innkeeper came into the dining room at that moment, as if summoned by Simon's thoughts. "Good evening, Mr. Byrd," he said jovially. "May I interest you in a cup of ale?"

"No, thank you. Tea, if it's not too much trouble. And a glass of wine for my wife, if you have one."

"Of course, of course."

"I see there are five seats at the table," Simon noted. "Will you and Mrs. Watt be joining us?"

"Oh yes. Mrs. Watt is quite keen to hear how you and Mrs. Byrd met. I'll apologize for her now—she's excessively romantic, the silly woman. Our other guest will also be in attendance. An older fellow, Mr. Alby."

"Brilliant."

"I'll just fetch the drinks." Mr. Watt bobbed his head and took himself off.

Simon went to the window and looked out into the dark yard. Their travel days were short due to the abbreviated daylight, but they'd been blessed by clear weather so far. One could only hope that would continue.

It had only been a day, but he'd enjoyed spending time with Miss Kingman. They'd read and dozed in the coach, and their conversation had kept entirely to what they were reading, the weather, and the difficulties of traveling. He longed to ask more intimate questions, such as why—specifically—she felt the need to run from her father, but expected there'd be plenty of time for that. He wondered if she felt the same. Was she burning to ask him about his horrid reputation? He couldn't blame her and acknowledged that he'd likely have to share *something*.

"Good evening." The arrival of the other guest—Mr. Alby—interrupted Simon's thoughts. Mr. Alby, leaning on a cane as he made his way into the dining room, was perhaps nearing seventy. Spectacles perched on his bulbous nose and white, bushy brows peeked over the top of the silver rims.

"Good evening. I'm Byrd." Simon offered his hand but belatedly realized Alby was using his to hold on to his cane.

The older man raised his left hand instead for an awkward, but firm handshake. "Pleased to make your acquaintance. I understand your wife will also be joining us."

"Indeed she will." He moved to one of the chairs and held it out. "May I help you get settled?"

"Very kind of you, my boy," Alby said, pitching himself into the chair with a subtle "Oof." He leaned his cane against the table.

The rustle of a skirt drew Simon to turn back to the doorway. Miss Kingman was still dressed in her traveling costume, but she'd removed the matching hat and discarded her gloves. Her dark hair was knotted into a simple bun at the back of her head, but she'd teased a few strands to curl about her face. Well, not curl exactly, but wave gently. She was incomparably fetching, even though she'd slept in that dress. What would she sleep in tonight, he wondered?

Hell, he shouldn't think of things like that when they were in company. Why, because he might become aroused? He didn't do that anymore. Rather, he hadn't until he'd kissed the woman standing in front of him at that house party. She'd reawakened the man buried inside the shell he'd become, and now he was to spend days on end with her without a chaperone. And he had to pretend to be infatuated with her.

No, that wouldn't be difficult. She breathed a life into him he'd long forgotten, and he'd take it. If only for a short time.

He smiled at her and moved to take her hand, guiding her into the room. The moment their bare flesh connected, awareness tingled through him. "Here's my wife. Mrs. Byrd, allow me to present Mr. Alby. Mr. Alby, this is Mrs. Byrd."

Miss Kingman let go of his hand—disappointingly—and dipped a brief curtsey. "Pleased to meet you, Mr. Alby."

Mr. Watt came in then, carrying a tray with their drinks. "Well, good evening, Mrs. Byrd! Dinner is just about ready." He unloaded the tray onto the table, setting Miss Kingman's wineglass at the seat across from Mr. Alby. He set the teapot and cup in front of the seat beside hers. Then he turned to Mr. Alby. "May I bring you some ale or Madeira? The latter is what I've delivered for Mrs. Byrd."

"Ale, thank you."

With a nod, Mr. Watt departed once more.

Simon held Miss Kingman's chair out as she sank onto the cushion, then pushed her toward the table before taking his own seat.

Alby blinked at him from behind his spectacles. "Is the tea for you, Byrd?"

"It is." Simon picked up the teapot and poured the brew into his cup.

Alby turned his head to Miss Kingman. "Is your husband ill? Or do you forbid him from drink?"

Miss Kingman shot him a look of alarm. Perhaps he should've prepared her for this. It hadn't even occurred to him. Hell, what else hadn't occurred to him? Maybe this would be more difficult than he'd anticipated.

"I don't take spirits," Simon said smoothly. "I prefer to keep a clear head at all times."

Alby looked horrified. "No ale or wine or spirits of any kind?"

Simon shook his head.

"Bloody strange," Alby muttered as he shook his head.

Miss Kingman lifted her glass to take a sip and peered sideways at Simon, her gaze curious. He busied himself with drinking his tea and was saved from further interrogation by the arrival of Mrs. Watt.

She bustled in with a tray of food and went about setting it on the table.

"I don't suppose you're serving pheasant?" Simon asked hopefully.

Mrs. Watt's face fell. "I'm afraid not. It's beef."

"I'm sure it's wonderful," Simon rushed to say, not wishing her to feel bad.

She brightened. "There are turnips and fresh-baked bread, as well as some greens. Oh, and the sauce. Mr. Watt makes an excellent mushroom sauce."

He arrived again then, bearing another tray with Alby's ale and other dishes for the table, as well as a bottle of wine and two empty glasses, likely for them. Mr. and Mrs. Watt set to serving everyone from the dishes they'd brought to the table.

Miss Kingman looked at him, her gaze reflecting surprise and uncertainty. Yes, he should have prepared her for this type of meal as well. She likely hadn't ever dined in this fashion. So far, he wasn't much of a husband.

"Do tell us how you came to be wed," Mrs. Watt said as she went around the table pouring sauce on everyone's beef. She looked at Miss Kingman. "You made an excellent catch. I'm sure there were several broken hearts in your wake, Mr. Byrd."

"Not very many," he said. "Or perhaps none at all. I really can't say. I paid no attention to anyone save my lovely wife. For years and years. Until she finally agreed to marry me."

Mrs. Watt sat down at the end of the table, next to Miss Kingman, and blinked at the younger woman. "Whyever did you make him wait?" She looked utterly incredulous, and Simon might have found it amusing if he wasn't tensely awaiting Miss Kingman's response. He hoped she wasn't put out by all this, but it was necessary to maintain their ruse.

Miss Kingman gave her a placid smile. "He's a bit older than me, as you can tell. I simply wished to wait until I felt I was ready for the marital estate." She turned her head to Simon and fluttered her lashes demurely. "Mr. Byrd was kind enough to be patient," she said softly.

"I had no choice. There is simply no other woman in the world for me."

Miss Kingman's eyes widened briefly, and Simon suspected he'd gone a touch too far. Ah well, it would please Mrs. Watt.

"How romantic," she said.

"Indeed it is," Mr. Alby said quietly, surprising Simon, and apparently everyone else since they all directed their attention at him. "I recently lost my wife. We were married for forty-eight years. There was no other woman for me either." He lifted his cup in a toast. "To our women."

Simon and Mr. Watt joined him, raising their vessels. "To our women."

Casting a look at Miss Kingman, Simon sipped his tea. She dropped her gaze to her plate and focused on her meal.

"When were you wed?" Mrs. Watt asked.

"Last week," Simon said, scooping up some turnips. "This is our wedding trip."

Mrs. Watt smiled at him and Miss Kingman. "Lovely. Where is your destination?"

"Wales." Simon wondered how long the interrogation would continue. Perhaps he could divert the conversation. He smiled across the table at Alby. "Where are you going, Mr. Alby?"

"Hounslow, to live with my daughter. Her husband runs a school there. Now that I'm alone, she wants me to come." He waved a hand. "I agreed since it will make her happy."

Simon smiled before taking a bite of the delicious beef. Mrs. Watt was right—her husband made an excellent mushroom sauce.

"How nice for all of you to be together," Miss Kingman said. "Do you have grandchildren?"

"I do." His tone carried a note of pride. "Two beautiful girls and a strapping lad."

Miss Kingman smiled, and it was as if the room was granted additional illumination. "They will love having you with them, no doubt."

Mr. Alby's eyes twinkled behind his spectacles. "Truth be told, my daughter didn't have to ask me twice."

Simon's heart tugged. To have a family that loved you, hell, that wanted you, was a wonderful thing. He thought of his mother and two older sisters, all of whom had turned their backs on him when Miriam had died. Before that, really, if he'd cared to pay attention. Which he hadn't. Prior to wedding Miriam, he'd only been concerned with having a grand time, particularly after his father had died.

And just like that, his stomach churned and he lost all interest in his meal. He sipped his tea and cast a longing glance toward the bottle of wine. He didn't really have an urge to drink it. Just to forget.

Miss Kingman looked to Mrs. Watt. "Do you have children?"

The innkeeper's wife dabbed at her mouth with her napkin as she nodded. "We do. Our son works as a secretary in London," she said proudly. "And we've a daughter who's married to a miller in Dunstable." Mrs. Watt gave Simon a pointed stare. "I hope you're paying attention to your wife's interest in children, Mr. Byrd." Her eyes sparked with merriment, and she exchanged a gleeful glance with her husband at the other end of the table.

Simon peered askance at Miss Kingman. A faint blush stained her neck, but she kept her face carefully averted as she reached for her wineglass. Was she praying for this meal to end?

The conversation turned to Mr. Watt's mushroom sauce when Mr. Alby complimented its flavor. This led to a detailed instruction of the methods he employed to create and preserve the sauce.

Simon picked at his food but didn't eat much more.

"Mr. Byrd, you've hardly touched your greens," Mrs. Watt fussed. "I hope there is nothing amiss. You can't be ill on your wedding trip."

"I'm fine, thank you, Mrs. Watt. Just a bit tired from traveling. I suspect Mrs. Byrd feels the same, don't you, my love?" He turned his body toward Miss Kingman, who was just finishing her Madeira.

"I am." She offered Mrs. Watt a weary smile. "Would you mind terribly if we retired?"

"Not at all. Tired or no, newlyweds need their private time." She exchanged another knowing glance with Mr. Watt.

After saying good night, Simon escorted Miss Kingman from the dining room and upstairs to their room. As soon as they were inside, Simon leaned back against the door while she made her way to the window overlooking the front yard.

"That wasn't so awful, was it?" he asked.

She looked outside a moment, then pulled the curtains closed. Turning, she shook her head. "A bit awkward, but not awful."

He pushed away from the door. "My apologies. I should've prepared you for a few things."

"Such as this story you concocted of us being newlyweds on our way to Wales." She arched a coal-dark brow at him.

"I came up with that in the moment, actually. I thought I handled it rather well. As did you, explaining why I was pining after you for years."

A soft but guttural sound came from her throat. "You were a bit excessive. 'No other woman in the world' for you?" She looked at him as if he were daft.

Chuckling, he went to the hearth, where someone had stoked their fire while they'd been at dinner. "If I'm going to spin a tale, I'd much prefer an exceedingly happy one, wouldn't you?"

"I suppose." She joined him in front of the hearth, holding her hands out to the heat. "I'd heard you don't take spirits. I wasn't sure if it was true."

"It is. Obviously."

"What do you do after dinner with the other gentlemen when they drink port? At the house party, did you simply abstain? Does no one question your behavior?"

He turned to face her. "Honestly, no. That house party was the first polite invitation I've received in two years. I think most of the gentlemen there were content to keep our dialogues focused on the completely inane. If they even spoke to me."

Her eyes widened briefly. "Some of them didn't?"

Most of them, actually. "Your father didn't."

She made that sound in her throat again, but this one was clearly due to disgust. "That doesn't surprise me. He thought it was scandalous you were there in the first place. When he heard that we'd kissed—"

She abruptly turned her attention to the fire. Since her cheeks were already pink from the heat, Simon couldn't tell if she was blushing.

"It was a silly party game." Simon hoped to put her at ease, but when she whipped her gaze to his for a brief, surprised moment, he wanted to take it back. Maybe it had been more than that to her.

"Yes, it was."

Or maybe, in his desperation, he was looking for affection where none existed.

He turned from the fire and contemplated the bed. It was neither big nor small and would support a blanket between them. However, there was no dressing screen to allow for privacy.

He wasn't entirely sure how to broach the sensitive topic of disrobing, but since they would be spending several nights together, it had to be done. He looked back at her over his shoulder. "You aren't planning on sleeping in your clothes again, are you?"

She turned in front of the fire but didn't come toward him. "I'd rather not. But I'm afraid I'm in need of assistance. Unfortunately, my wardrobe depends upon a maid."

"I'd be happy to provide help. Just remember I've no experience as a ladies' maid."

"Did you never undress your wife?" She looked away, angling herself back toward the fire. "Forget I asked that."

He went back toward her and spoke softly. "Don't." She turned her head, her blue eyes dark and vivid in the firelight. "We are going to get to know each other much better than we ought, and I don't want you to regret things you might say. I assumed you would be curious about my wife. Yes, I undressed her. Many times. If I close my eyes, I can still feel her skin." But he didn't close his eyes. He couldn't. She—Miss Diana Kingman—held him captive with her gaze.

Miss Kingman exhaled. "You must promise not to look. Aside from what you must do to unlace my gown.

"I promise." He kept his voice and his gaze steady. "We must trust each other on this journey. Implicitly. That's why I won't shy away from your questions."

She nodded, then presented her back. "Will you leave while I undress? I'll need ten minutes or so. I'll be in bed when you return and will close my eyes while you disrobe."

It was a good plan, particularly since he thought a walk outside in the cold might do him some good. A beautiful woman's back presented to him for the purpose of assistance with disrobing was too reminiscent of a time gone by and yet wholly new. Miss Kingman wasn't Miriam, nor did he want her to be.

Simon quickly unlaced her gown and helped lift it over her head. He laid it across one of the chairs set at a small table and returned to help her remove her petticoat and unlace her corset. When he finished, he dropped his hands to his sides.

"I can finish," she said, without looking back. "Thank you."

He left without a word, closing the door firmly behind him. He inhaled sharply, taking perhaps the deepest breath he had in the last ten minutes.

Thankfully he didn't encounter anyone on his walk. He wasn't in the mood to made idle chatter. His thoughts were bad enough—railing at him for being attracted to someone who wasn't his wife.

But how could he expect to go through life as he had the past two years? A self-hating, forlorn monk. Oh, he put on a good face for everyone else, but no one knew how acutely his pain cut. Not even Nick, his closest friend.

Nick. Simon meant to send a note to inform him what had transpired with Miss Kingman. Nick had been concerned for her welfare, as he should be. He'd never meant to cause her trouble or pain, and Simon wanted to put him at ease. Miss Kingman would be fine—if he had anything to do with it. And, fortunately, he did.

Tomorrow, they would be on their way to Northampton, and hopefully, things would go as smoothly as they had so far. Being recognized as Mr. Byrd was a small bump in his plan, but not a threatening one. If they could just continue on this path until he delivered her to Lancashire, all would be well.

But first he had to spend the night in her bed. Again. Only with less clothing.

Thinking it had been well more than ten minutes, he made his way back upstairs. The lantern next to the bed had been extinguished, leaving just the light from the fire to illuminate the room.

Simon looked toward the bed. Miss Kingman lay near the edge of one side—as close as she could get without falling off, he noted—her back to the center of the bed, where it looked as though she'd rolled one of the blankets and placed it between them. He hoped there were enough coverings on the bed to keep them warm. Last night, they'd worn more clothing to bed.

Hell. He wore a nightshirt to sleep in or, most often, nothing at all. Tonight, he should probably keep his smallclothes on.

Shrugging out of his jacket, he hung it on a hook in the wall. He sat down to remove his boots, working as quietly and quickly as possible. When he'd removed everything but his shirt and smallclothes, he went to his side of the bed and crawled between the icy covers. He shuddered involuntarily and felt her jerk.

"Sorry," he murmured. "Cold bed."

"Very," she responded, her low, feminine voice rustling over him like a fine silk.

He considered making an offer to warm them both up—body heat would be most beneficial. But that was likely a bad idea. For so many reasons.

He turned to his side, away from her, but snuggled his back against the rolled-up blanket. That would help with the cold. And the warmer he got, the more easily he would fall asleep. And the sooner he fell asleep, the sooner he could put the proximity of Miss Kingman out of his mind.

Too bad none of that happened very quickly at all.

Chapter Four
✦Ɛ•3✦

AS THEY NEARED the end of day three of their journey, Diana sent up a silent prayer for a repeat of the accommodations they'd enjoyed last night in Northampton—two beds! After the prior night when they'd shared a bed in Luton and she'd awakened pressed to his side with only the meager rolled-up blanket between them, she'd been incredibly grateful for her own space. She doubted she'd be so fortunate again tonight, but she could hope.

The coach rolled into the yard of the Jolly Goat, and Diana arched her back against the squab.

"You're an excellent traveler," Romsey remarked. "You never complain."

"That's not something I was ever allowed to do." She wanted to take the words back because they were too revealing.

"Your upbringing was rather strict." It wasn't a question but an observation.

He didn't know the half of it. "Yes. You don't complain about traveling either."

"I travel quite a bit."

"You said you like it," she said, watching him stretch his legs and arms. "Where have you been?"

He relaxed his limbs as the coach came to a stop. "All over England, Wales, and Scotland. I'm planning to spend the summer in Ireland."

"I've never been there. Maybe that's where I should go and disappear."

He arched a brow at her in the gray afternoon light spilling in through the window just before Tinley opened the door. "Is that what you've decided to do?"

She shook her head as she pulled the wool blanket off her legs. "No. I'm still mulling."

"And you still have time," he said pleasantly before turning and stepping down from the coach.

He reached up and offered her his hand. She slipped her gloved fingers into his and tried not to think of how much time they were spending together or what would happen if anyone knew of their scandalous journey.

By now, her father would be well on his way to King's Grange. Once he learned she wasn't there, what would he do? More importantly, what was Diana going to do?

She'd meant what she'd told Romsey—she was still mulling. For now, she had to admit she was enjoying this reprieve. Never had she been able to go about her day without asking for permission for *everything* or having her every choice and movement thoroughly scrutinized. And often criticized. It was, in a word, heaven. She wasn't sure she could go back to her life, not after this. Yet the idea of leaving it—and everyone she'd ever known—behind forever was rather daunting.

As she stepped onto the hard earth, Romsey frowned. But he wasn't looking at her. He was looking at the inn and the other vehicles in the yard. "It looks crowded."

"Should we go somewhere else?" she asked.

The duke looked at his coachman, who shook his head. "I didn't see anything else for the last mile, and it's getting dark quickly. I think this is our best bet."

"I agree," Romsey said. He cast Diana a hopeful look. "We'll be fine. Let's get inside." As if to hurry them along, a brisk wind blew against them, icing Diana's spine.

He clasped her elbow and guided her quickly into the inn, where they were summarily greeted by a rather grouchy innkeeper.

"We're full," he said, clearly harassed. His dark, bushy brows nearly met across his forehead. He barely spared them a glance but said, "I've a larger room you can share with another couple, provided they don't mind. I'll go and speak to them."

While he lumbered his rather large frame across the common room, Diana turned to Romsey. "Share a room?"

"It's not uncommon. I've done it," he said with a shrug.

She pursed her lips. "Well, I haven't." Then again, she hadn't done *anything*.

"Let's just wait and see what happens. There's no sense getting upset until we know what we're dealing with."

The innkeeper caught their eye and waved for them to come over to the table where he stood. The occupants of said table were a young couple— an apple-cheeked blonde beauty and her dark-haired, blue-eyed husband who wore a wide grin. Or maybe it wasn't her husband. Maybe they were on a scandalous journey like Diana and the duke.

Diana and the duke. That sounded like the name of a horrid novel. And perhaps one Diana would like to read. If she were allowed to read them.

The innkeeper nodded at Diana and Romsey. "These are them." He turned his attention to the duke. "Mr. and Mrs. Ogden said you can have the pallet in front of the fire and pay a third of the fee."

A third! For a pallet while they had the bed? What would they offer if they knew Romsey was a duke? Of course, she couldn't tell them.

"That would be excellent," Romsey said. He inclined his head toward the Ogdens. "Thank you kindly."

"They've already paid," the innkeeper continued. "So go ahead and pay them, plus I'll need an extra charge for having additional people."

"Of course." Romsey didn't bat an eye as he paid what the innkeeper demanded and then paid the Ogdens.

"Dinner's in about an hour," the innkeeper said gruffly before bustling off.

"Charming fellow," Diana muttered.

"What's that?" Mr. Ogden asked, leaning forward.

Diana smiled. "Nothing at all. Thank you for sharing your room with us."

Mrs. Ogden nodded toward the empty chairs at their table. "Please sit."

Romsey held a chair for Diana. "I'm Byrd, and this is my wife."

Ogden offered his hand to the duke. "Pleased to meet you."

Diana didn't really care to sit again so soon, but she was too eager to be near the fire to quibble. She turned her body toward the flames and briefly closed her eyes in ecstasy.

"It's so cold today," Mrs. Ogden said. "Much colder than yesterday."

"Where are you headed?" Ogden asked Romsey.

"North. How about you?"

Ogden took a sip of ale—there were tankards in front of him and his wife. "Birmingham. We came from a visit to Mrs. Ogden's family. Her sister just had a babe." He smiled at his wife. "We're hoping that will be us someday soon."

She beamed back at him, and the love between them was palpable. At least Diana thought it was love. How would she even recognize that emotion? She swallowed and looked at the fire.

Romsey, who'd sat down beside Diana, put his arm around her. "Us too."

What was he doing?

Playing a part.

Her pulse picked up speed at his touch and familiarity, but she didn't say anything. She gave him a half smile, confident her eyes were probably communicating her alarm. Alarm? Was this alarming? No, it was just...different.

He patted her shoulder, then withdrew his arm. She was surprised to find that she was disappointed.

"Have you been upstairs?" Romsey asked. "Is this room truly large enough for all four of us, or will we be cramped?"

"It's plenty big," Ogden said. "Hope you don't mind the pallet—you will be closer to the fire, so there's that."

"We don't mind at all. We're just glad to have a place to rest our weary selves."

"There's a screen too," Mrs. Ogden put in. "So we can all have some privacy." She tossed her husband a rather suggestive look and giggled softly.

Diana didn't know whether to feel relieved or anxious. She could only imagine what the Ogdens might do with their privacy.

The conversation turned briefly to the weather, and then Mrs. Ogden told them all about her sister's delivery and her new baby. It was far more information than Diana might have wanted. Childbirth seemed a frightening prospect, but also distant—as in very, *very* far in the future. Though she'd planned to marry the Duke of Kilve, they'd agreed there would be no children for a while. She was sure most men would not have consented to such a thing. And suddenly, she was annoyed all over again at her predicament. Why did it seem as if nothing was in her control?

Because it wasn't.

Until this trip. For the first time in her life, she was making her own choices. Yes, she ought to focus on that. She took a deep breath.

"You need some ale or maybe a whiskey," Ogden said, turning his head to look for the innkeeper.

Instead, a serving girl came toward them. When she was near the table, Ogden gestured to Romsey. "Bring the man a drink. Do you have whiskey?"

Before she could answer, Romsey gave her a charming smile. "I'd actually like tea, if it's not too much trouble."

"For me as well," Diana said, prompting the duke to slide an inquisitive look her way.

When the girl had gone, Ogden blinked at Romsey. "You don't drink spirits?"

Diana put her hand on Romsey's arm. "I prefer tea, and he joins me. Isn't that lovely?"

Romsey gave her a look that was nothing short of incredulous, but he masked it quickly. "Quite lovely," he murmured.

"Well, if you change your mind, the ale is delicious," Mrs. Ogden said.

A few minutes later, the serving girl brought tea and said their dinner would be out shortly. Then Tinley came over to tell them their things had been delivered to their room and that he'd see them in the morning.

Over dinner, Mr. Ogden asked Romsey about his occupation. Diana realized they'd come this far without discussing that. She was quite curious to hear what he'd say.

"I'm fortunate to have inherited a small estate," Romsey said easily. "Nothing terribly fancy."

"I wondered," Mrs. Ogden said, her gaze narrowing on Diana's traveling costume. "In fact, I wondered if you might be peerage, judging from your clothing." She exhaled, smiling. "I'm glad you're not. I've never met a peer, and I'm not sure what I'd say!"

Diana stifled a smile. If Mrs. Ogden only knew...

"Still, they're gentry, my dear," Mr. Ogden said, flicking a glance toward the duke that indicated he was perhaps not quite as comfortable as he'd been a few minutes before.

"Barely, really," Romsey assured him.

"Perhaps you should have the bed," Mrs. Ogden offered.

Her husband shot her a wide-eyed glance, and she blushed slightly.

Romsey was quick to say, "Heavens, no. We insist you take the bed— you were here first. The pallet will suit us just fine."

Mr. Ogden looked relieved. "You are very kind."

"We already established that you are the kind ones—offering up your extra space."

A yawn suddenly escaped Diana's mouth. She brought her hand up and tried to hide it, but everyone at the table noticed. She knew this because now they were all doing it.

Mrs. Ogden laughed. "I guess we should think about turning in!" She exchanged a warm look with her husband, and he leaned over and pressed a kiss to her cheek.

"Pardon us," he murmured.

Diana averted her gaze to her unfinished dessert—a wonderful bread and butter pudding with succulent currants. It was, she reflected, her favorite part of the meal. But perhaps that was because she wasn't often allowed sweets.

Romsey helped her up from the table as Mr. Ogden performed the same service for his wife. They went toward the stairs, and Romsey gestured for the other couple to precede them. "You first since we've no idea where we're going."

Ogden nodded. "Right." He guided his wife up and around the sharp corner to a large landing before leading them to the left to a room at the end of the corridor. "This is it." He opened the door and moved inside, quickly stepping aside to allow Romsey and Diana to come in.

It was the largest room they'd stayed in thus far, with a bed against the left side, a fireplace opposite the door, and a table and chairs in front of a window on the right side. The pallet looked like a nest of blankets situated on the floor in front of the right side of the hearth. There was also, as Mrs. Ogden had stated, a screen standing in the corner near the table.

"We'll just move this," Ogden said, going to the screen.

Romsey rushed to help him, and each man picked up one side before carrying it to the other side of the fireplace, where they placed it near the hearth on the left side between the pallet and the bed. This allowed privacy but didn't completely cut the Ogdens off from the heat source.

Mrs. Ogden stood near the center of the room and surveyed the placement of the screen. "Perhaps Mrs. Byrd and I can prepare for bed, while you two excuse yourselves."

While Diana wasn't terribly enthused about undressing with a stranger, it was perhaps better than being undressed by Romsey. Except, truth be told, she didn't mind being undressed by him. He was gentle, careful, and surprisingly adept.

"An excellent notion," Ogden said, turning toward the door. "Come, Byrd, let us have a nightcap." He glanced over at Romsey, his brow furrowing. "Or something."

When they were gone, Mrs. Ogden came bustling over. "Now we can gossip about them!"

Diana fought to keep from showing her distaste. She didn't like to gossip, but it was hard to avoid in London's social whirl. She could tell Mrs. Ogden things that would likely make her eyes the size of the ocean. "I'm sure I have nothing of interest to say about Mr. Byrd." But about the Duke of Ruin? She quickly put that from her mind.

"I doubt that." Mrs. Ogden's eyes twinkled as she walked to a narrow bench at the end of the bed and sat down to remove her shoes. "Mr. Ogden and I have been married eight months. In truth, I suspect I may be carrying a babe, but I haven't told him yet. What about you?"

Self-conscious but not knowing what else to do, Diana sat in one of the chairs at the table and took off her half boots. "We were married just last week. I am *not* carrying a child."

"Yet," Mrs. Ogden said with a wink. "That Mr. Byrd is as handsome as they come. Why, if Peter looked like that, I'd never let him out of bed!" She laughed as she stood and unbuttoned the drop front of her gown.

Diana averted her eyes and pulled the pins from her hair, setting them in a neat little pile on the table.

"Did I embarrass you?" Mrs. Ogden asked. "I'm terribly sorry. Sometimes I'm too plainspoken. Or so my mother says."

Diana lifted her eyes and saw that the other woman was removing her petticoat, which she draped over the end of the bed along with her dress.

Mrs. Ogden came toward Diana, her deep brown eyes tinged with concern. "Perhaps you don't think he's attractive? Were you…forced to marry him? I heard that happens sometimes with the gentry." She nodded knowingly. "It happens sometimes in my station too."

"No, I wasn't forced. As you said, he's quite attractive." Diana couldn't dispute that. While she hadn't seen him undressed—he was always careful to disrobe in the dark and was up and dressed before she even awoke— she'd become well acquainted with the feel of his thigh pressed along hers in the coach, the touch of his hand against her, the feel of his lips moving over hers. Perhaps not *well* acquainted with his lips since they'd only kissed that one time during that silly game at the house party of course. However, the more time she spent with him, the more she wondered what it might be like to kiss him again. And for longer.

Needing a distraction, she began to braid her hair.

"So you married for love, then." Mrs. Ogden smiled softly. "It wasn't precisely love with me and Peter. More like lust." She laughed again. "And when my mother caught us in the stable, well, we had to get married. It's all worked out, though. I do love him, and he loves me."

"How wonderful." And truly it was. Diana yearned for something simple and true, but knew she was unlikely to find it. Even if she did muster the courage to start a new life, she doubted love would fall into her lap. Or that she'd meet it in a stable.

Finishing her braid, she decided to take advantage of the other woman's presence. "I'm afraid I need help removing my gown. Mr. Byrd usually helps me, but it might be nice if I was already abed when he returns."

Mrs. Ogden's eyes lit. "I know where your mind's at! Of course I'll help. Turn around."

Diana pivoted, and the other woman yanked at the ties of her gown until it was loose, then helped take it over Diana's head. She draped it over the top of the screen while Diana removed her petticoat, then returned to help with Diana's corset.

"This is very fancy." Mrs. Ogden's voice carried a hint of awe. "Must've cost a fortune."

Diana didn't know what to say. It *had* cost a fair penny. "I think I might prefer something simpler like yours. Something I could take off by myself."

"We could swap," Mrs. Ogden offered. "On second thought, there's no way yours would fit me. You're a tiny thing."

Mrs. Ogden did have probably three inches of height on Diana, and her bosom was far more impressive. In fact, Diana suffered a bit of envy at the woman's curves.

Diana pulled the undergarment from her body and, standing in just her chemise and stockings, nearly choked at the sight of Mrs. Ogden using her hands to lift her breasts, as if she were weighing them. Looking down at the globes, the woman said, "This is why I'm fairly certain there's a babe. They aren't usually this big." She grinned at Diana. "Though Mr. Ogden seems to like them!"

Once again speechless, Diana turned to find her bag in order to fetch her night rail. Finding it, she said, "Well, good night, then. Thank you for your assistance."

"Happy to help," Mrs. Ogden said, going toward the bed.

Diana moved behind the screen and removed her chemise and stockings. Donning her night rail quickly, she was glad for the proximity of the fire. She hoped Mr. and Mrs. Ogden would be warm enough in the bed, but then it looked as if it had plenty of blankets. In fact, she ought to ask for one of them so she could roll it up to put between her and Romsey, but she didn't care to explain why she wanted it—not when they had the fire and the Ogdens didn't.

Settling herself into the pallet and drawing the blanket up to her chin, she closed her eyes and prayed that she would fall asleep quickly, preferably before Romsey returned.

That prayer, like so many others, went unanswered.

Hearing the men enter and bidding each other good night, Diana turned toward the fire. A few minutes later, the blanket moved, and she felt the warmth of Romsey's body close to hers. The pallet, damnably, wasn't very large.

She felt more awake than ever, her body screaming with awareness, both because of Romsey behind her and the other couple in the room. After a moment, she heard noises coming from beyond the screen. A sigh. A giggle. A soft moan.

Oh my goodness.

Diana closed her eyes tight and pulled the blanket up a bit more to nearly cover her ear.

But it wasn't enough. A few minutes later, the moans became louder and more drawn-out. Then came a keening cry.

Diana jumped, flipping to her back, her eyes wide.

"Shhh," Romsey said softly.

Diana looked at him. His dark eyes reflected the light of the dying fire. "What's wrong with her?" she asked urgently.

"Nothing."

The cry intensified and stopped. Diana began to exhale, but then Mrs.

Ogden let out several successive whimpers. Diana tensed. "Surely there's something wrong. She sounds as if she's in pain."

"She is not," Romsey whispered. "I can assure you, she is *not*."

"Then what's wrong with her?"

Romsey took a deep breath, his gaze never leaving hers. "Have you no idea what goes on between a man and a woman?" He kept his voice low so that she had to strain to hear.

"Yes, of course I do." Her mother had told her in painstaking detail how a man would put his... *member* between Diana's legs, and it would hurt. He would grunt and pant and deposit his seed, and she would be grateful. It sounded awful, and her mother had simply shrugged and said that all women must endure it. But then she'd also described kissing as a horrid activity akin to having one's skin peeled off. Diana knew that to be patently false and now wondered if the rest of her mother's descriptions had been lies as well. Although, it did sound as if Mrs. Ogden were being put on the rack...

Something entered Romsey's eyes, and they narrowed slightly. "You think it's unpleasant." He shook his head. "It's not. At least, not when it's done right. In fact, you can take pleasure all on your own—you don't need a man. Did you know that?"

Struck speechless yet again, she simply stared at him.

"I see," he murmured.

She could give herself pleasure? Where she cried out like Mrs. Ogden? She wasn't sure she wanted that, and yet judging from the chorus of "yes," coming from the bed, perhaps she ought to reserve judgment.

She recalled her earlier thoughts, about how she'd never been able to choose anything. This was something she could choose. As long as she was rebelling, she might as well make it memorable.

Diana turned toward him, anticipation curling through her. "Would you show me?"

His nostrils flared, and his eyes darkened until they were nearly obsidian, save the gold flecks that gleamed in the firelight. "Diana, do you have any idea what you're asking me?"

The shock of her audacity gave her a moment's pause, but only a moment. This was beyond the pale, and she should be overcome with shame. Except she wasn't. Nor did she want to be. "Not really. That's why I need you to show me. Unless you can't. Perhaps I should ask another woman?"

"No, no." His voice was tight, strained. "I can show you. Or guide you." He took a deep breath and let it out, then propped his head onto his hand, settling his elbow into the pallet. "It's best if you roll to your back."

She did that, and suddenly, the sound of the bed violently hitting the wall filled the room. Her jaw dropped, and Romsey leaned over her, his finger coming to his lips.

"It's all right," he whispered. "I don't expect it will be long now."

Diana had no idea what he meant. "Until what?"

"Until they finish."

"How can you tell?"

"There's a progression…an intensifying of sensations…a build-up of pleasure that reaches a climax."

Diana thought she understood. "Ah, that's when he leaves his seed inside her."

"Yes, but more importantly, that's when the pleasure is at its most spectacular."

Her limbs felt lighter suddenly, her breasts heavier. These changes to her body were strange but not unpleasant. "Does this happen to women? We don't have any seed."

"No, you don't, and yes, it does happen to women, although if a man doesn't know what he's doing and a woman doesn't know her body well enough to understand what she wants, it's possible, nay *likely*, she won't achieve the same pleasure. It's called an orgasm."

This was all so intriguing. Diana nearly forgot about the sounds coming from the bed. "Is that what you're going to show me how to do? Have an orgasm?"

"*Yes.*" His voice sounded strained again, as if *he* were on the rack.

"Is this going to be a problem for you? You don't sound very enthused," she said. Too bad, because she was warming to the idea of learning what an orgasm felt like.

His mouth curved into a small but seductively charming smile. "I'm plenty enthused, actually. Shall we begin?"

Before she could answer, the sounds from the bed intensified. Mrs. Ogden let out a high wail while her husband grunted, then moaned loudly. Then the bed stopped hitting the wall.

"Are they finished?" Diana whispered.

"I think so."

"Then I suppose I should start. What do I do?"

His Adam's apple bobbed as he swallowed. "This is going to involve your sex. Or we can call it your pussy. Or your cunny. It has a variety of names. Do you have a preference?"

Heat flooded her face. "I don't." She resisted the urge to turn and hide from him. No, she was going to do this.

"Put your hand on it—your sex," he clarified.

Diana reached down beneath the blanket and gently touched between her legs. "Should I lift my night rail?"

"Yes."

She did that and rested her hand against her curls. A mixture of embarrassment and curiosity set her nerves rattling.

"Now, there are parts to your cunny. Would you like to know what they are?"

"If I must."

He smiled again. "It would help. There are lips on the outside. They shield what you protect on the inside."

Lips...she supposed that made sense.

"Touch them. You'll need to part your legs a bit. Truthfully, the more you part your legs, the more you may enjoy it."

The heat that had just begun to fade from her face came rushing back. She faltered. "I don't..."

"Do you want me to help?" The question was so low, she barely heard it.

She couldn't bring herself to make the words, so she nodded.

His free hand moved beneath the blanket, and he found her hand. "Part your legs, just a bit, and open those folds."

Folds. Lips. The vocabulary began to jumble in her brain.

But then his hand guided her, his fingers moving over her fingers, parting her flesh. She gasped. "I'm...wet. Is that normal?"

"That's not just normal, that's wonderful. That wetness is what helps a man's cock—sorry, another word for you—glide inside. It will also increase your pleasure. When there's no moisture, it's not very pleasant."

She tried to imagine a—*cock*—sliding into her, and that heat that had suffused her face flushed through the rest of her body. Her pelvis twitched, and she suddenly wanted to press her fingers inside herself.

He seemed to know because that was what he guided her to do. Positioning his index finger over hers, he pushed hers inside, causing her to gasp once more. "That should feel pleasant at least."

"It feels... I-I don't know what it feels like." She was caught in wonder, trying—and failing—to understand everything. And her control was slipping.

"The most important part of your anatomy here is this." He guided her finger up to the top of her sex, where the...lips ended. "This is your clitoris. If you just rub this, you might even orgasm—without putting your finger inside. Some women do."

She squinted up at him. "You have a great deal of experience."

His expression turned wry. "A fair amount."

Diana felt a burst of irrational jealousy. "Have you done this before?"

"Taught a woman to pleasure herself? No, Diana, this is a first."

He'd called her Diana. She should be shocked, but that seemed laughable given their current state. Instead, it had sounded like a caress, and only served to heighten her desire. Yes, desire. She wanted this.

"What do I do to make that happen?"

He swallowed again, and she realized his breathing was a bit shallow. Was he all right?

Before she could ask, he used his fingers over hers, massaging her flesh. "Rub yourself. Here. Can you feel that little nub? Try to find it with your finger."

She searched until she found something that felt...nubbish, she supposed. "There."

"Close your eyes." His voice was soft and dark, lulling her into a state of seductive excitement as his hand instructed hers how to move. Slowly, softly, then faster with more pressure.

The pleasure he talked about—how it would build—started there. She sucked in a breath and opened her eyes. He was still watching her, his gaze impossibly dark and his face stretched taut.

His motions grew larger so that her fingertips slipped down along her folds, to where the moisture had gathered even more. She was quite slick now, and the sensations shooting through her were becoming more intense.

Her hips twitched. She wanted to arch up with the motion, to meet her hand—and his. Her breasts tingled, and the comment Mrs. Ogden had made about her husband liking her breasts rooted in Diana's mind. She opened her mouth to ask what that meant, to maybe ask Romsey to touch her there, but a shock of pleasure shot through her and she gasped instead.

He picked up speed, pressing her fingertips against her clitoris and moving their hands so quickly over her flesh that wave after wave of ecstasy came over her. She began to see, to understand...

She wanted more. She wanted him to touch her, to put himself inside her, to at least thrust his fingers into her. She ached to be filled, to be...satisfied.

"*Simon*." His name fell from her lips, but she couldn't find a single other word to say, to beg for what she wanted.

But then it wasn't necessary. He moved their hands down once more, slicking them again and repeated his frenzied attack on her clitoris.

Then his hand was gone. She fumbled, pausing for a moment and losing the thread of what had been barreling down on her.

"Don't stop," he urged. "Harder. Faster. Let your legs fall open. Give yourself what you crave."

She did what he'd taught her to, ravaging her flesh with hard, desperate caresses. Without thinking, she thrust her finger inside and cried out as it happened. *Orgasm.* Her belly pitched, and her muscles clenched so hard, she marveled at her own body. Or she would have if she hadn't been so utterly wrapped up in delicious darkness, a cocoon of rapture so lush and so gratifying that she never wanted to come out.

And yet she did.

She'd no idea how long it took, but she emerged from the other side, opening her eyes as her breathing started to slow. His lips were parted as his own breath came in harsh rasps, as if he'd come with her on the journey.

"Did you...orgasm too?" she asked softly.

"No. I don't think that would be wise."

Why not? She'd never felt anything so wonderful, so fulfilling, so bone-meltingly satisfying. Her limbs felt heavy and sated, as if she could sink completely into the pallet.

She blinked, noting that his face was still drawn with tight lines. "Why not? Can't a man pleasure himself?"

He smiled again, his lips spreading into a heart-stopping grin. That's just what Diana's heart did for a brief second—it stopped and flipped over before picking up its rapid pace once more. "Yes, we can. In fact, I think I must. But not here. Go to sleep. I'll see you in the morning."

He pulled the blanket back and sat up. The firelight splashed across his naked torso, revealing for the first time the smooth plane of his masculine flesh to her. She didn't look away. She couldn't, not when she wanted to touch the muscles sculpted into him, the arc of his shoulder blade as he turned away from her.

She reached out and grabbed his arm, her fingers closing around his bicep. "Where are you going?" The question came out a bit louder and harsher than she'd intended.

He turned his head. "To...take care of things."

"But—"

"We've had enough lessons for one night. Please, Diana, let me go."

She uncurled her fingers from his flesh and lay back against the pallet, her gaze never leaving his body as he drew his breeches on over his small clothes and pulled his shirt over his head. Then he went to the table, where he put on his boots. A moment later, he was gone from the room, leaving Diana to wonder what she had done to drive him away.

Chapter Five

❦

HE'D BARELY SLEPT at all.

As the first tendrils of gray morning light crept beneath the curtains on the window, Simon blinked. But he *had* slept. Otherwise, he wouldn't now find himself tangled with Diana.

Her back was pressed to his chest, her leg thrust between his. Despite frigging himself in an embarrassingly short amount of time last night, his cock was hard and eager against her hip. This was bloody torture.

He eased himself away from her, putting scant, but necessary, inches between them. He rolled to his back and draped his hand over his eyes to block out not just the burgeoning light, but the memory of last night.

And failed miserably.

The eagerness of her enticing arousal and the innocence of her ardent response had completely undone him. He'd nearly spilled himself as he lay beside her. He sensed that she wouldn't have minded if he'd finished himself right then, but he couldn't bring himself to do it. He'd already gone too far. How in the hell were they going to spend today together in the close confines of the coach? Let alone the rest of the days? Thankfully, they were about halfway to their destination. Maybe three or four more nights. He prayed the weather continued to hold.

Removing his arm from his eyes, he looked over at her again. Her beauty stole his breath. She was now on her back, her dark lashes fanned over her pale cheeks, and her dark pink lips beckoned for his kiss.

He practically jumped off the pallet in his eagerness to be away from her. He dressed quickly and quietly, then pondered what to do next—wake her or steal outside to frig himself again?

He didn't get to decide because Ogden chose that moment to leap out of bed stark naked. "Morning, Byrd. I trust you slept well!" He chortled, then shuddered. "Damn me, it's cold!" He quickly found his shirt and drew it over his head.

Simon turned from him and peeked around the pallet to see if the ruckus had awakened Diana. She was rubbing her eyes and pushing herself up to a sitting position. The blanket fell to her waist, exposing the thin lawn of her night rail. Simon could make out the gentle curve of her breasts and quickly jerked his gaze up to her face. That wasn't any safer. Her lids were still heavy and her lips parted. She looked as if she'd just been shagged. Or maybe that was only his wishful thinking.

Shit, he was in trouble. He never should've done what she'd asked last night.

And now he had to help her dress. His actions had consigned him to hell. A hell he likely deserved for taking advantage.

But had he? She'd asked him to show her. He hadn't taken anything from her.

"Shall we go downstairs and let the women dress?" Ogden asked.

Simon looked over at the man, who'd just sat on the bench at the end of the bed to draw on his boots. Before answering, he took a step toward the pallet. Diana's gaze lifted to his. A gorgeous blush stained her cheeks, and she simultaneously tipped her head down and pulled the blanket up to her chin.

"Just a moment," Simon said, moving behind the screen. "Do you want me to stay and help you?" he asked softly, then winced at the words that could be taken a number of ways, given the way he'd "helped" her last night.

She shook her head and answered quickly. Too quickly, almost. "No, Mrs. Ogden is a fair ladies' maid. I'll see you downstairs."

He nodded, hating this distance between them. He'd thought they'd become good travel companions, if not friends. Turning, he grabbed his hat from a hook on the wall and left the room with Ogden on his heels.

Ogden elbowed him as they strode down the corridor to the stairs. "Sorry if we bothered you last night. I'm afraid Mrs. Ogden can get a bit noisy."

Simon said nothing but flicked him a half smile.

"Sounded like Mrs. Byrd was enjoying herself," Ogden said with a grin.

Yes, it had sounded like she did. It had looked like it too. Watching the flash of ecstasy on Diana's face had given him the first burst of pure joy he'd felt in over two years. He was both delighted and angered. He didn't deserve to feel that again. Somehow, it sullied Miriam's memory, and that was something he had to protect above all else.

They descended the stairs and met with the innkeeper, who'd prepared packages of food for them to take along. Simon found his coachman and told him they'd leave within the half hour. He wanted to get as far away from this inn as possible.

A few minutes later, the women arrived downstairs, and the innkeeper sent a boy up to fetch their luggage.

Mrs. Ogden went directly to her husband's side, smiling warmly up at him. Diana, on the other hand, could barely look in Simon's direction.

Eager to be on his way, Simon turned to Ogden and shook his hand.

"Thank you again for your kindness last night. Safe travels to you." He looked at Mrs. Ogden. "And to you."

"To you as well, Mr. Byrd," Mrs. Ogden said. She turned to Diana and gave her a fast, tight hug. "Goodbye, Mrs. Byrd."

Diana's eyes glazed with surprise. "Um, goodbye."

Simon put his hand under her elbow and escorted her out into the cold yard. She shivered, and he blamed the cold.

"Come, let's get into the coach. Tinley is fetching coals for the box. We'll have you warmed up in no time."

She cast him a wary look, and he realized they'd need to have a frank discussion as soon as they were in the coach.

A scant ten minutes later, they were situated inside, the warming box beneath their feet and the wool blanket draped over their legs.

"I must beg your forgiveness this morning," he said without preamble.

"There's nothing to forgive." Her voice was tight and small.

He had a hard time believing that. She could barely look at him, and she was pushed up against the side of the coach in an effort to ensure she didn't touch him at all.

"Then why are you acting so skittish?"

The coach rumbled forward, taking them out of the yard and onto the road.

"I'm not."

She wasn't making this easy. In fact, she was frustrating the hell out of him. "You won't look at me. You're not even completely under this blanket, which can't make you comfortable. You're upset with me."

She looked at him then, her blue eyes vivid and intense in the dim light of the gray December morning. "I am not. I'm upset with *me*. I never should have asked you to do that last night."

Of course she regretted it. Any well-bred young woman would. Which was why he never should have done it.

"The fault is mine."

Instead of calming her, his words seemed to have the opposite effect. Her shoulders puffed up, and her eyes sparked. "It is *not*. I put you in an unconscionable position."

She blamed herself? He thought for a moment, considering everything he knew of her, of her upbringing. Of course she blamed herself. She would've been taught to do that. "Not unconscionable," he said lightly. "I would say enviable."

She pursed her lips and stared at him.

"Any man would've killed to do what I did."

"I'd wager none of them would have been as good at it."

Oh God, nothing she said could've been worse. Or better. Hell, this was a tangle.

"Miss Kingman," he began, forcing himself to revert to a more appropriate form of address. "What happened last night was wonderful—to me, anyway."

"It was to me as well," she said hastily, and again, color rose in her cheeks.

He found her hand beneath the blanket and gave it a squeeze, releasing it quickly for fear he wouldn't let go. "You mustn't be embarrassed. Not with me."

She was quiet a moment and managed to hold his gaze, which he sensed took great courage. "I'll try. It was…a singular event for me, which, of course, you know."

"As it was for me, which I think you also know." He curled his lips into a slight smile. "Let us remember it fondly—our night at the Jolly Goat—and let us not speak of it. Unless you want to."

"No, that's fine."

He thought so too. Better for them to go back to the way things were. "Good. Can we continue as we were?"

"I'd like that."

He pulled the blanket over so that it completely covered her, which left a bit of his leg exposed. She scooted closer to him—not so they were touching, but so that the blanket could cover them both. They were quiet for a few minutes, and Simon wondered if it was really going to be possible to pretend last night had never happened.

She finally spoke. "You play the role of Mr. Byrd quite well. Since you travel under this alias, may I assume that is how you've developed the particulars? The estate, for example."

"It's much easier to travel as a simple country gentleman instead of as a duke. Particularly the Duke of Ruin," he said wryly.

Her blue eyes were dark with concern. No one looked at him like that, and he wasn't sure what to make of it.

"I doubt the Ogdens would know about that unfortunate nickname."

"Probably not. Sometimes I think it might be nice to be Mr. Byrd permanently."

Her brows climbed. "You'd like to run away and disappear? Is that why you suggested that course to me?"

He lifted a shoulder. "Regardless of what I may pretend, I am who I am, and I can't run away from being a duke." Nor could he run away from being the Duke of Ruin. Unfortunate as it may be, that *was* his identity.

"And here I thought there was nothing more confining than being a woman."

He laughed then, because of the irony in her tone. "I would argue that there isn't. I may be tied to a dukedom, but really, there are far worse things."

"Yes," she said quietly, turning her head to look out the window.

Damn. He wanted to ask what those things might be, certain that she'd experienced some of them, but wasn't sure she'd answer. They were getting closer, perhaps, to such revelations.

After another minute, she looked back at him. "Tell me about your *real* estate."

"Lyndhurst? It's, ah, quite a bit larger than Byrd's fictional home."

"How large?"

"Forty-seven thousand acres."

Her eyes rounded. "My goodness. I didn't realize. Usually a peer's wealth is roundly discussed or at least speculated about." Her gaze flicked away, and he sensed she wished she hadn't said that.

He didn't want her to censor herself. He was sure he'd heard every bad thing that could be said about him. In fact, some of the worst were things he'd said himself. "But not with me. Because of my reputation. No one cares about my wealth, not when they think I'm a murderer. Apparently, there is a line some won't cross when it comes to seeking power and privilege."

"You aren't a murderer."

There it was. People sometimes said that to him, but more often they simply avoided the topic as if they might somehow catch it, like an ague. As if discussing it could result in their death too.

"You don't know that," he said softly. "*I* don't know that." He turned his head toward the window and stared out at the passing hedges. The sky was gray, a bit darker than yesterday. In fact, the clouds were dark enough that he began to worry about precipitation. That wouldn't be good.

"How long have you been the duke?"

She'd decided on avoidance. He couldn't blame her. He tried not to bring it up, truly, but it was sometimes impossible. He was, as he'd noted earlier, the Duke of Ruin, the man who'd killed his wife and unborn child and didn't remember a bit of it.

"Four years."

"What happened to your father?" she asked.

Simon thought back to that dark period. It had been the worst time of his life, but paled in comparison to what had happened just a couple of years later. "He died suddenly—an accident. He'd been out touring the estate with the steward. His horse went lame, throwing him, and he had the grave misfortune to crack his head on a rock." He'd died instantly, according to Nevis, and grief had stolen over Lyndhurst.

"How awful. Were you close?"

"Yes, I suppose we were." But Simon knew he'd disappointed his father a bit, that his indulgences had exceeded even what the former duke had expected when he'd advised his son to sow his wild oats. When his father died, Simon had gone from the Marquess of Lyndhurst, rakehell extraordinaire, to Duke of Romsey, and there had been no question that he would leave his raffish behavior behind and somberly focus on becoming the duke. Simon had been committed to preserving his father's legacy. So he'd gone home, finished his education of managing the estate that his father had started, and soothed his mother. His sisters, married by then but still distraught, hadn't required his attention. As they were seven and nine years older than him, they'd never been particularly close.

"Is your mother still with you?"

"She's still alive, yes." But she wasn't "with" him. She'd abandoned him completely after Miriam's death.

Though he tried not to think of his wife, she was always somewhere in the back of his mind. This conversation brought her to the forefront, sharpening the pain that was always buried within his heart.

After mastering the estate, he'd turned his focus to finding a duchess. When the London Season earned him nothing for his trouble, he'd gone back to Hampshire. It was that summer, when he'd attended a local assembly, that he'd met her—Miriam. With her pale gray eyes, honey-blonde hair, and winsome smile, she'd stolen his heart. He'd never met anyone so sweet or kind or loving. They'd married that fall, and for the next year, he'd inhabited a state of bliss he'd never thought possible. He allowed the memory of that joy to wash over him, closing his eyes lest he spring too quickly into what had come next—unimaginable misery and sorrow.

"Do you want to sleep?" she asked, startling him from his reverie.

He was grateful for the interruption before he could tumble headfirst into the abyss of the past. "No. I was just thinking." Damn, he shouldn't have said that. Now she'd ask.

She moved her feet from the warming box. "About your family."

He exhaled in relief, glad she hadn't asked about Miriam. But why would she? He made sure everyone knew he believed himself responsible for her death. That shocked and frightened them, and they never broached the subject with him again. Except for Nick, but his best friend had learned to curb his inquiries. Instead, he offered silent support, for it was the only thing Simon would allow.

He yawned then, and Diana swung her gaze to his. "Are you sure you don't want to sleep?"

No, he wasn't. He'd gotten precious little last night, thanks to the temptress beside him. "Perhaps I should. For a bit anyway."

"I'm going to read."

"Here." He leaned forward to where a basket sat on the floor. Inside was the food from the inn and the books he'd brought. He found what she was reading, *A Gossip's Story* by Jane West, and handed it to her.

"Thank you."

She opened the book, tilting it toward the window. The light filtered across her face, arcing over the smooth plane of her cheek and the lush bow of her lips. He thought of those lips, rounded into an O as she'd found her release last night.

He closed his eyes tight in an attempt to banish such thoughts. His cock was already hardening, and he was glad for the blanket covering his lower half.

He couldn't afford to indulge such fantasies. He *wouldn't*. He would see her to Lancashire and perhaps somewhere else, if that was what she decided, but he had to keep his distance.

Which was easier thought than done. With each moment they spent together, he liked her more, he admired her more, he enjoyed her company…more.

None of that mattered, however. He couldn't have more from her—not now. Not ever.

Chapter Six
✤℈3✤

THE LAST TWO days had passed in a blur. The day before had been exceptionally long as they'd traveled through Birmingham, and they'd gone on as long as they could before finally stopping at an inn when it was already pitch-dark. Exhausted, Diana had fallen into bed fully clothed after dinner. Part of that had been her not wanting to ask Simon to undress her.

Simon.

She had a hard time thinking of him as Romsey now. After the other night.

They hadn't spoken of what had happened since the morning after in the coach, but she felt its presence between them, as palpable as the blanket she'd rolled up and placed in the bed the night before.

"Damn."

Diana turned her head sharply. She'd thought Simon was dozing, but he looked toward the window, his lips pressed into a thin, hard line.

"What's the matter?" she asked, growing concerned.

"It's snowing." He thumped on the roof with his fist, and the coach rumbled to a stop.

"What are you going to do?" she asked.

He looked over at her. "I'm not sure, but I need to confer with Tinley." The door opened, and the coachman stood outside. White flakes landed atop his hat and shoulders.

"It's snowing, Your Grace."

"I see that," Simon said, frowning. "Any idea how far we are from an inn?"

The coachman shook his head, his features drawn with a bit of concern. "No."

Diana had come to know Tinley quite well over the past several days. A burly man in his forties, he was quick to smile and lend a hand to other travelers. She'd never seen him look worried. She hadn't seen Simon look worried either.

Simon inclined his head. "Pick up the pace a bit, if you can. Stop at the first inn you come across. I don't want to be caught in this."

"Yes, sir." Tinley nodded before closing the door. They were quickly on their way again.

"It's going to be dark soon anyway," Diana noted, looking outside.

"Sooner than it ought, because of the storm," Simon said, his voice as grim as the steel-gray sky.

"I'm sure we'll find something." Diana wanted to reassure him even if she was also concerned. What would they do if they became trapped in the snow?

Simon settled back against the squab and let out a long breath. "I usually like it. It didn't snow terribly often at Lyndhurst, but I remember one occasion when we had a snowball fight. My father and I joined up with some of the tenants." His lips curled into a warm smile.

She'd never have been allowed to do that, even if it had occurred to her. "Didn't you get wet?"

"Of course, but it's terribly fun. Perhaps I'll pelt you with a snowball when you aren't looking."

She arched a brow at him. "Perhaps I'll get you first."

He shook his head, chuckling. "Miss Kingman, you are one of a kind."

She'd preferred him calling her Diana but wouldn't say so. Instead, she opened up her book to read, but quickly abandoned the occupation because the light simply wasn't good enough.

"Should I light the lantern?" Simon offered.

"It isn't necessary. I'm tired of reading anyway."

He cocked his head to the side. "I didn't think of bringing another activity for you. Such as needlepoint. Do you stitch?"

"On occasion. I don't particularly enjoy it." Because her parents had ensured she was exceptionally good at it—just as they had with dancing and playing the pianoforte. She'd been schooled in everything they'd deemed necessary to the point of guaranteeing she'd loathe every single thing they'd pressed upon her.

"Then it's good I didn't bring any."

The coach began to slow, and Diana wiped the condensation from the window to see outside. "There's an inn."

Simon exhaled again, his relief evident. "Good."

A few minutes later, they were stopped in a busy yard outside a large inn. Tinley opened the door. "We're a bit outside Brereton, Your Grace. This isn't the type of lodging you prefer, but it may be a while before we find something else, and the snow is coming down quite hard."

Diana looked to the ground, which was completely white. "We should stop."

"Yes," Simon agreed. He stepped out of the coach, then turned to help Diana down. "The inn is larger than I'd like, but it should be fine. We're so far from London now. I doubt anyone would know you out here."

"And they'll only know you as Mr. Byrd," she presumed.

"Perhaps. If they know me at all. Come, let's get inside." He took her arm and escorted her quickly into the common room. As soon as they were over the threshold, a small person barreled into them.

"Matthias!" A woman rushed toward them and picked the child up. He couldn't have been more than five. She looked aghast at Diana and Simon. "I'm so sorry. He's tired of being in the coach all day, I expect."

Diana smiled at the boy. "Me too. And snow is exciting, isn't it?"

The boy nodded. "I like snow. Mama won't let me go outside, though." He pouted.

"It's nearly dark," his mother said. "Tomorrow, if the weather is pleasant, you can go outside."

The boy had warm brown eyes the color of sherry. Dark lashes spiked out from them as he blinked at her. "Promise?"

"Promise." She tweaked the end of his nose and dropped a kiss on his head.

Diana's heart twisted in the presence of such maternal love. For the first time, she wondered what it might be like to have her own child. She'd love him or her so very much. She'd never force them to do anything or to be something they weren't. She'd love them just as they were.

Except she'd probably be married to a man who wouldn't let her.

Another child, this one a bit older than the first, came to the woman's side. "Mama, our room is ready."

"Oh good." She sounded weary as she flicked a look toward Diana and Simon. "Thank you for being so understanding."

After they were gone, Diana noticed that Simon appeared as tense as he had back in the coach when they'd first discovered it was snowing. "Do you not like children?" she asked.

He shook his head slightly and blinked, as if she'd disrupted his thoughts. Perhaps she had.

"I don't like or dislike them," he said. "Let me see about a room." He went to the innkeeper, who was just finishing up with the family.

Diana watched as they spoke for a few minutes and then Simon handed him money. Relief collapsed her shoulders, and she realized she'd been holding her breath. "There's a room for us?" she asked when Simon returned.

"The last one, as it happens."

"But what if more travelers arrive? Perhaps we'll have to take someone into our room, like the Ogdens did in Coventry." She fought the blush that started up her neck.

"We needn't worry about that. Our lodging is a rather small room on the uppermost floor. In fact, the rest of the chambers up there belong to the innkeeper and his family. He wanted to make sure we didn't mind cramped quarters. I assured him we were grateful for *any* quarters."

Diana couldn't disagree, but she did wonder what "cramped" meant. She hoped the bed was large enough for them to have space between them at least.

"Shall we go and see?" Simon asked. "Dinner won't be for a while yet."

She nodded, and he excused himself to dart outside. She turned and went to the window. Simon made his way to the stables, where Tinley had undoubtedly taken care of their team of horses. When Simon returned, he had their luggage. They climbed two flights of stairs to a landing where the top of Simon's head barely cleared the low ceiling. He gestured toward a door on the left. "There, I think."

She tried the latch, and it opened into a small, dim, cold room. She wrapped her arms around herself and shivered.

Simon set their cases inside and went to the compact fireplace. "Let me get the fire going."

Diana took stock of the space while he worked. It was their smallest lodging yet, with a rather narrow bed opposite the fireplace and a single chair in the corner between the hearth and one of two tiny windows.

"Oh, it's so dark in here!" A woman walked in—Diana had neglected to close the door—carrying a lantern and a basket of wood. "Here's more wood for you, and some light." She took the basket to Simon and set it on the hearth, then went to place the lantern on the small table in the corner next to the bed. Turning to Diana, she smiled. "I'm Mrs. Woodlawn. Welcome to The Happy Cat."

Diana hadn't paid attention to the sign in the yard. "I like the name you chose for your inn."

"We have several cats—all of them happy. I suppose we should have called it The Happy Cat*s*." She laughed softly. "Don't be surprised if one of them tries to sleep with you. Most folks don't mind, especially on a cold night like tonight. They're nice little warmers." She frowned at the bed. "Let me go fetch you another blanket or two. We don't often have guests up here, and you're going to need more covering than that." She turned and left, closing the door behind her.

Diana went to one of the windows and peered outside. It was nearly dark, but the lamp in the yard illuminated the white ground as well as the snow descending in fat white clumps. "I can't believe how much it's snowing. I've never seen such big flakes." She squinted. "Or maybe that's a bunch of flakes stuck together." She began to worry about how long they might be trapped here.

Turning from the window, she went to the hearth, where Simon had started a nice fire. She held her hands out to the warmth that it was just starting to generate.

He stood and brushed his hands on his breeches as he went to the window closest to the fireplace. His exhalation made her turn partially toward him.

"It doesn't look good, does it?" she asked. "What if we can't leave tomorrow?"

"There isn't much we can do if that happens. At least we're here and not stuck out there with no place to stay."

Yes, that was a blessing. But that didn't mean she had to be happy about staying here. "I will hope for a speedy thaw."

He rejoined her at the fire, peering at her askance. "I own I'm looking forward to the cat on the bed. Do you like cats?" His mouth tilted up. "Kitty?"

She laughed softly at her alias. "I suppose I should." She threw a glance at the too-small bed and wondered if the cat would be kind enough to act as a barrier. "I've never had one." Her father always had a pack of large hounds. The animals showed their allegiance to him and him alone, which was the way he preferred it.

Simon arched a brow at her. "Indeed? Not even in the kitchen to chase the mice away?"

"I don't know. I was never allowed in the kitchen."

"Never? Not even to sneak a cake?"

She'd tried once, when she was five, but that had earned her a week of nothing but bread and broth, and she hadn't been allowed cakes for a month. "My parents didn't like me spending time with the retainers." That was true enough. Long-buried memories rose to the front of her mind, and she flinched.

"Cold?" Simon asked, apparently noticing her movement.

"Y-yes. Warming up, though." She shoved the thoughts away, annoyed that her parents and her upbringing had intruded on her so much. She longed to focus on the future, to hopefully put her past behind her and maybe be like the cats here…happy.

"Good."

A rap on the door was followed by Mrs. Woodlawn greeting them again. "I've brought extra blankets." She set them on the bed. "I'll make sure one of my boys tends your fire while you're downstairs for dinner. That is, if you're coming down for dinner?"

Simon's stomach growled, causing Diana to stifle a smile. He was always ravenous when they arrived at their evening destination. "Goodness yes, why wouldn't we?"

Diana was fairly certain it had been a rhetorical question, but Mrs. Woodlawn answered it nonetheless. "There's a couple who arrived before you, and they've asked to have dinner in their room. It's no trouble to bring yours up, if that's what you prefer."

"All the way up here?" Simon shook his head. "Absolutely not. We look forward to dining in the common room. Your hospitality is beyond compare, Mrs. Woodlawn."

She blushed, and her chest seemed to puff up. "Thank you, Mr. Byrd. We'll see you downstairs shortly—the mutton smells delicious!" She flashed them a smile as she took herself from the room, closing the door behind her.

Diana turned, warming her neglected backside. "You're a kindhearted gentleman. I think that's a rarity for men in your class."

"Is it?" he asked softly. "I aim to be pleasant and unobtrusive." He turned his attention to the fire, and she wondered if that was a hint of color stealing up his neck, or if it was merely a reflection of the flames.

He wanted people to like him. And why wouldn't he when the majority treated him as if he carried the plague? "I find you quite pleasant," she said.

When his gaze found hers, his eyes were intensely dark, the color of the coffee her father drank, with just a few of the gold flecks smoldering in their depths. The moment stretched between them until she felt warm all over and was fairly certain it wasn't due to the fire.

Finally, she blinked and looked away. "Shall we go downstairs?"

"Yes, I think we must." He opened the door for her and waited for her to pass, giving her a wide berth and trailing her down the stairs.

There were several people in the common room already. A couple in their fifties greeted them and introduced themselves as Mr. and Mrs. Emerson.

"I'm Byrd, and this is my wife," Simon said, smiling, as they moved farther into the common room. His hand lightly grazed the small of her back, and she realized she'd become accustomed to his light touches. Just as she'd become comfortable with playing the part of his wife. If it weren't for him calling her Miss Kingman when they were out of earshot of others, she might have forgotten that was really her name.

"Pleased to meet you," Mrs. Emerson said. She possessed kind, light blue eyes and a warm smile. "You sound as if you're from the south."

Simon nodded. "Indeed we are. And you have the lilt of a northerner."

"Leeds," Mr. Emerson said, his still-dark brows in contrast to his mostly gray hair. "On our way to Birmingham to see our son for the holidays. Or we were until the snow put a stop to our journey." He sounded a bit frustrated.

Mrs. Emerson touched his arm. "It will be all right. I doubt we'll be stuck here long. In any case, it looks to be a happy group. Whom I've met anyway. Apparently, there's a couple who aren't coming down to dinner." She pointed to a pair of women seated in the corner. "That's Mrs. Haskins and her daughter. They seem lively. They asked if we played cards." She blinked at Diana and Simon. "Do you?"

"Somewhat." Simon cast a reassuring look at Diana. He hadn't yet taught her to play.

"And those gentlemen over there are brothers," Mrs. Emerson continued, inclining her head to the pair of men standing near the hearth with cups in their hands. "The Misters Pickford."

The sound of several feet clambering down the stairs drew them all to turn their heads. "Ah, this must be the charming Taft family. Please excuse me, I must go see that darling girl."

Girl? Diana only recalled the two boys, but perhaps she'd missed something.

Mr. Emerson pivoted toward the bar that ran along the back wall. "I'm going to fetch an ale. Do you want one, Byrd?"

"No, thank you." Simon's gaze was trained on the base of the stairs, where the Taft family had just emerged. Mrs. Emerson greeted them, much the way she had Simon and Diana. She immediately took a small girl, perhaps two or three years old, from the mother's arms, and spoke to her animatedly.

The boys dashed off to one of the larger tables, where they sat down and pulled out toy soldiers. Diana started to take a step toward the family. "Shall we go and welcome them?"

He grabbed her arm tightly, almost painfully. "No."

She turned her head and looked at him sharply. "That hurts."

His eyes widened, and he blanched, dropping his hand from her immediately. "I'm terribly sorry." The apology was soft and raspy, almost anguished.

Something about his demeanor worried her. It was worse than the concern he'd displayed earlier when the storm had started. "Let's go and sit down, then."

When he didn't move, she gently touched his arm and guided him to turn. He allowed her to lead him to a table in the opposite corner from the Haskins'. She sat so that she could see the room, while Simon's chair pointed toward the corner. Whatever was bothering him, hopefully he could put it out of his mind.

"Is it too late to have that ale, I wonder?" he murmured.

She'd heard him, and it only added to her growing alarm. She leaned across the table. "You want ale? I can get it." She started to rise, but he reached over and briefly touched her hand.

"No, I wasn't serious. I'm not going to drink any ale."

"Tea, then. I'll get some tea." She got up and hurried to the bar, where she asked the innkeeper for a pot of tea. If he found the request odd, he didn't say so, for which she was relieved. Simon's drinking habits weren't normal, but they were perfectly respectable.

She'd heard he didn't drink spirits, and he'd confirmed that. What they hadn't discussed was why. The rumor was that it was because of his wife's death, that he'd been stinking drunk when she'd tumbled down the stairs. If that were true, she could well understand why he would abstain. Why then would he suggest he might want an ale now?

A high-pitched squeal drew her to turn to where Mrs. Taft sat with her daughter at the largest table in the room. The boys were there playing with their soldiers, and a gentleman, perhaps Mr. Taft, seemed to be the reason for the child's excitement. He had a doll in his hand and was hiding it beneath his jacket only to pull it back out with a grand flourish. He did this three times before delivering her the toy. And each time, she squealed and laughed happily.

Diana made her way back toward the table. Simon had turned his head and was staring at the family again. She sat down and when he still didn't avert his attention away from them, calmly asked.

"Is there something wrong?"

He looked at her, appearing startled. "No."

She didn't believe him. His color was off, and she could tell he was tense. "I think you've mistaken me for someone who doesn't know you. Something is definitely wrong. You seem upset."

"You know me, then?"

"As well as you know me." Her mind jolted back to Coventry and just how well he'd come to know her. Perhaps she *didn't* know him as well as he knew her.

"It's the child." He turned his gaze away from her, staring out the window into the dark night. "She reminds me of… Never mind. Where's the tea?"

"It's coming." Suddenly, she knew the reason for his distress. The child reminded him of the child he lost. Along with his wife. Though she couldn't quite fathom the depth of his emotion, she felt a surge of empathy. "I'm so sorry. I think you must have loved your wife very much." That detail was never part of the tales surrounding his past.

"I did."

Without hesitation, she reached over and clasped his hand atop the table. His gaze snapped to hers. She said nothing, just gave his fingers a squeeze.

He arched a brow at her. "Careful. You're behaving like a wife."

"Or a friend." She withdrew her hand as the innkeeper deposited a tray with the tea service on the table.

Mr. Woodlawn wiped his hands on his apron. "Dinner will be out in a few minutes."

"Thank you." Diana poured their tea.

"You're managing me," he said.

"I'm helping. You're not going to be an arrogant toad, are you?"

He let out a laugh that warmed her. "God, I hope not. You're welcome to cuff me if I behave in such a manner."

"I'll do that." She wanted to ask about his wife, but, seeing that his mood was starting to pick up, abandoned the topic. Some day there would be an appropriate time for them to discuss what had happened and, more importantly, his feelings about that.

She hoped.

Perhaps they'd part ways before that happened. Wanting him to know she cared, she said, "I'm here should you ever wish to unburden yourself."

He gave her a saucy look, and it seemed he was back to his regular self. "That could be taken any number of ways, Mrs. Byrd."

She rolled her eyes as she lifted her teacup. "Here comes our dinner."

They kept the conversation light as they ate their meal, but she noticed he avoided the children and seemed relieved when the Tafts went upstairs. Not long after, they said good night to the remaining patrons and made their way up to their small second-floor room.

Diana allowed him to help her disrobe, but they were quick about it. He presented his back while she finished dressing for bed, and didn't turn around until she had the covers pulled up to her chin. The familiar rolled-up blanket was situated between them but she realized she was very near the edge of the narrow bed.

A few minutes later, he climbed in beside her and pulled the blankets up. "Ah, I'm afraid I don't have much space," he said gently. "Can you move over a bit?"

"Unfortunately, I can't." She winced, knowing what was coming next and frustrated with herself for not having the courage to suggest it first.

"We could remove the blanket. Honestly, it's cold enough that I think I would appreciate the extra covering. What's more, combining our body heat without the barrier is probably smart."

He said it so matter-of-factly, as if there weren't a multitude of things that could arise from sharing a bed so intimately. But really, what was she afraid of? He wouldn't take liberties, of that she was certain.

Then what was it?

That she'd want him to.

Oh, yes, that was a true fear, and one she mustn't think about. Fears only became worse if you entertained them.

He broke into her rambling thoughts. "It's all right, I'll make do." He started to turn, and the bed creaked with his movement.

"No, you're right. We should move the blanket." She pulled it up from beneath the covers and sat up to unroll it.

He joined her, and their hands touched as they both reached to spread it out across the bed. Their gazes locked in the dim light from the fire—and held.

She didn't know how long they sat like that, but it was long enough for a thrill to steal across her shoulders. She shivered.

He held up the covers. "Back into the bed with you. I'll apologize now if I get too close in the night, but it's only to keep warm, I assure you."

She settled into the mattress, snuggling deep beneath the covers and staying as close to the edge as she dared. Still, she felt his heat behind her, and instead of being scandalized, she felt…pleasant.

As she drifted off to sleep, she thought it might not be bad if he cozied up with her, not because he was cold but because he wanted to.

Chapter Seven
⋆ℰ⋆3⋆

A LIGHT RAP on the door pulled Simon's eyes open. He was aware of two things: someone was coming into their room, and Diana's body was pressed up against his, her hand resting on his chest with two of her fingertips breaching the V-neck of his nightshirt so that they were flesh to flesh. Simon gently took her hand and tucked it to his side before bringing his head up from the pillow.

The intruder was a boy. He glanced toward the bed, and seeing that Simon was awake, pointed at the fireplace. Realizing the boy was here to tend the fire, Simon nodded. He raised his finger to his lips and gestured toward Diana with his head. The boy bowed and went about his work.

Simon lay back and stared at the low, pitched ceiling. Diana moved softly against him, her hand moving over his arm and resting on the underside of his elbow. It seemed she wasn't content unless she had a hold of him. He didn't mind that. No, in fact, his cock was quite pleased to have her touch.

Shit. This was Coventry all over again. Well, not precisely. At least last night, he hadn't completely overstepped propriety and showed her how to pleasure herself. He'd permitted one transgression with her. He wouldn't allow another.

Just one?

What of stealing her away to the north of England and utterly changing her life? She couldn't go back to her family without facing certain outrage and castigation, not to mention the public scorn she may endure. He hoped she would choose beginning her life anew in a place where she wasn't known. Lord knows he would've done that if he could. Dukes, however, couldn't disappear. But they could wander, especially when no one much cared.

The boy finished and left. Regretfully, Simon removed Diana's hand once more before slipping out of the bed. The room was cold, but the replenished fire was beginning to warm it up. Eager to see if they could leave, he went to the window. His heart sank, for the yard and road beyond were completely covered in a thick blanket of white. The sky was dark and gray, and it looked as if it would snow again.

Blast it all.

"What is it?"

He turned from the window to see Diana sitting up in bed, rubbing her eyes. He stared at her for a moment before answering. She was unbearably lovely, her dark hair braided into a thick rope that draped across her right shoulder. He followed the line of that braid and couldn't help but appreciate the swell of her breasts beneath her night rail. He jerked his gaze back to her face just as she was blinking at him, her features still creased and drowsy with sleep.

"There's quite a bit of snow on the ground," he said. "And it looks to snow again."

"We can't leave today?"

"I'm afraid not."

"Then I guess we get to have a snowball fight." Her lips curved into a smile that made his heart jump.

"I thought you were afraid of getting wet. It's not as if we have an endless supply of clothing. At least not with us. I imagine you have a vast wardrobe."

"Too vast, truth be told." There was an edge of distaste to her tone. Last night, she'd talked of coming to know him well. He'd come to know her too, and she did not like playing the role of debutante.

"Come, then, let's get dressed, and we can have a small snowball fight." He realized he wasn't dressed at all. He wore a nightshirt that hung to his thighs. And nothing else. He'd been careful to be dressed in front of her, and here he was standing here in the dim morning light, practically naked.

She knew it too. Her gaze had traveled slowly over his form and now she worked to keep her attention focused on the coverlet, which she clasped to her chin. "I'll just wait here until you're dressed."

"I'll be quick." He went about pulling on his breeches and the rest of his clothing. When he'd put on his waistcoat, he turned the chair away from the bed and sat down to tug his boots on. "I'm busy with my boots, and my back is to the bed."

"Thank you."

He listened to her movements, by now aware of what she was doing by the sound. So it didn't come as a surprise when her voice came from just behind him. "Can you help with my corset?"

"Of course." He rose and tied her undergarment, pulling it tight around her torso. He always strove to keep his knuckles from grazing her, but sometimes, he failed. Today, he brushed her spine and almost flinched in his hurry to pull his hand away.

"Let me help you with your petticoat and dress," he offered, as he did every day. He went to the hook on the wall where her garments hung and brought them back to where she stood. Laying the dress on the bed, he started with the petticoat. She lifted her arms like a supplicant, and he drew the fabric over her head. He repeated his movements with the dress, and once she settled the garment around her slender frame, he laced it closed, tucking the ends inside when he finished.

She smoothed her hands over the skirt. "Thank you. While my wardrobe is too large, I do miss the variety. I'm a bit sick of this gown."

"You have another, do you not?"

"Just one, yes."

"Then I shan't worry about getting you wet."

"Not too wet," she cautioned, her blue eyes sparkling. "I don't have another petticoat or corset, and I don't want this gown to be wet when we depart tomorrow."

If they were able to depart tomorrow. No, he wouldn't think of that. Anyway, weren't there worse things than being trapped with a beautiful young woman whose company he enjoyed more than anyone he'd met in the past two years?

She sat down and put on her stockings and half boots while he shrugged into his coat. He waited near the fire as she wound her braid into a circlet at the back of her head, using her discarded pins from yesterday. The glass hung near the hearth, and when she finished, she pivoted toward him.

"You look beautiful." He'd thought the words every morning of their journey, but today was the first time he said them.

She blushed and looked at the fire. "Thank you," she murmured.

They grabbed their cloaks, hats, and gloves and went downstairs to the common room. Only Mr. Taft and the two boys were present.

"Slow down, Matthias, the snow will still be there." The man chuckled as his younger son continued to shovel food into his mouth. Simon remembered what it felt like to be a boy filled with excitement for the day ahead. There was nothing else, just the very next thing. It was an excellent metaphor for the life he'd been living the past two years. Minus the excitement, of course.

This time with Diana was the most forethought he'd given to much of anything, save the house party he'd attended last fall with Nick. He glanced over at his companion.

That event had ended poorly, at least for him. During an excursion to St. Andrew's Cathedral in Wells, Nick's fiancée—well, his *other* fiancée—Violet, had tripped and fallen. Because she'd been alone with Simon, everyone had assumed the worst. Or so it had seemed. Simon hadn't stayed to find out. He'd fled the cathedral, returned to the house, packed his things, and departed immediately.

What had Diana thought of that? He shouldn't ask, but he was always perversely interested in what people said of him. *Probably,* a small voice in the back of his mind whispered, *because you keep hoping something will finally be kind.*

He guided her to the table where they'd had dinner last night. Mrs. Woodlawn came over directly with tea and toast. "I'll bring some ham, kippers, and some eggs."

"Thank you," Simon said while Diana poured. She'd taken to drinking tea with him at all times of day, though she'd also sipped a sherry or two. He didn't fault her for it. He was humbled that she sought to join him at all.

"Were people surprised when I left the house party this past fall?" Apparently, he wasn't able to contain himself. He was, as his mother had told him after his father's death, weak.

She looked up at him in shock, blinking after a brief pause. "Surprised? I don't think that's the proper way to characterize it."

When she didn't offer the *proper* way, his curiosity got the better of him. "And how was that?" She blanched, and he realized he knew. He picked up his teacup in a show of nonchalance lest she think he was upset—he wasn't. This was what he'd become accustomed to. "They were relieved to be rid of me finally. I'm sure they blamed me quite thoroughly for Lady Pendleton's tumble."

Except being accustomed to people thinking the worst of him was nothing compared to actually having the worst happen. *Again.* One moment, Lady Pendleton had hold of his arm, and the next, she was gone, sprawling beside him while he did nothing but gape in horror.

The vision of his wife at the bottom of the stairs, her body broken, filled his head now as it had then. It was the only thing he remembered from that night aside from holding her and begging her to live. His hand began to shake, and he hurriedly put his teacup back down.

"She wouldn't let them," Diana said. "Lady Pendleton was quite vocal in her defense of you. And of course the Duke of Kilve supported her." She looked at him squarely. "I didn't believe it. Neither did my friends."

No, the younger set had been quite genial. Maybe, in time, people would forgive him. Not that it really mattered since he would never forgive himself.

"That's kind of you."

She leaned forward, her eyes gleaming. "What Lady Nixon and Mrs. Law fail to realize is that every time they say something about someone, we younger people are inclined to believe the opposite. That is, the younger people with sense. They're horrid old hags."

Simon barked with laughter. He couldn't help himself. It was the most he'd ever seen Diana let down her guard. "Is that what you called them?"

She sat back and picked up her tea. "Among other things." She arched a brow before she took a sip, and though the cup blocked her mouth, he suspected she was smiling.

"I like this side of you." And upstairs she'd said she wanted to have a snowball fight. This was a Diana he hadn't seen, a Diana he doubted *anyone* had seen. He felt privileged to spend time with her.

"Now, about this snowball fight," Simon began.

Mrs. Woodlawn interrupted them with the arrival of their breakfast. "Did I hear you say snowball fight? The Taft boys will be thrilled. They've been discussing having one all morning."

Simon tensed, and the despondent feeling he'd battled all last night during dinner while the Taft family taunted him from the center of the room came rushing back over him. It was impossible to look at them, especially the young girl, without thinking of Miriam and their child. He'd no idea what she was carrying, of course, but he'd been confident the baby was a girl. With shining honey curls and pale gray eyes like her mother.

They aren't your children.

No, but they could be. He wanted them to be. Not *them*, of course, but he wanted children. He'd wanted Miriam's children. His heart ached, and his throat burned for a quick moment.

He coughed lightly as he got a handle on his emotions. "Then we'll have to make sure they get one." He smiled up at Mrs. Woodlawn, who grinned in response.

After she was gone, Diana's brows pitched low over her eyes. "You don't have to do that."

"Do what?" He sliced into the tender ham.

"You also don't have to be obtuse," she said lightly. "It won't bother you to spend time with the children?"

It might. But he was determined to rise to the challenge—and emerge victorious. "It will be good for me. I think," he added quietly before shoving a too-large bite of ham into his mouth.

When they were nearly done with breakfast, Mrs. Woodlawn returned with a blanket. "This is for you to wear outside while you watch the snowball fight."

"Oh, I'm not watching," Diana said with a fair amount of grit. "I'm participating."

Mrs. Woodlawn's eyes widened. "I see. Well, then I know who I'm cheering for." She winked at Diana as she folded the blanket over the back of Diana's chair.

Diana sat forward until the wool was situated, then thanked Mrs.

Woodlawn for her thoughtfulness.

A moment later, the younger Taft boy came over to their table. He had dark brown eyes and sandy-colored hair—the kind that had probably been nearly white when he was born but darkened over time. Simon's had been that way. "I'm Matthias. Mrs. Woodlawn says you're going to throw snowballs with us. Is that true?"

"It is. Have you ever made a snowball?" Simon asked.

The boy shook his head. "Is it hard?"

"It depends on the snow. We'll have to see what it's like."

"Let's go now." Matthias reached for his hand, which Simon had rested on the edge of the table. His inclination was to withdraw, but he steeled himself for the boy's touch.

Simon's gaze flicked toward Diana. She was watching him with the hint of a smile lighting her eyes.

"I suppose I've had enough breakfast," Simon said.

"Matthias!" Mr. Taft came to the table and took the boy's other hand, prompting Matthias to let Simon's hand go. The father looked at Simon apologetically. "He's yet to learn all his manners."

"I think his manners are just fine," Simon said. He looked over at Diana. "We were just about to go outside for a snowball fight." She nodded slightly, encouraging him. He returned his attention to Mr. Taft. "I know Matthias is keen to join us. I hope you will too. And your other boy." Simon stared past the man at the older boy, who was now finishing the rest of the food on his brother's plate.

"They'd like that," Taft said. "I'll just fetch Jonathan."

Diana put on her hat, then rose, picking up her gloves, which she donned. Simon did the same after getting to his feet. "Come, Matthias. I'm Mr. Byrd, and this is my wife, Mrs. Byrd."

"I like birds," Matthias said. "There's a harrier nest in a tree near our house. I like to watch them hunt."

"I'm sure that's quite exciting." Simon moved to help Diana with her cloak and then arrange the blanket over her shoulders. Not that she needed his assistance. He realized he was simply looking for a reason to touch her—or almost touch her, as it were.

While they'd dined, the other guests had come down to the common room, save Mrs. Taft and her daughter. They arrived at that moment, just as Simon opened the door.

The chilly air swept over him, and he shivered slightly. It was quite cold. Their snowball fight was going to be short-lived. They'd best make it memorable, then.

"Are you ready, Master Jonathan?" Simon asked.

The older boy jumped up from the table, and he and his father moved toward the door.

"Where are you going?" Mrs. Taft asked. The high pitch of her tone seemed to indicate she wasn't in favor of this excursion.

Mr. Taft waved them on. "Go ahead. I'll be out shortly."

Simon didn't linger to watch the parents discuss the issue. He ushered Diana and the boys outside into the gray morning.

Not gray, precisely, because the white snow lent a brightness that wouldn't have been there otherwise. The blanket of white was pristine and perfect.

And then the Taft boys ran out into the yard, spoiling the flawlessness. Simon laughed.

"What?" Diana huddled beneath her blanket.

"I just remember what it was like to be that age." Carefree and invincible. As if nothing could harm him. "Are you sure you want to do this? You look to be freezing."

"I am. But I'm not letting this opportunity pass me by."

"We won't take too long. It is rather cold, and I'm confident it will start snowing again soon."

She looked up at the sky and winced. "Then let's hurry."

"How is this snow, Mr. Byrd?" Matthias asked.

Jonathan shook his head at his brother. "It's cold and wet, silly." He bent down and scooped up a handful, which he immediately tossed at his brother, hitting him in the shoulder.

"That wasn't a snowball!" Matthias said. "Only snowballs. Papa said!"

Simon went farther into the yard where the boys were facing off against each other. "You have to listen to your father."

Matthias pointed at his brother, his small face haughty. "I don't want to be on his side."

"I don't want to be on your side either." Jonathan crossed his arms over his chest.

"He's on my side." Matthias jabbed his thumb toward Simon.

Jonathan opened his mouth, likely to protest, but their father joined them just then. "I'll be on your side, Jon." Matthias immediately pouted, and Mr. Taft shrugged. "It's only fair, Matthias. I daresay Mr. Byrd may be better at this than me."

Jonathan looked horrified. "He *can't* be, Papa."

A feminine cough drew them all to turn.

"What about me?" Diana asked. "What team am I on?"

"Ours." Jonathan stared smugly at his brother.

"No fair," Matthias whined. "They have more people."

"I'll be on your team," one of the Pickford gentleman—the elder of the two—offered. Matthias stuck his tongue out at his brother.

"Then what side am I to be on?" the younger Pickford asked. "It will still be lopsided."

"Oh, well, I don't have to participate," Diana said.

Simon heard the edge of disappointment in her offer, and even if he hadn't, he wasn't going to let her bow out. "Of course you do. We'll find someone else to join us." He looked at the younger Pickford. "Whose side?"

"It seems to be brother against brother." He winked at Jonathan. "I'll be on theirs."

Matthias looked pleadingly up at Simon, his brown eyes wide and limpid. "We need someone else."

"Can I be on your team, Matthias?" The boys' mother had come out, and so had Mrs. Haskins and her daughter, who'd taken charge of the Tafts' daughter.

"What about Mary?" Mr. Taft asked before glancing back toward the inn, where Miss Haskins held the girl in her arms.

"She's fine," Mrs. Taft said. "So how about it, Matthias?"

He looked torn. Simon could tell he loved his mother, but that he maybe didn't think she'd be good at this endeavor. Crouching down to the boy's height, Simon whispered, "Are you worried that your mother won't be able to make snowballs?"

Matthias shook his head. "She's not a good thrower," he said gravely. And not too quietly. A quick glance toward Mrs. Taft and the quirk of her lip showed that she'd heard her son.

"I bet she makes excellent cakes. Am I right?" Simon asked.

Matthias nodded. "The very best."

"Well, then I wager she'll be exemplary at making snowballs. Shall we charge her with that duty? It's always best to have someone keeping up our supply."

The boy's eyes lit, and his lips spread into a wide smile. He looked at his mother. "Mama! Mama! We have the best job for you!"

She laughed and patted the boy's head. "So long as you promise me this will be quick. It's too cold to be out here long, and I swear I just felt a snowflake on my nose."

Simon looked up and was rewarded with a wet droplet landing square in his eye. He dropped his head down to his chest and blinked rapidly.

"Are you all right?" Diana's hand touched his bicep, jolting him to awareness.

He wiped his fingers over his eye and blinked some more. "Fine, thank you."

She nodded at him and walked away from him to join her team.

Everyone turned toward Simon and seemed to be waiting for him to take charge. It had been ages since anyone had looked to him. He hesitated, but only for a moment.

Clearing his throat, he addressed the group in a loud voice. "Since it's so cold, there will be a time limit on the fight. Five minutes." The Taft boys' faces instantly fell, but Simon jumped to reassure them. "It sounds short, but it will be a vast amount of time once you begin to get wet."

"I'm not going to get wet," Jonathan announced. "I'll be too fast to hit."

Simon smothered a smile at the boy's confidence. "Even so, you'll find it's plenty long enough. No throwing snowballs in people's faces—that will get you tossed out." The Taft boys looked even more dejected, and their father gave them both reproving looks. "If at any time you wish to remove yourself from the game, simply step over to the overhang. Or, if you're terribly freezing, go on inside." He looked around at everyone. "Is that acceptable?"

There were nods all around, albeit reluctant ones from the young boys.

Their mother put her hands on her hips. "Perhaps we should just go inside right now."

The boys immediately stood straighter and shook their heads. They lost their air of gloom, and anticipation crept over their features.

"We'll take one minute to make snowballs before we begin. Go!" He hurried to the doorway of the inn and asked Mrs. Haskins if she could keep time.

"I think Mr. Emerson has a pocket watch," she said. "I'll just run in and get it."

With a nod, Simon returned to his team, who were busily making snowballs under the guidance of Mr. Pickford, the elder.

"Mama, you need to make them faster if you're to be our snowball maker," Matthias said rather sternly for a child his age. His admonition was tinged in irony because he was having the devil's time with his own snowball.

Simon crouched down once more. "Here, let me show you." He scooped a handful of snow and curled his hand up around it. Then he covered the snow with his other hand and squeezed his palms together, keeping them rounded, to make the ball. "You want to press tightly to keep the snow together, but not *too* tightly or it will fall apart. It takes a bit of practice."

Matthias concentrated on doing precisely what Simon said. When he was finished, he opened his hands and smiled widely. "I did it!"

"Indeed you did." Simon stood and looked over at the small arsenal Mrs. Taft and Mr. Pickford had created. "And look how fast your mother has gotten. You must be very proud."

"Mama, you're doing ever so good!"

"Ever so well," she corrected with a smile.

"It's time to start," Mrs. Haskins called.

"Mama!" The girl, Mary, now standing in the snow next to Miss Haskins, clapped and grinned at her mother.

"I forgot one last thing," Simon said, looking about. The men who worked in the stable, as well as his own coachman, had gathered to watch. Tinley waved, and Simon nodded in response. "No leaving the yard. Ready? Go!"

It was as if the sky had decided to join in, because whereas small flakes had peppered him off and on, now large flakes floated down, adding to the mayhem. And it was mayhem. The other side had accumulated quite a few snowballs, and Mr. Pickford the younger was an excellent shot.

It wasn't long before Simon had taken a snowball directly in the gut. He looked for Diana and saw her making snowballs behind the others. She'd been given the same job as Mrs. Taft, apparently. Well, that wouldn't do. He knew she wanted to participate in the actual fight. He could think of one way to provoke that.

Throwing together a fresh snowball and grabbing one from their diminishing stash, he crept to the side and skirted the other team as they were focused on Mr. Pickford the elder—he was as skilled as his brother, hitting each of his opponents in equal measure. Jonathan was already rather wet. So much for his prideful prognostication.

Diana's attention was also on their advance, so she didn't see Simon coming. His snowball hit her square in the shoulder, causing her blanket to slip down.

Gasping, she turned. Her eyes narrowed at him. Without hesitating, she lunged for one of the snowballs she'd just made and tossed it at him. Unfortunately, it fell short.

He moved closer and threw his other snowball, this time hitting her in the behind as she bent to get another ball.

She jerked upright and gaped at him briefly before throwing two balls at him in quick succession. The first missed its mark again, but the second splatted against his chest. She laughed gleefully and grabbed two more snowballs. "Help me with Mr. Byrd!" she cried.

Oh damn. This wasn't going to be good.

Both Mr. Taft and Jonathan turned their attention toward him, pelting him with snowballs. Trying to back away, Simon slipped. He fell backward into the snow. Jonathan approached him with a snowball and smashed it into Simon's chest. "Did we win?"

Simon looked past the boy and saw that Matthias and Mr. Pickford the elder stood over Mr. Pickford the younger, who must have fallen also. "It doesn't appear so." He pointed across the yard.

"Time's up!" Mrs. Haskins called.

Simon looked over as Mary ran toward her mother. She didn't get very far as her little legs sank into the snow. Mrs. Taft hurried to her and swept the child into her arms.

"I like snow!" Mary declared.

Mrs. Taft retrieved the last snowball she'd made and handed it to her daughter, whose eyes widened with wonder. Simon's heart tugged. He could so easily imagine his wife and daughter...

"Can I help you up?" Mr. Taft asked the question, but Simon's gaze fell on Diana, who was staring at him in concern—and something else. Perhaps a bit of admiration. And damn, if that didn't feel strange.

"Yes, thank you," Simon said, grasping the man's hand and clambering to his feet.

The boys were now simply playing in the snow, leaving no corner of the yard untouched.

"Just another minute," their mother cautioned.

"You're quite wet," Diana said, joining him as she wrapped the blanket around herself more securely.

"You're barely so," Simon observed.

"A bit." Her lips curved into a winsome smile. "That was fun."

"It was, wasn't it?" It was perhaps the most fun he'd had in two years. Unless he counted the house party. Before things had gone to hell, he'd enjoyed himself, especially when they'd played Kiss the Nun. He couldn't keep himself from staring at her lips for a moment. "I wonder if we could persuade the others to play games, after we change clothes and warm up."

"Kiss the Nun?" Her eyes sparkled as a snowflake landed on her cheek. Her mind had been in the same place as his. How extraordinary.

With his fingertip, he brushed the snowflake away from her flesh. "Probably not that," he said softly.

The charged moment broke when Mrs. Woodlawn called from the doorway. "I've hot tea and coffee for everyone! And cakes, of course!"

"Come, boys, time to go inside."

When they didn't immediately come, Mrs. Taft added, "There are *cakes*." This drew their attention, and they ran toward the inn.

Simon escorted Diana inside where Mrs. Woodlawn was addressing the group. "I've set up two areas with hot water to get everyone out of their wet clothes and cleaned up as quickly as possible. I've gathered new clothes from your rooms—the women can go into the kitchen, and the men can stay out here."

Mrs. Woodlawn had pushed two tables together, and on them sat several bowls of steaming water, toweling, and some blankets—and clothes were piled on several chairs. He noticed a table with breakfast dishes, but it wasn't where any of them had sat. He wondered if the mystery guests who hadn't come to dinner had eaten breakfast while they'd been outside. They must prefer to keep to themselves.

"Come, ladies," Mrs. Woodlawn said, turning toward the kitchen.

Diana gave him a charming smile before disappearing toward the back of the inn with Mrs. Taft, Mary, and Mrs. Woodlawn.

Simon watched her go, feeling more content than he had in ages.

"You and your wife seem very much in love," Mrs. Haskins said approvingly. "I hope my daughter can make such a fine match one day."

He pushed a smile onto his face. "Thank you." Too bad it was all a lie.

Chapter Eight
❦

DINNER WAS A lively affair, with all the tables pushed together and the guests sharing the meal as if they'd planned to be snowed in together. Afterward, they played cards—which Diana fumbled through with Simon's guidance—while Miss Haskins read to the children by the fire. When Mrs. Taft left to put Mary to bed, Mrs. Woodlawn appeared in the common room with a large, shallow bowl.

"Time for Snapdragon!" she announced, clapping her hands together.

The boys cried with glee, and Diana couldn't help but smile. Snapdragon could be terribly fun—so long as her parents weren't around. And luckily for her, they were not.

Mr. Woodlawn hurried to move one of the smaller tables away from the others, and Mrs. Woodlawn set the bowl in the center. She looked down at the boys, who stood on either side of her. "You've played Snapdragon, then?"

They nodded. "You're going to light the brandy on fire, and then we must grab as many raisins as we can and eat them," Jonathan said eagerly.

"That's right," Mrs. Woodlawn said with a smile. "However, we're not going to eat them in this version. I don't want anyone burning their mouths. Here comes Mr. Woodlawn now to set the brandy alight." She looked about the room. "Who else is joining us?"

"Me," Mr. Pickford the younger said, moving toward the table.

His older brother followed. "I will too." He looked back toward Miss Haskins, who'd risen from her chair by the fire.

She blushed prettily, and Diana wondered if a match was in the making. "I'll play too," she said, joining them at the table.

"Anyone else?" Mrs. Woodlawn asked. "Or is this just for the unmarried folks?"

Diana nearly raised her hand to say she wasn't married, but quickly bit her tongue. Simon seemed to catch on to her near mistake and chuckled softly. "Do you want to play?"

"I think I do," she whispered.

"Then by all means, do. Be careful—don't burn yourself."

She stared into his deep brown eyes, the golden flecks near the center glowing like the bowl of brandy soon would. "You aren't coming?"

He shook his head. "I'll watch."

Diana stepped toward the table, "I'll play."

The six of them stood around the table, the anticipation palpable as Mr. Woodlawn lit a spill from the hearth and brought it to the bowl. "Only one hand allowed—unless you're under the age of twelve." He winked at the Taft boys. "Ready?"

"Yes!" the young boys cried in unison.

The innkeeper lit the brandy and the bowl was immediately aflame. Dozens of raisins bobbed about the liquid. It should be relatively easy to grab a few, at least. But one had to brave the flames.

Diana sucked in a breath and plunged her fingertips into the brandy near the edge. Heat licked her fingers, and she pulled back without a single raisin. *Blast.* Exhaling to settle her nerves, she tried again, working to recall how she'd done this last time. That had been a few years ago, Christmas at Beaumont Tower, after Verity's husband had gone missing. Perhaps Diana would spend this Christmas at Beaumont Tower too. No, she couldn't afford to stay that long—her father would find her.

Shaking those thoughts from her brain, she refocused on the task at hand before the fire went out. Or worse, before there were no raisins left.

Tensing her muscles, she narrowed her eyes at the flames. The key was to set aside your fear. Don't think, just act. It was, she realized, the opposite of how she'd been taught to live.

That only increased her resolve.

She thrust her hand into the flames, using her thumb and forefinger as pincers to snap up as many raisins as she could. She didn't think, just acted, moving with quick audacity. She was vaguely aware of Miss Haskins sucking on her finger and no longer participating, and of Mr. Pickford paying her attention.

But Diana was intent on her task. She didn't count the raisins, just plucked as many as she could before the fire went out. The flames began to die down, and there were only a few raisins left. Diana moved quickly and was the last to steal a raisin from the bowl, just before the fire was gone.

"Huzzah!" Mr. Woodlawn clapped, and the adults joined in as the Taft boys began counting their raisins.

It happened that they had the exact same amount, a disheartening fact to both of them.

"I wonder if Mrs. Byrd has won, however," Simon said, drawing everyone to look at the substantial pile of raisins in front of Diana.

He set about counting them, and when he was finished, she had won.

The boys seemed pleased with this turn of events, but not so much when their father informed them it was time for bed.

They said good night, and Matthias even gave all the women, including Diana, a hug before chasing his brother up the stairs. The rest of the guests said their good nights, but Diana noticed the lingering glances between the elder Mr. Pickford and Miss Haskins. Soon it was just Diana and Simon alone in the common room.

She scooped up all the raisins and put them into the bowl. "Thank you, dear," Mrs. Woodlawn said, picking up the bowl. "Can I bring you two a nightcap?" She looked to Simon. "Or tea?"

He smiled at her thoughtfulness. "No, thank you."

"Thank you, Mrs. Woodlawn," Diana said.

When they were alone, Simon peered at her with interest. "You were shockingly good at that game. How are your fingers?" He reached for her hand and held it up so he could inspect her reddened flesh.

"A bit sensitive, but it will pass."

He blew on them gently. "Does this help?"

A shiver danced over her hand and traveled up her arm, then shot down her spine. "A bit." Whether it helped or not, she didn't want him to stop.

"Do you think we can leave in the morning?" she asked.

He blew again before answering. "I'm optimistic. We had a good melt this afternoon." After the snow had finished falling that morning, the sun had come out and turned the yard into a muddy mess. "We should rise at first light just in case."

"Mmm." She was having a hard time focusing on what he was saying because of the way his thumb was stroking her hand and the proximity of his mouth to her fingers. She fought an urge to trace his lips.

She couldn't do *that*. Searching about for something to distract herself, she said the first thing that came to her mind. "You did well with the children today."

Blast, she probably shouldn't have said that. She didn't wish to dredge up bad memories, not when this moment was so lovely.

"They're good children," he said softly. "Matthias seems quite taken with you. I think you have a mother's instinct."

She wasn't sure she agreed. "They were enthralled with you. They spent most of the day reliving that snowball fight, and you indulged them—quite happily, it seemed. You even acted it out again in here." That had been after luncheon. The boys had taken on the roles of Simon and Mr. Pickford, who'd both fallen down in the snow. Simon had told them they didn't have it quite right, so he'd demonstrated the *correct* way to slip and tumble on his arse.

He dropped her hand and moved to the fireplace, his back to her as he stared into the flames. "I was looking forward to being a father."

She almost didn't hear him, but was glad she did. Moving slowly, lest she make him tense, she joined him at the hearth. "You still could."

He flicked her a look filled with doubt—and something far more sinister: self-loathing. "That's unlikely. I'd need a wife."

"Yes, you would. Don't you want one?"

He focused on the fire, his face impassive. "I did."

She turned toward him and moved closer, so that they were barely a hand's width apart. "What changed?"

"I don't think any woman would have me, not when she heard of my past. And I would never enter into marriage without telling her the truth."

"I think you underestimate yourself," she said softly.

He turned toward her, his gaze naked and vulnerable. "Do I? Then let me tell you the truth. I'm afraid, Diana. I'm afraid to marry again."

The weight of her heart nearly buckled her knees. She surrendered to her desire and touched her sensitive fingertips to his jaw, rubbing lightly against his flesh and feeling the whiskers starting to emerge. She thought of her revelation during Snapdragon and whispered, "Don't be afraid."

A soft creak from the stairwell was followed by "Oh!"

Diana dropped her hand from his face and turned at the sound of one of the boys. Jonathan stood on the bottom step, his eyes wide for a brief moment. Then he rolled them back into his head and snorted. "You're going to kiss like Mama and Papa." He made an expression of disgust, then dashed to a table and picked up a handful of soldiers. "Good night!" He ran back up the stairs.

Diana exhaled with relief, then smiled, turning back to Simon.

He was still staring at her with a passion that stirred her soul.

"Diana." He breathed her name across her lips a second before his mouth sealed over hers.

She returned her hand to his face and cupped it, then slipped her other hand around his waist, clutching him as he kissed her. His lips were soft and instructive, moving over hers with intent. This was different from Kiss the Nun, which had been a fast peck that had lasted perhaps a moment too long.

This kiss already surpassed that—both in length and intensity. That first kiss had been an awakening. This was a promise. And she wanted him to deliver on it.

His hands came around her, pressing into her back and drawing her tight against his chest. He was warm and hard. She felt safe and protected in the circle of his embrace.

He tilted his head slightly, and she felt moisture against her lips. His tongue. She'd heard of this kind of kissing, but had no notion how to proceed. Guilelessly, she opened her mouth and awaited his direction.

The changes in him were subtle, but she caught them. He held her a bit tighter. An almost imperceptible sound lodged deep in his throat. His mouth opened with hers, and he gently thrust his tongue inside.

The sensation was overwhelming. Desire burst through her. She curled her hand around the back of his neck and tipped her head back, giving him access to whatever he wanted.

What had been gentle and tentative was now strong and sure. He kissed her thoroughly, igniting a need she'd never experienced. Her sex pulsed as it had in Coventry, when he'd taught her to pleasure herself. She thought of that night, of that release, and realized she wanted that now.

This was nothing like her mother had told her. *Nothing.* But then she oughtn't be surprised that she'd been lied to. She'd been nothing more than an instrument for her parents' own ends.

Well, no more. Now she was living for herself. This moment and all the moments to come were for *her.*

She dug her fingers into his neck and met his tongue with her own, sweeping against his with delicious abandon and never wanting it to end.

The creak in the stairwell sounded again. Oh dear, what else had the boy forgotten?

"My goodness, I thought everyone had gone to bed."

That wasn't Jonathan. In fact, that wasn't a voice Diana recognized at all.

Simon ended the kiss but didn't release her. He looked over her shoulder and said, "We were just heading upstairs."

"Well, don't let us stop you," the woman said. She sounded haughty and self-important, like so many people Diana's parents chose to spend time with.

"Your Grace?" This was a masculine voice, and the pair of words he uttered sent ice spiking through every part of Diana's body.

Simon kept one arm around her and tightened his hold. "Don't move," he whispered. "Keep your back to the room."

Then he was gone, moving away from her, and she fought to keep herself from turning around. What she really wanted to do was flee up the stairs. If they'd recognized Simon, how long would it be until they recognized her as well?

"I'm sorry, I don't recall your name?" Simon said genially. He wasn't even going to *try* to convince them he wasn't the duke?

"Sir Fletcher Dunford-Whaley, and this is Lady Dunford-Whaley."

"I'd no idea any of the other guests were Quality," the woman said in her high-pitched tone of superiority. "If I had, I wouldn't have felt the need to keep ourselves apart."

"We didn't *have* to do that, dear," the baronet said in a quieter tone.

Lady Dunford-Whaley sniffed. "Of course we did. And actually, I'm not certain knowing His *Grace* was here would have changed my mind." She lowered her tone to say the last, but Diana still heard what she said and the way in which she said it. Irritation curled along her spine, and she gritted her teeth lest she deliver the woman a well-deserved set-down and reveal herself. She couldn't do that.

"Care to introduce your, ah, lady friend?" Sir Fletcher asked.

"We can't ask to meet the Duke's paramour," his wife said, again using a tone that was probably meant to be a whisper but wasn't.

Simon sidled close to Diana once more, his side against her back. He leaned in and spoke softly against her ear. "Let them think you're my mistress. I'll distract them while you start toward the stairs."

She nodded slightly, then waited for him to step away once more.

"As I said before, we were about to retire," Simon said evenly. "Please excuse us."

It was at that moment that Diana made a fateful error. She took a step toward the stairs but must have turned too much or in just the right way for the light from the fire to splash across her features.

Lady Dunford-Whaley's indrawn breath struck fear deep into Diana's heart.

"My goodness, it's Miss Kingman! Fletcher, this is that young woman I told you about—the one who was engaged to the Duke of Ice, the Duke of *Kilve*. But he left London, and then she did too. Rumors abound at what happened." She had the audacity to step toward Diana. "I would be the envy of everyone if you could just tell me—"

"You can't think to be so rude," Simon said coldly. If Diana hadn't already been struck with abject terror, his tone would have made her shiver.

As Diana crept slowly toward the stairs, she saw Sir Fletcher pull his wife to his side. He kept his voice low, but Diana was able to hear what he said, "He is a *duke*."

"The Duke of *Ruin*!" Again, she used her not-whisper, her voice seething. "He's Kilve's closest friend. Can you imagine? Did he steal his friend's fiancée? When people hear—"

Diana couldn't stand another moment. Without care, she picked up her skirts and ran upstairs.

Yes, he was the Duke of Ruin. And now she was ruined too.

•℥•3•

BLOODY FUCKING HELL.

This couldn't be worse if a playwright had penned it for maximum drama. He bit his tongue lest he use it to lash at the sniping bitch before him. On second thought, what did he care? She more than deserved it.

"Women like you are a menace," Simon spat. He looked at her husband, who'd gone pale. "My apologies, but I can't abide gossip, especially when it causes pain."

Lady Dunford-Whaley sniffed as she pushed back her shoulders. "I'm not the one running off with my best friend's fiancée. If she suffers pain, it's her own doing. And yours."

Simon advanced on her, baring his teeth in his rage. "You've no idea what she suffers or what's her doing or not. You're a presumptuous, self-important termagant with no business in polite Society."

Her eyes widened, and she gasped. "You can't speak to me that way."

"Actually, I don't need to speak to you at all. As your husband so aptly pointed out—I'm a duke." He pitched forward with a sneer. "*Regardless* of my reputation."

Her lips opened and closed, but she said nothing.

"Go upstairs, dear," the baronet said quietly, but with a steel that brooked no argument.

She snapped her gaze to his and pursed her lips before stamping toward the staircase. Simon watched her go but felt no relief.

"I'm terribly sorry," Lord Dunford-Whaley said. "My wife does like her gossip."

"This isn't gossip," Simon said.

"Well, it is, I'm sorry to say. You and Miss Kingman have eloped. Headed to Gretna Green, are you?"

Simon startled. He stared at the baronet, nonplussed for a moment. *Well, of course they were.*

Simon took a deep breath. "Yes. And we'd like to keep things quiet, at least for a few more days. Is there any chance of that happening?"

The baronet tipped his head to the side and back upright again, seeming to dither. "A slight one. I'll do my best to keep my wife quiet—it helps that we're so far from London, of course. But I daresay she's upstairs drafting a letter to her sister already." He winced.

"You could burn it," Simon suggested.

"I could. But she'll write another." Sir Fletcher shook his graying head. "Never you mind. I'll take care of it. Get yourselves to the anvil, and by the time anyone is the wiser, she'll be your duchess."

Except she wouldn't.

Fuck, fuck, *fuck.*

It seemed Simon could only think in curse words.

He gave a slight nod in lieu of saying good night and hurried up to the second floor, anxious to see Diana and hopefully put her at ease. Did he really think that was possible? There was no good end to this scenario, not unless she decided to disappear.

He opened the door to the sight of her pacing in front of the fire.

She briefly looked up at him but didn't pause. "I-I-I c-c-can't ev-even p-p-pack."

Simon had never seen her so distressed, not even when he'd told her that her fiancé wanted to marry someone else. "Why can't you pack?" He strived to keep his voice even and his tone soft.

"B-b-be-c-c-cause the c-c-c-lo…thes are s-s-still in th-the k-kitch-kitchen." She stopped pacing suddenly and took several deep breaths.

Alarmed, he moved toward her, taking slow steps lest he agitate her further. "Are you all right?" When she didn't respond, he wondered if she'd even heard him. "Diana?"

Finally, her gaze swung to his. Her blue eyes were as dark as midnight. "I'm f-fine."

"You don't sound fine."

She turned from him then and stared at the fire. Inhaling deeply once more, she took a moment to repeat, "I am fine." The words came out slow and measured, as if it had taken great effort. Was speech a problem for her? He wouldn't have guessed and yet he seemed to recall a few other times she'd struggled… He swallowed the question before he could ask it. Now was not the time to broach the subject.

"I spoke with Sir Fletcher, and he made the assumption we were headed to Gretna Green. I said we were and asked him to keep quiet for a few days to buy us enough time to get you situated."

She kept her gaze averted from him. "S-s-so…that's…m-my…choice…then?" She shook her head. "Th-that's…no…choice…at-at…all. You've f-forced my h-h-hand."

He moved to her side and tried to take her hand, but she crossed her arms over her chest. "It doesn't have to be your choice. It merely gives us the time we need to get to Blackburn. Then you can choose where you want to start anew."

She remained silent, staring into the fire, her shoulders stiff and her body radiating tension. It was a far cry from the embrace they'd shared downstairs. Whatever happened, he would remember that kiss for the rest of his days. He'd never thought to experience that rush of excitement, of desire, of the promise of joy again. She'd given him a beautiful gift, and he would cherish it.

He took a step back. "I'm going to speak with Tinley and ask him to be ready to leave at first light. I'll make sure our belongings are ready too." He turned toward the door and added, "I'll ask Mrs. Woodlawn to come up and assist you. Try to sleep, Diana."

He wanted to comfort her, but there was nothing he could say or do to fix things. She'd had choice taken away from her—first by her parents and their demands for a lofty match, then by Nick when he'd decided not to go through with their marriage, and now by Lady Dunford-Whaley who would certainly tell everyone that Diana had run off with the Duke of Ruin. Even if she wanted to go back to her parents and manage the scandal of not marrying Nick, she now had a much bigger scandal to deal with. And this one would ruin her.

His nickname had never been more bloody apt.

He made his way back downstairs and came upon Mrs. Woodlawn sweeping the common room.

She started when she saw him. "Oh! I thought everyone had gone to bed."

"I need to speak with my coachman."

She nodded and made only brief eye contact. Something was amiss.

"We met your other guests—Sir Fletcher and his wife." The harridan.

"I suspected that had occurred," she said carefully.

"Did you hear the conversation? I won't be angry if you did."

She met his gaze then, her cheeks turning a pale pink. "I did, but I didn't mean to. Lady Dunford-Whaley has a rather loud voice." There was a wealth of disdain buried in that true statement.

"She does indeed."

"Would you think terribly of me if I told you I'd hoped they would keep to their room until they left?" She winced, and tiny lines fanned out from the corners of her eyes. "I could only imagine what her presence would've done to our pleasant activities."

"I think my opinion of you, and of this entire establishment, just improved tenfold." He leaned forward with a wink. "And it was already quite good."

Her blush deepened. "Pshaw! You're too kind, Mr. Byrd." Her eyes widened, and her mouth rounded briefly. "Begging your pardon, Your Grace." She dipped into a curtsey.

He waved a hand, gesturing her to stand up. "Knock that off. I prefer Mr. Byrd. I travel with that name whether I'm eloping or not." Just saying that he was eloping sent a little shiver up his neck. He ignored the sensation. "Would you have a few minutes to go up and help Mrs. Byrd prepare for bed?"

"Of course, Your—Mr. Byrd."

"Very good. And remember, she's *Mrs. Byrd.*" He gave her a pointed look.

Mrs. Woodlawn nodded enthusiastically. "Certainly. And may I say, whatever your names and your current situation, you are a delightful couple."

Again, a shiver raced up his spine. *A delightful couple. Diana* was delightful. He was only delightful by association. And they weren't a couple, not really. But the fact that Mrs. Woodlawn believed they were filled him with a sense of satisfaction and at the same time left him feeling hollow.

"Thank you. We do appreciate your hospitality. However, I hope you'll understand when I sincerely pray we'll be able to leave at first light."

"I absolutely understand. I'll make sure to pack up plenty of food for you to take along."

Simon nodded, about to turn, then recalled what else he needed. "Our clothing is still drying in the kitchen, I believe. Will you be able to pack that up too?"

"It would be my pleasure. I think it's about dry now. I'll take care of it directly. After I see to Mrs. Byrd." She offered a smile before leaning her broom in the corner and heading toward the stairs.

Simon opened the door and stepped outside. A gust of cold wind stole his breath, and he pulled his coat tighter around himself as he walked briskly to the stable. While still chilly, it wasn't as cold as it had been last night. He hoped the temperature wouldn't drop too much more, if at all. He looked up, thinking they needed some divine cooperation. "For her, not for me," he whispered.

A young man greeted him at the stable door. "Can I help ye?" He opened the door wide to allow Simon to enter.

"I'm looking for my coachman, Tinley," Simon said, moving inside, where it was much warmer without the wind.

"Here." Tinley came from a doorway at the back. That had to be where the grooms and coachmen were staying.

The young man slipped away, leaving Simon and Tinley alone. The sound of a whinny from a nearby stall broke the silence before Simon spoke. "Will you be ready to leave first thing? And I mean *first* thing—as soon as we have enough light."

"I can be ready whenever you tell me to be, but it all depends on the weather. It was a bit muddy this afternoon."

"Yes, but the temperature has dropped enough to harden much of it. Anyway, it doesn't matter. We have to leave in the morning, even if we only transfer to another inn."

Tinley's brows rose. "Problem?" he asked quietly.

Simon's lip curled. "Couple of bloody scandalmongers."

Tinley grimaced. "They recognize you?"

"And her." Simon exhaled. There was nothing to be done about it now. He could wallow in frustration and anger, or he could push it to the recesses of his mind along with the other emotions he chose not to deal with.

"Well, that's a bloody mess."

"It could be, but hopefully it won't. We have a bit of time, but only a bit."

"Which is why we need to get on the road tomorrow." The coachman nodded sharply. "I'll be ready."

Simon clasped his retainer's bicep. Tinley was one of only a small handful of his staff that had stayed on after Miriam had died. "Thank you, Tinley."

Departing the stable, Simon looked up at the second-floor windows of the inn. He couldn't see anything—or more importantly, anyone—but decided to give Diana a few more minutes to ensconce herself in bed.

He slowly made his way to the inn. If he'd still been a drinking man, he'd find Woodlawn's supply of liquor and give Diana many, many minutes.

But he wasn't that man anymore. When he thought of the time he'd wasted—the women, the gambling, the drinking… It made him angry. And sad and agonizingly full of regret.

He'd always been glad that Miriam hadn't met him in London. She never would have given him a second glance, let alone allowed him to court her. He suspected Diana would've felt the same. She had little tolerance for the life she'd been raised to lead. How could she choose anything other than leaving it behind completely?

The choice seemed clear to him, and it wasn't a trip to Gretna Green. Though, he'd offer that if she wanted it.

Would he? Could he take her as his duchess? Live with her at Lyndhurst in the shadow of Miriam's death?

Simon's heart began to pound, and sweat speckled the back of his neck. It wouldn't come to that. She'd been horrified by the very idea of it.

And he didn't blame her one bit.

Chapter Nine

❦

DIANA EDGED CLOSER to the fire. She was so cold. From the inside out, she was just *cold*. And hollow.

Numb.

That was a familiar emotion. She'd schooled herself to feel that way with such frequency and ferocity that it was second nature. It usually provided respite and protection. Tonight, however, she was vulnerable in a way she hadn't been in a very long time.

She took a deep breath and forced herself to think. Unlike the past, she had choices. She wasn't being forced into marrying Simon at Gretna Green. She was, however, being forced into *something*.

Throughout their journey north, she'd considered two options: starting over somewhere new or returning to her parents to weather the scandal of her broken engagement and her father's fury. She still hadn't quite decided but had been leaning toward starting over. Just the thought of facing her parents after she'd run off made her feel sick.

But to face them now? Now that all of Society would know she'd run off with the Duke of Romsey? Her stomach churned. She didn't want to contemplate it. Which meant she had to disappear from her life forever.

Simon had promised to help her, and she'd no doubt he would. Even if it meant disaster for himself. With his reputation, it wouldn't be a stretch for people to believe he'd killed Diana, as he'd killed his first wife.

She could guess how it would play out. She'd disappear. He'd go back to London, and the rumors of their flight would greet him. As would her father's rage. Very clearly, she saw her father accusing him of disposing of Diana the way he'd disposed of his first wife, assuming he'd even married Diana at Gretna Green.

The agony Simon would suffer, to have to relive his worst moments all over again under the scrutiny of the vicious gossipmongers and scandal-hungry vipers of the ton… It was unconscionable.

And what if he were formally accused of her murder? Could she stay silent in her new life and watch him tried for a crime that hadn't even occurred?

Of course she couldn't. But maybe it wouldn't come to that… Oh God, was she really thinking of throwing him to the wolves, just to save herself?

A soft rap on the door interrupted her dreadful speculation. Was he back so soon? She wasn't ready.

She trudged to the door and opened it just a small crack. "I'm not—" It was Mrs. Woodlawn, not Simon.

The innkeeper's wife smiled warmly. "Mr. Byrd asked if I'd come attend you."

She'd forgotten, as if their conversation had happened hours ago instead of a few minutes. Opening the door wider, she tried to smile but failed. "Come in, please."

"At least it's nice and toasty in here," Mrs. Woodlawn said, closing the door behind her.

Diana went to the chair and sat to take off her half boots. Did Mrs. Woodlawn know anything about what had transpired? Diana decided she didn't have the fortitude to ask. She also didn't particularly care. Everyone would know soon enough.

Standing, she presented her back to Mrs. Woodlawn, who unlaced her gown. "Your other gown is dry," Mrs. Woodlawn said. "Mr. Byrd's clothing isn't quite. I'll have it all packed up and ready for you in the morning. I'll just take your bags downstairs with me when we're finished."

A bit of the tension leached from Diana's frame, and she relaxed under Mrs. Woodlawn's care. "You are too kind," Diana said.

"I'm happy to help. You and Mr. Byrd are such a fine pair."

This praise gave Diana a thought: perhaps she ought to reinvent herself as an actress. Her lips quirked up, and she had to swallow a laugh.

Mrs. Woodlawn helped take the gown over Diana's head, then assisted with the petticoat before setting to work on Diana's corset. "It's been so lovely to have you and the Tafts and the others here during the snowstorm. I so enjoyed watching the children play. My own wee ones aren't so wee anymore. My first grandchild will be here in the spring."

Grateful for a subject that didn't involve the scandal she was now facing, Diana looked over her shoulder at Mrs. Woodlawn. "How wonderful."

"Oh, it is indeed. My daughter has had some difficulty—she's lost a few babes—but this one seems to have rooted."

And there was another reason Diana wasn't overly enthusiastic about the state of marriage. There would be children, and while she wasn't opposed to them, the begetting of them could be quite harrowing. Furthermore, what if she was a terrible mother? What if she'd learned how to treat a child from the way her parents had treated her?

Mrs. Woodlawn stepped back. "All done, I think."

Diana could finish undressing and get ready for bed on her own. "Thank you, Mrs. Woodlawn."

"I hope I'm not being presumptuous, but you seem to have a bit of a dark cloud tonight. I hope everything is all right with you and Mr. Byrd. He'll be a good helpmate to you, far better than most of the gentlemen who come through here. It's clear he loves you very much."

Perhaps Simon should join her on the stage. Too bad dukes couldn't disappear. He'd tried, hadn't he? Traveling about as Byrd and yet being recognized as Romsey in spite of his efforts.

Diana merely nodded in response. "We appreciate your hospitality very much."

"I do hope you'll stop on your way back—if you come this way."

Of course they wouldn't. Diana wouldn't want to risk running into anyone like Sir Fletcher and his wife. And this inn was too large, too easy to get to. If not for the storm, they never would've stopped here. Instead, they would've found their usual small, out-of-the-way lodging, and their masquerade would be intact.

Mrs. Woodlawn stoked the fire up and found their bags before going to the door. "Good night, Mrs. Byrd."

"Good night," Diana said. "And thank you again."

She finished preparing for bed, swapping her clothing for her night rail hanging on the hook on the wall. As she slipped into the cool bed, she shivered and burrowed deep beneath the blankets. Rubbing her hands together to generate heat, she drew her legs up until she likely resembled a round lump.

Only a few minutes passed before she heard the latch click. Peering over the edge of the blankets, she made out Simon's shape as he closed the door and moved quietly into the room. Normally, she would close her eyes and will herself to sleep before he joined her, but tonight, she didn't. She watched him as he undressed in front of the fire, the light from the flames dancing across his bare torso as he stripped down to just his breeches.

He grabbed his night shirt and drew it over his head before removing the lower half of his clothing. Pity, she'd hoped to catch a glimpse of him nude.

She had?

And why not? She was curious. Their journey would be over soon, and then she'd likely never see him again. She'd expected to perhaps feel sad— she'd come to like him more than she'd anticipated—but after the kiss they'd shared, it was more than that.

That kiss... She'd spent far too much time thinking of her plight rather than relishing that glorious experience. It was another reason to loathe Sir Fletcher and his wife, for they'd interrupted a truly spectacular moment.

The desire that had sparked in her belly earlier that night kindled anew as she watched him. She recalled his hands on her back, the press of his chest against hers, the thrill of his tongue in her mouth. Suddenly, she wasn't cold anymore.

She stretched her legs out—she had to in order to give him room—and heard him move toward the bed. Closing her eyes, she decided to feign sleep. The mattress dipped with his weight, and she caught the scent of spice and leather. She could reach out and touch him, restart what had been stolen from them earlier...

"I can't just disappear." She whispered, but her voice was heavy in the quiet room.

"Of course you can. Don't worry about money or anything else. I'll take care of it."

"I can't let you do that. You'd be blamed for my...disappearance."

He inhaled sharply but said nothing. He lay on his back staring at the ceiling.

Diana gazed at his profile. He was an exceptionally handsome man, with a strong nose and a mouth that could deliver so much delight.

"I'm the subject of blame every day," he finally said. "This won't alter anyone's perception of me."

She propped her head on her hand, jutting her elbow into the pillow. "It could make it worse. Besides, you aren't guilty of anything."

He turned his head toward her. "Aren't I?"

"Oh, stop with that! I've no idea what you're guilty of because you won't say. But for me, you're guilty of nothing save trying to help me. Y-You've done more for me than anyone I've ever known. You are not a m-murderer."

He propped his head up, mirroring her pose. "You don't know what I am."

"Because you won't say." She wanted to know. She needed to know. "Did you kill her?"

He stared at her a long moment. Her pulse raced as she both anticipated and dreaded his answer.

He rolled over, presenting his back to her, then got to his feet.

Her stomach fell. He wasn't going to tell her. She should've expected it. She knew him well enough by now—he didn't discuss what happened to his wife. Not with *anyone*. Not even with his pretend wife. "Where are you going?" she kept her voice even, without demand.

"I just need to walk. Or something." He drew his breeches back on, followed by his stockings and boots. "Go to sleep. We need to be up before dawn."

And with that, he left.

She flopped back onto her back, frustration roiling through her—both because of his attitude and because she was still physically aroused. She could always do what he'd taught her…

Mrs. Woodlawn had said he was a good helpmate. She'd no idea.

If they were so bloody good at playing husband and wife, perhaps they should just go to Gretna Green and make it official. That would solve everything. Her parents might not be thrilled at her choice of duke, but he was still a duke, and Diana would still be a duchess. Moreover, her father's grandson would be a duke, and that would make everything else that had come before palatable.

For that reason alone, Diana hated the idea. Anything that would make her father that happy was surely a disaster in the making.

Only, she *didn't* hate the idea. She liked Simon. She was fairly certain he liked her. They seemed to be attracted to one another. Everyone else believed they were happily wed, so maybe they could be.

She knew he wanted a family. But he was afraid. He might not be *able* to marry her.

Furthermore, she wasn't entirely sold on marriage. To live in such a close relationship with another person… She wasn't sure she was capable of such a thing. Of love.

She was sure of one thing, however. She couldn't choose what she really wanted—the independent life with a new identify. If she did, Simon would truly be what everyone said: ruined.

⟞⟋ᴇ·3⟍⟝

THE LAST TWO days had been grueling. Simon stifled a yawn as the coach hit a rut, jostling the interior. Diana, who'd been asleep beside him, sucked in a breath, clearly startled. She rubbed at her eyes and slowly pushed herself up.

He didn't know how much she'd slept in Manchester last night—she'd tossed and turned for quite some time. He knew that because he hadn't slept much either, not because they'd shared a bed. After a long day of travel from Brereton, they'd found a tiny inn on the outskirts of Manchester. He'd introduced them as Phineas Byrd and his sister Miss Kitty Byrd. Diana had looked at him in surprise but hadn't said a word.

The innkeeper had given them a room with two beds. Diana had taken her meals there, choosing to remain out of sight as much as possible. Though he'd been careful to lodge away from the main road, he didn't blame her reticence.

"That's Beaumont Tower," she said a bit hoarsely, her voice craggy with the remnants of sleep, as she gestured toward the window.

Simon leaned over her, careful not to get too close—they'd maintained a polite distance since leaving Brereton. Outside the window rose a hill, and atop it sat a large fortress. "It's a castle."

"Yes, it dates to the twelfth century and was substantially rebuilt in the sixteenth. Shakespeare stayed here once."

"Indeed? Will I be given his room?"

Her lips curved into a rare smile—they'd become scarce the past two days. "I'm sure that can be arranged."

The coach turned from the road onto a narrower track. They gradually began to climb up the hill toward the tower.

"When was the last time you were here?" he asked. Their conversation had been stilted since leaving Brereton. She answered his questions with brevity and a seeming disinterest, never putting in effort to continue an exchange. He kept thinking of the other night and how flustered she'd been. He wanted to ask about the stuttering. She hadn't done it to that extent since, but he couldn't believe that had been the first time, not the way she'd behaved. She'd measured her words and tried to speak more slowly but had still struggled. He suspected it was an ongoing battle.

If he were honest with himself, he'd acknowledge that he wasn't making much of an effort either. She'd rattled him with her questions about Miriam's death. That, and he knew their time together was coming to an end. Better to keep her at arm's length. No revealing discussions or sharing of thoughts. And definitely no kissing.

Except that was all he could seem to think about when he closed his eyes. Which would explain his exhaustion. He yawned again and stretched his hand over his mouth, angling his head away from her. He didn't dare sleep, not when she was so close, and his body could reach for her without conscious thought.

She smoothed her hand over her hair. "Thank goodness for hats," she murmured.

"You look lovely." Perhaps he shouldn't have said it, but the words had tumbled from his mouth before he could stop them.

She flicked a glance in his direction. "You're too kind. *Truly.*" The last word carried a hint of humor, and he was glad for it. The air between them had been so heavy and dark, whereas the time at The Happy Cat before they'd been recognized had been full of light and charm. He'd remember that snow for as long as he was blessed to breathe.

They crested the hill and passed through a gatehouse. The coach rumbled to a stop, and a moment later, Tinley opened the door. Another man, the gatekeeper, apparently, stood a few feet away.

Simon climbed down. "Good afternoon, we're here to see Her Grace, the Duchess of Blackburn."

"I'm her cousin."

Simon looked back to see Diana poking her head through the door.

"I remember you, Miss Kingman. You and Her Grace always did look more like sisters than cousins." The gatekeeper shot a look toward Simon, and his brow furrowed. "I beg your pardon, perhaps you are no longer Miss Kingman."

Simon would let her handle that however she saw fit. They were in her world now, and he meant to let her take the lead. She smiled warmly, and Simon felt a visceral pull toward her.

"It's fine. May we continue up to the house?" An excellent diversion.

"Of course. Welcome to Beaumont Tower."

"Thank you." Simon climbed back into the coach, and they were quickly on their way. The sound of a bell tolling from the gatehouse chased them up the drive.

Simon rubbed his palms together before plucking his gloves from the opposite seat and drawing them over his cold hands.

Diana reached for her hat, which was also on the opposite seat. The coach hit a bump, and she pitched forward. Simon reached for her, clasping her waist and drawing her back. She landed half on him and half on the seat.

"Sorry, I didn't want you to fall." He released her almost immediately.

She slipped from his thigh and moved away from him as she smoothed her hand over her skirt. "Thank you."

He grabbed her hat and handed it to her, then did the same with her gloves.

The coach passed through the inner gatehouse and stopped in a cobbled courtyard. Through the coach window on Diana's side, Simon saw a liveried footman rush forward to open her door. He pulled down the step and helped Diana alight. Simon followed her out.

"This way," the footman said, leading them up a short flight of stone stairs. They passed through a gateway in a low stone wall and were greeted with a lawn and garden. Everything was a dull green or brown, ready to suffer the cold winter months ahead. Even so, Simon imagined it was a beautiful place to pass the time in finer weather.

The path cut straight down the middle of the garden until they met a second, longer set of stairs. At the top, they continued forward through another gatehouse into the inner courtyard of the castle.

"Are we going to the drawing room?" Diana asked.

"Yes, miss," the footman replied.

She gestured in front of them toward the upper floor. "It's up there.

We'll go in and take the stairs."

They walked into a grand receiving room with a staircase to their immediate right.

"This is the King's Hall," Diana said.

It *was* fit for a king and quite medieval, heavy with wood and tapestries. "I'm afraid I've nothing that compares to this at Lyndhurst." He wanted to explore the room, but there'd be time later. He trailed Diana up the stairs.

She looked back at him. "And this is nothing compared to the Great Hall." Her eyes held a sparkle that had been absent the past two days. In fact, he wasn't sure he'd ever seen them quite so animated.

The reason for that became apparent as soon as they entered the drawing room to the right at the top of the stairs.

"Diana!" A taller version of Diana rushed forward. Simon blinked. They could indeed be sisters.

They wrapped each other in a fierce hug that lasted long enough for Simon to see the affection between them. He shifted his weight, feeling as though he were intruding.

When they broke apart, they continued to hold hands. Diana looked radiant. Happy. She deserved to look like that every day for the rest of her life.

"Romsey, allow me to introduce my cousin Verity, Her Grace, the Duchess of Blackburn."

He bowed. "It is my distinct pleasure."

"Verity, this is His Grace, the Duke of Romsey."

She curtsied. "Pleased to meet you, Duke."

"Please, call me Romsey," he said.

The duchess had the same nearly black hair as Diana and the same pale, lush skin. Her face was a touch longer, and her eyes had more of a tilt. They were also brown, a warm chestnut color, instead of Diana's vivid blue.

The duchess turned to Diana. "This is such a surprise." Her gaze flicked toward Simon. "For so many reasons."

"Yes, I have many things to tell you," Diana said.

"Do you want to rest first?" the duchess asked with deep concern. "You've just completed such a long journey."

"I'm fine. I'd rather talk to you." She smiled again, and it lit her whole face. "I'd love some tea, however."

"Of course, of course." The duchess shook her head. "I'm so surprised to see you, I forgot my hospitality—we don't get many visitors." She let go of Diana's hand and went to the bellpull.

Simon edged closer to Diana. "I think I'll go to my room," he said softly while the duchess was occupied.

"Why? Surely you want tea or something to eat?"

"I'd rather let the two of you speak in privacy. I'll see you at dinner later, I presume." He turned toward the duchess with a bright smile. She'd just finished speaking with one of her retainers. "I'd like to retire for a bit. I've been promised Shakespeare's chamber, if it's available."

Diana laughed, and the duchess slid her a playful look. "Is that right?" Her lips curved up as her attention redirected to Simon. "I wouldn't want to disappoint you. Let me take care of that directly." She went back to the bellpull, and the same retainer returned a moment later.

"You seem much improved now that we're here," Simon said to Diana, again keeping his voice low.

"How can you tell? We only just arrived."

"You're pleased to see your cousin—the tension has left your shoulders, and the tiny lines that reside between your eyes have vanished."

She didn't immediately respond but stared at him intently. "I'm sorry about the last couple of days. Things did not turn out as I'd hoped."

"Nor for me either." He'd wanted her to escape from this entire damnable situation as uninjured as possible. He still hoped the damage could be mitigated, but it was ultimately up to her what step she took next.

The duchess swept toward them. "Romsey, this is my butler, Kirwin. He'll see you to your chamber."

With a final look at Diana, Simon bowed again to his hostess. "Thank you for your kind hospitality."

"Thank you for delivering my cousin to me."

"We'll go this way, Your Grace," the butler gestured to the other door, which led to a corridor. "Your chamber is the second."

To Simon's right, windows overlooked the courtyard below. To his left, they passed a door and approached a second—his room. "Is this the one?"

"Indeed it is," the butler said, moving abreast of him to open the door. "Your things will be delivered momentarily."

Simon moved into the chamber. He was instantly struck with how cold it was but knew they'd rectify that shortly. He took in the dark wood and the heavy, emerald-green bed hangings. As with most buildings this age, there was just one small window, which only emphasized the lack of light, even though the draperies had been pulled open. "Thank you, Kirwin. Might I trouble you for a tea tray?"

"Her Grace already requested one. Will you require the services of a valet?"

Simon thought of Graff, his valet, whom he'd left behind—as he always did when he traveled, and this time in particular in the interest of privacy.

He was an accomplished valet, but his absence only served to remind Simon that he didn't really need one. He'd gone without for a year after Miriam had died. His prior valet had left his employ, as several of his retainers had done, and Simon hadn't bothered to hire one until Nick had finally talked him into it.

He realized Kirwin was awaiting a response. "No, thank you."

Kirwin arched a thick gray brow but merely nodded. "Will there be anything else?"

"Not that I can think of."

"Very good. You have only to ring if you require something." He gestured toward the pull between a door and the fireplace on the wall opposite the door. "Ah, here's your luggage."

A footman had arrived at the door, and Kirwin took the bag and nodded for the other retainer to go. The butler took the bag to the doorway at the back of the room. "This is your dressing chamber. There's a passage to a set of stairs if you'd like to go down that way. Your tea tray will come up from there, as will a boy to start your fire."

Kirwin emerged from the dressing room a moment later. "I nearly forgot to mention dinner will be at six." He offered Simon a bow before taking his leave.

Simon went into the dressing room, where his bag sat near a small table. There was an armoire and a chair and another narrow window.

A soft rap was followed by a lad poking his head in. He carried a basket of fire-starting implements, and Simon nodded for him to go about his work. Crossing to that narrow window, he gazed down at another garden like the one in the courtyard on their way in. This one was larger but just as manicured. Dormant rose bushes marched along one side.

The door to the passage downstairs was ajar, and from the side of his eye, he caught the arrival of his tea tray. Rushing to open the door wider for the maid, he waved toward the bedroom. "In there is fine. Thank you."

"Just so, Your Grace. Would you like me to pour for you?"

"No, thank you, I'll manage." He was quite used to taking care of himself. To that end, he removed his coat and cravat, then pulled his boots off, wiggling his toes when he was finished.

The maid left, offering a curtsey on her way out. A moment later, the boy followed, executing a perfect bow. Pushing himself up from the chair, Simon meandered back to the bedroom. He felt disjointed now that they were here. Likely because he'd no idea what was going to happen next.

He should've embraced this sensation—he lived his life without knowing what he was going to do next. He'd gone from looking forward to a wonderful, specific future to sadness and regret. And in an effort to avoid those things, he took each day as it came and tried to just live in each moment. No future, no past. No ties to anything.

Which was probably why he felt disjointed, he realized. For the first time in two years, he felt tied to something. To someone.

To Diana.

Oh, it was a temporary thing, but he cared about what happened to her. And he suspected he always would.

He poured himself some tea and nibbled from the food on the tray. He really had no idea what she planned to do. She'd been so upset and then adamant that she couldn't endanger him by disappearing. *I can't let you do that,* she'd said. It was perhaps the most thoughtful thing anyone had ever said to him.

But he'd meant what he'd said. He dealt with the stain of his wife's death every day. Living with the scandal of Diana's disappearance wouldn't be any different.

Except it would. People, namely her father, would blame him. Simon would have to say he'd brought her here and that he didn't know where she'd gone after. Then it would fall on Diana's cousin to cover things up. Hell, he wasn't going to do that to the duchess.

Which meant Diana had to "disappear" somewhere around Manchester—after they'd seen Sir Fletcher and his nasty wife. That also meant the duchess and her staff would have to lie about Diana being here.

Bloody hell, this was a disaster.

Stop and think, he told himself. *You've managed disasters before.*

The hell he had. He'd burrowed himself into a ball and hidden from the world. Even now, though he tried to reengage with people, with Society, he held a part of himself back. He always would. That part of him was dead. He couldn't offer something that no longer existed.

He removed his waistcoat and threw it over the chair near the fireplace. The room was slightly warmer now that the fire was going, but still cold enough to cause him to shiver. The bed, with its heavy hangings and thick blankets, beckoned him. He peeled his stockings and breeches away and climbed beneath the coverlet.

He'd find a way to ensure Diana disappeared without putting the duchess and her household in the way of trouble. He, on the other hand, was likely doomed. Diana had made an excellent point—everyone would assume he'd killed her. And this time, he might not escape prosecution. This time, he might even hang.

Perhaps that was the ending he deserved.

Chapter Ten
⊷ℰ∘ℨ⊷

FAIRLY BURSTING WITH anxious energy, Diana paced in front of the windows overlooking the garden and lawn at the back of the castle while she waited for the maid to arrange the tray of tea and food. Finally, she left, and Verity, whom Diana hadn't seen in almost two years, poured her cup precisely the way she liked it—a bit of cream and a large spoon of sugar when her mother wasn't around.

Verity sat in a wing-backed chair, looking up at Diana. "Are you going to sit or hover?"

Diana sank onto the settee perpendicular to Verity's chair. "It's been a trying week."

"I can only imagine." Verity sipped her tea and, setting it down, picked up a cake. "I'll endeavor to hold my tongue so you can disclose the entire tale. It looks to be fascinating."

That was one word to describe it. Many others crowded Diana's mind: desperate, exciting, disastrous, astonishing to name just a few. Life changing was perhaps the best.

"Just a moment." Diana was rather famished, so she wolfed down a cake in a manner she never would have done at home. Taking a sip of tea, she set her cup down and began to speak.

"As you know I was engaged to the Duke of Kilve."

"Yes. But you arrived with the Duke of Romsey." Verity flinched and held up her hand. "My apologies. I did say I wouldn't interrupt."

Diana smiled. "You said you'd try. I know better." People found the two of them reserved or perhaps even aloof in Diana's case, but together, they were animated and talkative, as if they couldn't possibly say everything they wanted to. Perhaps they saved it up for when they saw each other, despite the fact that they corresponded regularly. It certainly felt like that to Diana. With her cousin, she could be absolutely herself, in a way she couldn't with anyone else.

Verity laughed softly, her eyes glowing with warmth. "It's so *good* to have you here."

"It's good to be here." And it was. Oh, how she wished that staying here—away from her parents, away from the pressures they placed upon her, away from Society, away from scandal—was a choice she could make.

"So tell me about Romsey." Verity picked up another cake and winked at

Diana. "If I keep eating, I can't talk."

"The story is more than just Romsey," Diana answered. But he was a central part of it. Without him, things would have gone very differently. He'd promised Kilve he would look after Diana and protect her from scandal to the best of his ability. She'd believed in his promise, but now, after what had happened in Brereton, scandal would find them.

Diana worked to start back at the beginning. "The Duke of Kilve is in love with someone else and is going to marry her instead."

Verity's jaw dropped. "What? The scoundrel!"

"Try not to blame him—it was my idea to marry, not his. And I believe I caught him at a rather vulnerable time."

Twisting her lips into an unsatisfied grimace, Verity grunted softly. "I will still blame him. A little." She took a breath. "So how did Romsey become involved?"

"They are friends, and he delivered the news to me."

"Kilve didn't even have the grace to face you himself?"

"Apparently, Lady Pendleton—the woman he's to marry—had an accident, and he was anxious to reach her. And before you say anything against her, don't. I've met her, and I actually like her very much." Truly, Diana wanted them to be happy. They certainly deserved to be. "Looking back, it seems obvious to me now that she and Kilve were in love. And they have been for quite some time. In truth, it's a rather sad story."

Verity shook her head. "I'll trust you—perhaps you can tell me the details another time, if you wish. So Romsey took on the unenviable task of messenger."

"Yes, but also savior. He offered to help me in any manner I required, in order to mitigate the scandal."

Verity's eyes narrowed. "And why did he do this?" Like Diana, she'd no reason to trust a man. Her father and Diana's were brothers and very alike. Their example hadn't exactly recommended the males of their species. Furthermore, Verity had married a cold autocrat who saw her as little more than a broodmare.

Simon was, however, different. "Because he possesses a kind heart." And was perhaps looking for absolution.

"I should say so," Verity murmured. "He possessed no ulterior motive whatsoever?"

"Not that I can tell." Diana shook her head firmly, certain of him—at least about this. "No."

"Remarkable. However did you end up here?"

"My choices were few," Diana said. "I could do nothing and suffer Father's wrath."

Verity winced. "You thought running off with Romsey would help you avoid his anger?"

"No, but it gave me time to think about what to do. Romsey suggested I could disappear, that I could start my life over in some village using a different name."

"An intriguing idea, but you'd have to turn your back on who you are. We wouldn't be able to see each other."

"Perhaps not right away. But after my father gave up looking for me, I could find my way to Blackburn and we—"

"If you think my father or your father wouldn't hear of that, you're deluding yourself." Verity's tone had gone cold, making Diana shiver. She was, terrifyingly, correct.

"I know," Diana said softly. "It was sophistry."

Verity reached over and touched Diana's arm. "You were in a horrible situation. It's just too bad the duke—Romsey, I mean—didn't offer to marry you. That would've *truly* made him a savior."

"He suggested it, actually." Diana picked up her teacup and took a long, fortifying sip.

Verity stared at her, clearly waiting for the *why* it hadn't happened.

"You aren't aware of his reputation?" Diana asked, putting her cup back on the table in front of them. Of course she wasn't. Verity disliked gossip as much as Diana, and, living so far from London and actively ignoring information that might filter its way to Beaumont Tower, it was entirely possible she knew nothing of the Duke of Ruin.

"He is rumored to have killed his wife," Diana said dispassionately, still refusing to believe it even though Simon said nothing to defend himself. "Since he doesn't remember what happened, he doesn't deny it."

Verity's eyes rounded. "My goodness. I see why you didn't want to marry him. Is it all right for him to stay here?" She glanced toward the door he'd exited earlier.

"Of course it is!" Diana pitched forward slightly in agitation. "The problem isn't that stupid rumor—at least not to me. It's that my father finds him wholly unsuitable. I met him at a house party two months ago, and Father didn't even want me to speak with him. Marrying him would have made him as furious as if I'd simply cried off with Kilve."

"But you didn't cry off."

"No, but I would have if my father was a reasonable person. Since he's not, I fled. With Simon."

There was a beat of silence as one of Verity's dark brows arched into the semblance of a question mark. "Simon?"

Diana felt the heat rise up her neck and worked to ignore it, praying her cousin would do the same. "R-Romsey. We became a bit, er, f-familiar during our journey."

"That's to be expected, I suppose." Verity eyed her warily. "How familiar?"

"We needn't marry, if that's what you're intimating," Diana said with a bit of exasperation.

"I'm on your side in this, Diana, whatever happens. You will always have a home here."

Diana supposed that was an option she hadn't really considered. Because she didn't think her father would allow it. He saw her as a valuable commodity, and after the scandal died down, he would try to make the best match possible. But that had been before Brereton. Before *this* scandal. With Simon. This one wouldn't die down. She'd be ruined forever. Perhaps she *could* just live here...

"But your plan is to start over with a new life," Verity said. "I will support that too."

"Unfortunately, I don't think that plan will work any longer." Diana squeezed her hands together on her lap. "If I disappear, Simon will be blamed." She needed to back up a bit to explain. "Though we posed as a married couple and traveled under an alias, someone recognized us in Brereton. My running off with Romsey—the Duke of Ruin is what they call him—will shortly be *the* scandal on everyone's lips."

"So people will know that you were together, and if you go missing, he will be seen to be at fault." Her face creased into a deep frown. "I see the problem clearly."

It wasn't a problem. It was a potential disaster. For Simon. "He's already widely believed to be a murderer, and though he wasn't charged with the crime, this time, he may very well be. I can't let that happen."

"So you'll live here in disgrace?" Verity asked, her dark gaze full of love and empathy.

"If I must."

"You could marry him," Verity suggested softly. "You said the rumor about him—I believe you called it stupid—didn't matter to you."

"It doesn't. I know in my heart he didn't kill her."

"In your heart? Diana, is it possible you've fallen in love with him?"

The air left Diana's lungs. Love? She hadn't considered that. She didn't even know what that felt like. She glanced toward the windows, breath fighting its way back to her. "I don't know."

"Where does Uncle think you are? Or did you just leave without a word?"

"I left a note that I was going to King's Grange. He likely arrived a

couple of days ago. I can't imagine what he's doing now. Besides fuming."
Diana had tried not to think of it. Imagining her father's reaction to not
finding her at home made her stomach seize, and she feared she would
toss up her accounts.

"He's methodically determining where you might have gone." Verity's
face darkened. "He'll come here first."

"If he travels by horse, which I think we can assume he will, he could be
here in a few days."

"Yes," Verity's tone was grim. "Unless the weather slows his pace."

Diana sent up a silent prayer.

The tension growing in the air shattered upon the arrival of Verity's son.
Augustus "Beau" Beaumont, all of five years, tore into the drawing room
as if his feet were on fire. "Mama, Mama! The puppies are here! The
puppies are here! Come see!" He ran straight for his mother, snagging her
hand in his and pulling. He'd grown so much since Diana had last seen
him nearly two years ago. He wasn't a baby anymore but a boy.

Verity laughed. "How wonderful. Beau, did you not see we have a
guest?"

He turned his head and looked at Diana. "She can come see the puppies
too. Come *on*, Mama!"

"Beau, this is your Aunt Diana. You remember her, from that time she
came for Christmas?"

Beau narrowed his green eyes—those hadn't changed one bit—at Diana.
"Maybe. It's nice to see you, Auntie." He offered a quick bow, and Diana
had to commend his manners, especially in the face of such excitement.

"As it happens, I do want to see the puppies," Diana said. She could use
seeing something exceedingly adorable. "Do you mind if I join you?"

"No. But let's *go*." He pulled so hard on his mother's hand that he tipped
backward.

Verity reached out and steadied him, then rose gracefully to her feet.
"Let's not keep them waiting." She looked over at Diana. "Are you sure
you're up to it? I know it's been a long journey."

She far preferred puppies to being alone with her own thoughts at the
moment. "Absolutely. Let us see the puppies!" She grinned at Beau, who
smiled back. Clasping his mother's hand tight, he skipped forward, forcing
her and Diana to laughingly keep up.

To enjoy such a simple life… Diana wanted nothing more. She'd never
had that. And she feared she never would.

•ℰ•3•

BECAUSE HE'D SLEPT through dinner, Simon devoured a tray of food in his room. He was sorry to have missed the meal, for a variety of reasons. He had no idea if Diana had come to a decision. He'd been looking forward to getting to know his hostess.

And he missed dining with Diana.

After spending so much time with her over the past nine days, he felt rather alone. Looking at the clock, he wondered if she and the duchess would still be about. But the bath the footman had offered when he'd brought the dinner tray was awfully tempting.

In the end, he opted for the bath, but when he was finished, he was too restless to go to bed. He dressed and went back to the drawing room, hoping to find either Diana or Verity. But the room was empty. Perhaps they were downstairs. He retraced the way he'd come that afternoon and found himself in what Diana had called the King's Hall. Unfortunately, that was empty too.

He meandered about the room, looking at the paintings which were an interesting mix of portraits, perhaps of past dukes and their families, and landscapes. One in particular looked as though it was a representation of the countryside surrounding Blackburn.

Spying light at the end of a passageway behind the stairs, he walked into a massive library with a huge stone hearth occupying a full third of the back wall. Windows on either side of the fireplace looked out toward the back of the tower, but he couldn't appreciate the view since the curtains were drawn. It was also quite dark, he reminded himself, thinking the late nap had thrown him off.

The collection of books was awe-inspiring. Some Duke of Blackburn must have been a well-read gentleman. Or perhaps they all were. Simon suffered a brief pang of regret at having disposed of most of his library, but brushed it away. The books he'd donated would get far more use than collecting dust at Lyndhurst.

His eye caught a grouping of toy soldiers on a table, and he was instantly reminded of the Taft boys. He smiled to himself, thinking of what a splendid day that had been. At first, being around the children had summoned too much pain, but their joy for life had given him a glimpse of hope.

For what, exactly?

That he couldn't answer.

"Good evening, Romsey."

The feminine voice came from behind Simon. He turned to see the duchess moving into the library and offered a small bow. "Good evening."

"You found Beau's soldiers." The duchess came toward him, her lips curved into a smile.

"You and Di—Miss Kingman look very much alike," he said. "You could be sisters."

"Just call her Diana. She refers to you as Simon. It's to be expected after you've spent so much time together."

He nodded, wondering just how much Diana had told her cousin. He was probably better off not knowing. "Who is Beau?"

"Diana didn't tell you about my son?"

"No." She'd said precious little about her family, just that she and the duchess were close. Simon picked up one of the toys. "He likes soldiers?"

She cocked her head to the side. "He likes to pretend his father is a soldier."

"I thought he..." Simon let his voice trail off rather than bring up any unpleasantness.

"I've told Beau that his father will likely never come home, but he likes to imagine that he went off to war and is protecting us." There was a sad lilt to her tone.

"I'm sorry for...you." He'd been about to say "your loss," but if the duke was merely missing, even for such a long time, perhaps he would return. It wasn't the same as Simon's loss. Maybe it was worse—the not knowing. "That must be difficult. To not know what happened."

"Somewhat." She lifted a shoulder in a half shrug. "He's been gone a long time now. Sometimes I wonder if I even remember him. We were married for only a few months before he disappeared—just long enough for...Beau."

Simon understood. He and Miriam had been wed long enough to make their baby. But not to see her into the world. His throat burned for a moment as he nodded slightly and averted his gaze.

The duchess turned toward a sideboard on the wall opposite the fireplace. "Would you like to have a drink with me?"

"No, thank you. I don't drink spirits."

Her eyes widened briefly. "My husband drank to excess. We may not have been together long, but that was one of the things I recall quite clearly."

Simon could see she *hadn't* loved her husband. Or so it seemed based on the derision in her tone. But perhaps it was something else.

"Is there a reason you don't drink?" She quickly waved a hand. "Ignore my impertinence. I'm afraid I'm rather sheltered here at Beaumont Tower. Sometimes I think my social abilities have faltered."

"I used to drink to excess." For some reason, the words fell from his mouth unplanned. "Then my wife tumbled down the stairs, and I've no recollection of what happened, just that I was there, cradling her at the bottom of the steps and begging God to give her back to me. I haven't had a drink since."

Her forehead creased, and her brown eyes warmed with sympathy. "That can't have been easy."

"On occasion, it can be difficult to find an alternate beverage," he said drily, knowing that wasn't what she'd meant but wanting to bring a lighter tone.

"I'll ensure you have whatever you desire while you're here."

He appreciated her consideration. "I regret missing dinner and, presumably, the discussion of what Diana wants to do next."

The duchess gave a slight nod. "Kirwin said the footman wasn't able to wake you. I'm sure you were exhausted. Diana and I had a small, informal dinner in her chamber. She's already asleep."

Damn, there went his hope for seeing her this evening. He couldn't be sure what Diana had told her cousin, and he didn't want to reveal anything she wished to keep secret. So he said nothing.

"She hasn't entirely decided what to do next," the duchess said. "But she's going to have to make a decision in the morning because she's running out of time."

He had to assume she knew the story of what had happened in Brereton, then. "Because the rumor that we eloped will get out." Simon didn't mask his bitterness. If only they hadn't been seen by Lady Dunford-Whaley.

"Eloped?"

Damn, perhaps she hadn't known the story. But he couldn't think of a way to hide it from her now. Anyway, it would soon be common knowledge. "We were recognized in Brereton. I told them we were on our way to Gretna Green and asked the gentleman to keep things quiet for a bit—to buy us some time to get here."

"Smart. But it's more than that, I'm afraid." She winced. "Her father could be here in a few days."

Damn. "She seems terrified of him." It sounded like hyperbole, but it wasn't. From their first discussion in Green Park, she'd been clear that her father's anger drove every decision she made.

"She has every right to be. He and my father are horrid men." She said this with an even tone, as if she were remarking on the weather.

"I'm sorry to hear that." He'd loved his father very much. And his mother, but then she'd made things difficult since Father had died. A thought occurred to him, one that had plagued him from time to time whenever Diana mentioned her father. "They didn't...hurt you, did they?"

"Not physically. Well, that's not precisely true." She shook her head.

"It's not my place to tell. My father is maybe not quite as cruel as my uncle. But cruelty is their currency, make no mistake. If he finds Diana here, I worry what he will do."

Simon's muscles tensed. "I won't allow him to do anything."

The duchess's face softened. "I was hoping you'd say that. I'm quite concerned about her plan to change her identity. I honestly don't know what she was thinking. She is who she is, and I don't think she'd like to be alone without support, regardless of how strongly she yearns for independence."

"Those aren't really the same things, though, are they? She could have independence and still have people to support her."

"You're quite right. I've managed to find that here, managing things in my husband's absence. But that's not what Diana would have—she wouldn't be Diana Kingman anymore."

"No, she wouldn't."

"There is that other alternative…"

Not changing her name and disappearing, and not awaiting her father. That left… "I don't think she's interested in marrying me."

"Have you asked?"

"I have."

The duchess blew out a breath and lowered her lids as she stared at him expectantly. "Did you really, or was it more of a suggestion?" She waved her hand. "Have you asked her *recently*?"

"Er, no." He didn't count the discussion they'd had at Brereton. They hadn't seriously discussed it as an option.

"You may consider doing that."

What did that mean? Had she and Diana discussed this? Was Diana expecting a proposal? Did she *want* to marry him? A cold sweat dappled his neck, and ice slid down his spine.

"She wants that?"

"Do you?" the duchess countered. She straightened. "I've meddled too much, probably. I just want, no, I *need* for Diana to be happy."

Then on that they were agreed. Simon just wasn't sure marriage to him was the answer. But neither was he sure it wasn't. "I want that too."

"If there's any chance you care for her—and it seems you do—please think about it. We have an excellent stable. You can take horses and be in Gretna Green in three days if you change a few times a day. I'll send a groom with you to help. Actually, I may come along myself. My presence will lend some prestige to the event. And please don't think I have a lofty opinion of myself—I'm a woman out in the country raising a son. But if I can use my title for some good, especially where it concerns Diana, I am happy to do so."

Simon couldn't argue with that. "Your offer is most generous, Duchess."

"I insist you call me Verity, especially if we're to be family."

She made it sound as if it had all been decided. Really, was there any other choice? He wasn't going to let Diana's father get near her, and the only way he could protect her was to make her his wife. He just hoped she would agree.

"You're a formidable woman, Verity. Diana is lucky to have you on her side."

Verity laughed. "I'm not sure I agree with formidable." She seemed to think about it for a moment. "But maybe you're right." She grinned. "I think I like you, Simon. I hope you don't mind, but I'm calling you Simon. Since we're to be family."

Yes, it had been decided—at least in Verity's mind. "Of course."

She scooped the toy soldiers from the table into her left hand. "We should rise early and leave by eight, I think. I'll have everything organized."

Simon gave her the soldier he'd been holding. "You really think she'll say yes?"

"Are you going to make her happy?"

"I'm going to try." But he honestly didn't know if he could. Hell, he didn't know anything anymore.

"Then she'll say yes. She's not stupid, but you know that. It's one of the reasons you admire her, I'm sure." She gave him a small, almost secretive smile, as if she knew more about their relationship than even they did. "Sleep well."

Simon watched her go and wondered if he and Diana had just been managed. Did it matter?

Not particularly. He couldn't say he was distressed by this turn of events. Nervous, worried, and incredibly apprehensive—yes, he was definitely those things.

What the hell was he going to do with a wife? He'd considered remarrying, had thought he wanted to, but now faced with doing so, he wondered if he could do it again.

He'd have to take Diana home to Lyndhurst. *Home.* It had ceased being that when Miriam had died. Now when he went there, it felt like a mausoleum.

The ice returned to his spine and spread through him like a sickness.

He knew what he had to do. He just prayed he'd be a better husband this time.

Chapter Eleven
✦℮✦

DIANA'S HAND FROZE just before she rapped on his door. She should wait until morning.

But they needed to leave as soon as possible. That is, if he even agreed to her plan.

What if he didn't?

Her shoulders slumped, and she pivoted from the door. This was foolish. Her entire mad dash from London had been incredibly ill-conceived.

Why, then, couldn't she regret it?

Clenching her teeth in determination, she turned back to the door and knocked before she could lose her courage once more. She bit her lip as she waited, trapping it between her teeth, then remembered she wasn't supposed to do that. Only her parents weren't here to admonish her. In defiance, she snagged her lip again and pushed her shoulders back.

He still didn't come to the door. He was probably asleep.

Defeat pulled at her spine, and she began to wilt.

The door opened slightly. Simon peered through the narrow gap. "Diana?"

He pulled the door open and ushered her inside. "Come in."

She lifted her skirt lest she trip over the too-long hem of her borrowed dressing gown and stepped over the threshold. "No one saw me," she said, sensing his anxiety.

He closed the door behind her. "Is everything all right?"

"Yes. No. Probably." She shook her head. "I don't know."

"Do you want to sit?" He gestured to the wing-backed chair in the corner near the fireplace.

"No, thank you. I shouldn't stay long." She shouldn't have come at all. She rubbed her hands together, then smoothed them over Verity's dressing gown. It was an item of clothing she'd wanted to bring but hadn't had room for. Stealing away in the night didn't allow for proper preparation.

Simon moved toward the bed and leaned against one of the end posts. This was far grander than any of the bedchambers they'd shared on their journey north. He wore his familiar night shirt and a pair of breeches. His feet were bare.

His lips lifted into a faint smile. "I'm delighted to see you, but it's rather late for a visit, isn't it?"

"Yes, but since you didn't come to dinner, there are things we should discuss." Dinner? They wouldn't have discussed any of this there, not in front of Verity. And Diana hadn't made her decision until a short time ago.

She was stalling. Better to just get it out. "I think we should marry."

He blinked as he pushed away from the post and walked toward her, stopping just a foot away. "Did Verity tell you that?"

"She suggested it. But, if you recall, it was your idea originally. I know a great deal has transpired since then, and perhaps now that you've g-gotten to know me, you'd rather not w-wed." She winced inwardly, thinking she hadn't needed to say any of that. It was an appalling show of weakness and doubt after years of learning to hold her tongue.

Her anxiety grew as he stared at her for a long moment, but then his features softened, and his mouth curved into a smile that made her heart pound.

"You stole my thunder." He took her hand. His flesh was warm. Electrifying. "I'd planned to ask you again in the morning."

Joy mixed with relief, and she relaxed. "You did?"

"It seems the best solution, don't you agree?"

Yes, it was a solution. Just as her engagement to Kilve had been a contractual arrangement, so was this. It was a means to an end. Precisely what her father had always intended. And, whether he liked Simon or not, Diana would be a duchess.

"I do. Are you sure you don't…m-mind?"

Furrows ran along his forehead, and he stroked his thumb across the back of her hand. "I can think of no one else I'd rather marry. Is it acceptable to you? Your speech—I notice it falters a bit when you're upset."

Self-loathing poured through her. She tried to take her hand away, but he held her firmly. She didn't want to talk about her speech, so she ignored what he said. "Yes, it's acceptable."

He tipped his head to the side, his gaze soft and compassionate. "Your father won't be able to hurt you anymore."

Again, she tried to withdraw. This time, he held her even more tightly and pulled her toward him so that they almost touched. "What did Verity tell you?" she asked, hating to think her cousin had laid her secrets bare.

"Nothing specific. And I don't wish to intrude. Just know that I will always do my best to keep you safe." His gaze was so intent and his tone so rich and candid that she couldn't help but believe him.

She wanted to ask him if he was sure he wanted this. Forcing him into something had never been her intent. But then she hadn't really *had* an intent. "I can't help but think we didn't plan this very well. I never should have dragged you into this."

He squeezed her hand and gave her a half smile. "I offered my services if you recall. Whatever anyone may think of me, I possess an unabashedly romantic nature. I wanted Nick and Violet to be together—they deserve their happiness. But it was equally important to me—and to Nick—that you not be left alone to bear the brunt of his stupidity."

"I should have realized our proposed marriage was doomed before it even started. Neither of us were very enthusiastic. Not really." All her excitement—every last dollop—had come from the idea of escaping her parents.

"Is this the same way?" he asked quietly, his gaze dropping to where their hands were still joined.

"I don't think so." She kept her voice low, as if speaking too loudly would ruin whatever was transpiring between them—this combination of comfort and anticipation. "It feels…different."

She hadn't given much thought to kissing Nick—or doing anything else with him. He'd given her a chaste kiss on the cheek once or twice, but she hadn't even touched his bare hand. With Simon, however, she could *remember* kissing him. Even before they'd embarked on this ill-fated journey, they'd kissed and she'd thought of it often. And after kissing him in Brereton, she wanted to do it again. And again. Not to mention whatever else he wanted to teach her in the bedroom. Nick had agreed to give her space, to postpone having children—meaning delay sexual relations. She and Simon had made no such arrangement.

She gathered her courage and asked, "Is this to be a true marriage?"

He pulled her closer until her chest met his. "If you're asking whether I want you to share my bed, the answer is an unequivocal yes. But only if that's what you want."

She took her hand from his and laid her palms against his chest. The cotton lawn of his shirt was thin enough that she could feel his heat through the fabric. Since she'd seen his bare chest in the firelight, she'd wanted nothing more than to touch him, to feel him.

She inched her hands up until they framed the opening in the neck of the shirt. "Yes, that's what I want."

Rising on her toes, she pressed her mouth to his. He swept his arms around her and crushed her to his chest. Their lips moved together, tempting and teasing, until, impatient, she opened and invited him inside. Rapture made her body pulse with need. She pushed up against him, seeking to feel him any way she could.

She wanted him now. Her body screamed for his. That sensation he'd built in her…cunny, that was what he'd called it, came roaring back.

His hands caressed her spine, then one crept up to her neck. He found her braid and gave it a gentle tug, pulling her head back slightly as he devoured her mouth.

She nearly melted in his embrace. Wrapping her hands around his neck, she held on for fear she'd simply dissolve into the carpet.

His hand cupped her hip, and he brought her pelvis flush against his. The hard rod of his cock surprised her, but it felt divine. She pressed into him, desperate for that sweet release he'd shown her too many days ago in Coventry. Her hips rotated, seemingly of their own volition, as she sought satisfaction.

His lips left hers, and she gasped, both from needing a deep breath that she didn't think she'd be able to find in her heightened state of arousal and because of the exquisite things he was doing to her body. One hand moved along her neck, teasing her flesh; the other massaged her hip and behind, spurring the frantic movements of her hips. And his mouth, God, his mouth. His lips slid across her jawline until he found her ear. He nipped the lobe, then licked at it before descending along her neck with long, lush strokes of his tongue.

"Simon, *please*." The words spilled from her mouth with abandon. She had no control, nor did she want any. She gave it freely to him and to her body.

His hand came up her side and brushed the underside of her breast. She sucked in a breath as the sensation pooled in her loins migrated north. Her breasts tingled. He slid his hand inside her dressing gown and fingered her nipple through the thin cotton of her night rail. It grew instantly hard, and she arched into his touch, aching for more.

His mouth was on her collarbone, just inside the edge of her gown. With a harsh, ragged breath, he lifted his head. "We'll be wed soon. This can wait."

The hell it could. She'd been waiting her whole life for this. For *him*. "I don't think I want to. What does it matter?" She clutched at his neck, not wanting to let him go.

He didn't release her either. In fact, his fingers continued their soft, gentle assault on her breast. His movements were quite at odds with what he'd said.

"I don't think I want to either." His lips spread into a self-deprecating grin. "*Clearly*." His hips twitched against hers, reminding her of the steel of his erection—as if she could forget. And his hand finally stilled. "Nevertheless, I'm going to wait until we're wed."

She groaned in frustration, tugging at the ends of his hair brushing over his nape.

He arched a brow at her. "Have you forgotten what I taught you in Coventry? You needn't go to bed wanting."

"Of course I haven't forgotten. But I haven't tried it alone. I'd rather you did it. I suspect that's better anyway."

Now he groaned, his head tipping forward as he brushed his lips against her forehead. "You are a temptress." He brought his hands to her face and cupped her cheeks. "And you're *mine*."

"Apparently, not yet," she said with dark disappointment.

With a flick of his fingers, he untied her dressing gown. Then he bent slightly at the knees, his hand whisking up the end of her night rail. She felt his fingertips against her bare thigh.

Gasping, she breathed his name. "Simon."

"Isn't this what you want?" He caressed her bare flesh, moving slowly but specifically toward her core. "If it's not, tell me now."

"It's what I want." So badly.

He lifted her and carried her the few steps to the bed, setting her on the edge of the mattress. His dark eyes stared into hers, his dark lashes fanning out over the narrowed slits. "Open your legs." The command was silkily seductive, and she obeyed it without hesitation.

"Do you remember what happens next?" he asked.

"Yes."

"This will be a bit different. I'm going to put my fingers inside you." His thumb found her clitoris and teased it. "You like it when I touch you here. You'll also like it when I'm inside—and this will give you an idea of what will happen after we're wed."

"Then you'll put your cock inside me," she said huskily.

He pushed out a breath that sounded a bit like a grunt. "Yes."

His fingers teased at her folds, coaxing her to open even more. She fully relaxed and yet tensed at the same time as her body reacted to the growing pressure and desire. Then he did what he said; he slipped his finger into her. She clutched his shoulders and gasped loudly.

He kissed her then, his mouth taking command of hers and driving his tongue into her. She met his thrusts with her tongue and with her hips. He felt so good inside her, as if they were meant to be joined.

His thumb grazed over her clitoris again, and she dug her nails into his shoulders. His pressure increased, and he used his hand relentlessly, pushing her to the edge of reason, that dark and beautiful place where she'd come apart before.

He tore his mouth from hers and kissed along her cheek before whispering against her ear, "Come for me, Diana."

Her body quivered and then shattered as her orgasm broke over her. His movements increased, taking her through those hysterical moments and guiding her to the bliss on the other side.

Their ragged breathing filled the room as her body sagged with satisfaction. She opened her eyes and blinked, focusing on him. His face was taut, his eyes dark with lust. "What about you?" she asked.

"Don't worry about me."

"You said that last time." And she wasn't having any of it. "Show me what to do." She reached for the hem of his shirt, her hand brushing against his cock.

Simon quirked a smile at her. "You're not going to let me refuse, are you?"

She shook her head firmly. "Absolutely not." She tugged the shirt up, and he helped her pull it over his head.

When his chest was bare to her, she smoothed her hands over the hard plane. "I've wanted to do this since you took off your shirt in front of the fire."

His breath caught as her fingertips trailed across his nipples. "You were watching me?"

She met his gaze and felt a bit of heat in her cheeks. "Guilty, I'm afraid."

His finger grazed the underside of her chin. "Don't ever feel guilty for anything you want where I'm concerned, and don't feel guilty for wanting pleasure."

"My mother told me that what happens between a man and a woman is a necessary evil to beget children. Even kissing isn't to be tolerated."

"Is that why you were so shocked when I kissed you at the house party?" he asked.

She continued to stroke his chest. She loved the feel of his muscles and was fascinated by the light sprinkling of hair between and around his nipples. She traced along his collarbones and back down over his chest. "No, I was shocked because I liked it." She lifted her gaze to his once more and saw the stark desire burning in their depths.

Trailing her hand over his abdomen, she felt his intake of breath more than heard it. She found his waistband, then the buttons of his fall, undoing first one side and then the other until the front of his breeches dropped open.

He was nude beneath, his cock jutting proudly toward her.

"I pulled these on in a hurry," he explained. "When you knocked on the door." He sounded hoarse, as if his throat were constricting.

"You're supposed to be telling me what to do," she said.

"Right." He reached up and raked his hand through his hair, coaxing the strands to stand on end. It made him look wild.

She leaned forward and brushed her lips against his chest, near his nipple. "You're terribly attractive."

"Are you sure you need direction?" he asked tightly. "You seem to be doing just fine."

She smiled against his heated flesh. "What should I do with my hand *down here*?" She brushed her fingers against the base of his shaft.

"The thing to know about a cock is that it likes to be touched—in pretty much any way. It likes to be buried inside you best of all, but absent that, your hand can mimic a fair imitation. So can your mouth, but we'll leave that for another time."

Diana was incredibly intrigued. "My mouth?" She looked down at him and ran her fingers along the length. He twitched, the flesh jumping in her hand. He was so warm and soft there, but hard too of course, beneath the velvet of his skin. She licked her upper lip.

"*Diana*. Not tonight," he rasped.

She looked up at him, intending to argue, but didn't. She'd do whatever she damn well pleased. She closed her hand around his shaft. "Is this right?"

"Yes. Now move it up and down. Remember when I showed you how to pleasure yourself, how important it was to keep up the pressure and move quickly, especially as your orgasm builds?"

She thought she understood where he was going. "I should move my hand rapidly up and down, from base to tip?" She did what she asked, enclosing her hand around him as tightly as she dared.

He groaned, and she glanced up to see his lashes flutter down over his eyes and his head tip back. Was he enjoying this? She loosened her grip slightly. "Too tight?"

"*No*, don't stop."

She leaned down and touched her lips to the end of his shaft where a tiny bead of moisture had pooled. She licked at it with her tongue and was surprised by the thick, salty flavor.

"*Diana*."

She looked up once more and narrowed her eyes at him. "My entire life people have told me what to do and when to do it. I want to put you in my mouth. You can tell me how or suffer whatever I manage to come up with."

A dark, warm laugh escaped his mouth. "God, you're amazing. It will be easier if you kneel in front of me. Take me as deep as you like. Or not, it's up to you. There's no right or wrong. Use your tongue. Hell, you can even use your teeth—gently, of course."

Her teeth? That never would have occurred to her, and she still wasn't sure how she would do that without causing injury. But the rest she could do. Her breasts tingled and her core throbbed again with need, as if she hadn't already had an orgasm. She slipped from the bed, and he pivoted so she could kneel before him.

"Simon, is it possible to have more than one orgasm?"

"Uh, yes, particularly for women. It's less common for a man—we take a bit of time to recuperate. Any man worth his salt takes great pride in making a woman come multiple times, and after we're wed, I'll show you precisely what I mean."

The desire pulsing through her rose to a crescendo, but she pushed it aside to focus on him. She wanted to bring him pleasure—to do for him what he'd done for her. What he promised to do for her over and over. Anticipation curled through her veins as she touched her lips to the end of his cock.

She gripped the base and opened her mouth, drawing his flesh slowly inside. He glided over her tongue, and she relished the silky softness of his flesh.

"God, Diana. Yes. That's"—he grunted—"*perfect.*"

She thought of what he'd said—take him as deep as she wanted. Opening wider, she sucked him farther inside until he neared the back of her mouth. He pulled back, then pushed forward slowly. She recalled the movements of his fingers inside her. His cock would move the same way. Which was why she was supposed to move her hand up and down the shaft. She did that now, pulling back with her mouth and bringing her hand up, then plunging forward again with her hand and mouth.

His moan filled the room and his hand wrapped in her braid, holding her head while she moved her mouth and hand over him. She felt him tense, then he withdrew from her completely. When she tried to draw him back, he caressed her cheek. "Diana, my orgasm includes spilling my seed."

She looked up at him. His eyes were opened to bare slits. "I know," she said.

"If you don't stop, I'm going to spill it down your throat."

"Is that a problem?"

"Some women don't like it."

She didn't like thinking of him with "some women." Or with any women. And yet he'd been married. Had his wife done this for him? Had she let him come in her mouth? She would never ask, and decided it didn't matter. There could be no place in their marriage for her jealousy, not of the woman he'd loved.

"I want you to." She gripped his hip with her free hand and drew him back into her mouth, not giving him a chance to talk her out of it. Increasing the pressure of her hand, she used her tongue, as he'd said, and licked along the underside of his shaft. Then she grazed her teeth over the tip. He swore passionately. Yes, that's what he'd meant.

She smiled as she took him back in. Then there was no time for thought, just losing herself in the rhythm of this joining, of the give and take of their bodies. He tensed again, and she tasted something at the back of her tongue. He shouted, his hand cupping her head, and then his seed coursed into her mouth, filling her with heat and rapture.

When he was finished, she felt him sag against the bed. The muscles in his thighs quivered. She pulled away and wiped her hand over her mouth, leaning back on her feet.

His hands cupped her elbows, and he drew her to stand. "That was astonishing. I am humbled by your generosity. And enthralled by your skill."

She laughed. "I can't imagine why. I've no experience whatsoever."

"Experience doesn't matter, not when you're naturally talented." He winked at her before retrieving his shirt and pulling it on over his head. "You should get back to your room. We'll be leaving very early."

She looked at him in surprise as she tied her dressing gown closed. "But we have to arrange everything first."

"Verity's taken care of everything." She realized he'd called her Verity earlier too. They'd spent a bit of time together at some point. Had she talked him into this?

"The two of you have already planned everything?" She put her hand on her hip. "What if I'd said no?"

"Then we wouldn't go. We simply wanted to be ready in case you said yes." He cupped her cheek. "You will always have choice, Diana. Say the word, and we'll stay right here. Or go anywhere you want to."

She wanted to go to Gretna Green. Did it matter if it felt a little bit like she'd been managed?

Had she really, though? Simon had assured her the decision was hers. Verity only had her best interests at heart, and she believed Simon did too. He'd never given her reason to doubt his intentions. It wasn't their fault that she was predisposed to distrust people's motives when it came to her happiness.

His brow creased with concern, and he stroked his thumb along her cheekbone. "Are you all right?"

She nuzzled her face against his hand, craving his touch. "Yes. It's just been a long day. You're right. I should go to bed."

"I'll escort you," he said, dropping a kiss on her temple. "Let me put my breeches back on."

When he was more appropriately covered, he led her to the door and into the corridor.

"I'm to the left." She gestured down the corridor where a sconce flickered on the wall at the corner. They made their way to the light, then turned right along another gallery that overlooked the courtyard. She stopped at the first door and opened it, then turned toward him. "Thank you for...tonight." She couldn't keep from blushing when she thought of what she'd done.

"Thank *you*." He leaned forward but hesitated before touching his lips to hers. "May I kiss you again?"

"Now you're going to ask?" She laughed softly. "Yes, please." She curled her hands around his neck and pulled his head down to hers for a searing, knee-melting kiss.

He drew back with a sigh. "Verity says we should be in Gretna Green in three days. It feels like a lifetime."

It did to her too. "It's rather ironic that we're in separate bedrooms after sharing one for over a week, and now we actually *want* to share a bed."

He grinned. "Indeed. Well, we'll ride as fast as we can."

She gave him a suggestive look. "We'll have to stop for two nights probably."

"Verity will be with us, so we'll have to behave. Besides, I told you I'm waiting until we are wed, and I meant it."

She let out a soft snort. "We could repeat what we did tonight."

He kissed her hard and fast. "Incorrigible. Don't ever change. Good night, Diana."

"Good night, Simon."

She watched him back away from her door and reluctantly turn. When he reached the corner, he looked back at her. She curled her lips into a smile, and he placed his hand over his heart.

With a giggle—truly a sound she didn't think she'd ever made—she went into her chamber and closed the door.

For the first time in her life, she looked forward not just to tomorrow, but to all the tomorrows. The future was no longer a gray, grim unknown. She glimpsed peace and happiness.

As she shrugged out of her dressing gown and climbed into bed, a voice in the back of her head reminded her she still had to face her father at some point and that he would still be furious she'd run off and married the Duke of Ruin. The worst of it was that her father would only be angry because Simon was a pariah. The reason behind his reputation mattered not. Father would have no quarrel with Diana marrying a murderer, *if* that murderer was popular and admired and would advance their family's position.

However, she *wasn't* marrying a murderer.

Chapter Twelve
❦

IT HAD BEEN a grueling three days that saw them to Gretna with cold temperatures and a persistent drizzle on the middle day. Even if Verity hadn't been traveling with them, Simon doubted he and Diana would've had the energy to continue what they'd started the night before they'd left.

And if he believed that, he'd clearly forgotten what it was like to be hopelessly attracted to someone.

In fact, he had. He'd spent the last two years in deep mourning, not just disallowing himself to want another woman, but not even finding the urge to do so. The kiss he'd given Diana at the house party had reawakened his body. The kiss at Brereton had reawakened his mind. The events at Beaumont Tower had sent him into a haze of desire so strong that barely an hour went by that he didn't think of her and all the things he wanted to do to her once they were wed.

It would likely have been even more often than that, but he was also busy loathing himself for feeling this way. He didn't deserve to find such bliss, not when Miriam was cold and dead in a grave.

Christ, he was a maudlin prick.

He wiped a hand over his face as they rode into the yard at the blacksmith shop. He looked over at Diana, and Verity rode up beside her. The groom lingered behind them on his horse.

They'd discussed their plan last night at dinner. They would ride directly to the blacksmith shop and be married. Then they'd find an inn. Their coaches—Simon's and Verity's—would hopefully arrive late tomorrow. Then Simon and Diana would travel south to Lyndhurst while Verity would return home. Though he'd only spent a few days with her, Simon was already quite fond of his soon-to-be-wife's cousin.

Soon-to-be-wife.

His heart pounded in his chest, and he hoped for the thousandth time that he was doing the right thing. Not that he would change his mind. He was quite past the point of no return.

Their groom, Paddon, helped Verity dismount, while Simon moved to help Diana. From the moment he clasped her waist, awareness tripped along his flesh and up his spine. Their eyes met, and he saw desire reflected in the blue depths.

Reluctantly, he let go of her but offered his arm, which she took as they made their way to Verity. She took Simon's other arm, and he guided them into the blacksmith shop. Paddon remained in the yard to look after the horses.

Inside, a young man rushed to meet them. "Good afternoon, are ye here to wed?"

"Indeed we are. I am the Duke of Romsey." There was no need for aliases any longer. Indeed, he *had* to be the duke now. "We have a witness with us, the Duchess of Blackburn, cousin to the bride. Will you be able to provide another, or should we fetch our groom from the yard?"

The lad bowed a bit awkwardly to the duchess and then to Diana. "Mrs. Elliott can serve as your other witness. Ye just need to pay the fee." His brogue was thick but understandable. "Mr. Elliot is finishing up with another wedding. May I take your hats, gloves, and cloaks?"

"Thank you," Verity said, withdrawing her hand from Simon's arm and removing her gloves.

Diana followed her actions, and Simon resisted the urge to take her hand, to keep her close. In a very short time, she'd be bound to him forever. Cold sweat broke out along his neck. Miriam was supposed to have been forever. He didn't see how he could love two wives. And he would always love Miriam.

The sound of a hammer hitting the anvil came from the room next door.

Verity smiled. "Someone is newly married."

Simon handed his items to the boy, and Diana and Verity did the same. Arms laden, the lad opened a door into an adjoining room, where the sound of the hammer had originated.

Verity turned to Diana. "I'm sorry you aren't getting married in a splendid gown in front of an audience."

"I couldn't give a fig about an audience. Everyone I care about is right here." She smiled at Verity, and Simon knew she was speaking of her cousin and only her cousin. It wasn't that she didn't care for him—he assumed she did, at least somewhat. But it wasn't the same, and he didn't expect it to be.

Diana looked down at one of the only two gowns she'd brought with her. This one had a bit of decoration along the neck. "A new gown might be nice—or perhaps just one I haven't worn to death and never wish to see again."

Verity gave her a sympathetic nod. "Tomorrow, my maid will arrive with the gowns that she's altered to fit you for the journey to Lyndhurst. You'll feel better then."

A young, very pretty woman came from the room next door. "We're ready for you," she said, nodding toward the room. "Go on in."

"So quickly?" Diana asked, looking mildly surprised.

Was she nervous too?

He stepped toward her. "We can take a few minutes, if you like."

"No, you can't," the woman said apologetically. "Another couple will be along shortly, and then you'll have to wait."

Diana looked to Simon. "Then we'd best go in."

She took his arm again as they made their way into the next room. A couple was just leaving through another door, and the young man was closing it behind them. A second man came toward them with a broad grin.

"Welcome to Gretna! I'm Robert Elliot. I understand I have the distinct honor of marrying a duke today."

Simon nodded. "I'm the Duke of Romsey. This is my bride, Miss Diana Kingman, and her cousin, Her Grace, the Duchess of Blackburn."

"My goodness, such esteemed company." Elliott puffed up his wide chest and stood a bit taller. "Have you paid the fee?"

Simon took his arm from Diana's grip and reached into his coat for the money, then handed it to the man. "I believe this is more than sufficient."

Elliot looked down. "Yes, indeed, thank you." He handed it off to the woman who'd greeted them in the other room. "This is my wife. Is there anything you require before the ceremony?"

"Is there a ceremony?" Diana asked. They'd been told at the inn in Carlisle last night that they could simply declare their wish to marry, and as long as they had two witnesses, that was all it took.

It was laughably simple, once you made the arduous journey to get there.

"There can be," Elliott said. "You're welcome to recite vows. But it isn't necessary. I just need your names and your witnesses for the register."

Simon turned to Diana. "What do you wish to do?"

She was quiet a moment then asked, "What do *you* want to do?"

"I've been married before," he said. "You haven't. I will do whatever you wish."

"You've been married before?" Elliott asked, sounding a bit alarmed.

"His wife is deceased," Verity said softly.

Elliott nodded. "I'll be over at the register while you decide." He moved to a table where a book lay open.

Diana looked at Verity. "Does it matter if we say vows? It feels…strange to do so in a blacksmith shop. But then maybe it would feel strange regardless."

"Say the vows," Verity said with a small smile. "You won't regret it. And if you don't, well, you may decide later that you wish you had."

That was an excellent point, and yet Simon was a little frightened about repeating them. Miriam had never felt more present, and he didn't like the sensation.

Diana took a breath and turned determinedly toward the register. "Let us sign our names, then."

Simon touched her arm. "What about the vows?"

"I appreciate what Verity said, but I don't need to say them, nor do I need to hear them. They're just words." She tipped her head to the side. "Unless you really want to. It's just... I thought..." She looked away. "Never mind."

He stroked his thumb along her forearm. "What?"

She returned her gaze to his. "As you said, you've done this before. Had a wedding and recited vows. This one is quite different—so why not make it so in every way?"

The apprehension bubbling inside him settled. Yes, it was quite different. "What a thoughtful sentiment."

They went to the register, where they signed their names. Verity signed hers next, then she handed the pen to Mrs. Elliott. "Thank you for serving as witness."

"Happy to, Your Grace." Mrs. Elliott put her name to the paper.

Elliott blinked at Simon. "Do you have a ring?"

He'd thought of that, but there'd been no time. Still, he regretted not having one. "No."

"If you like, we have hammered iron bands for purchase."

"That isn't necessary," Diana said.

Simon nodded at Elliott. "Yes, the daintiest, most feminine one you have, please."

The anvil priest turned to his wife, but she was already on her way out. He smiled at Simon. "She knows just what to get. That will be two pounds."

Diana curled her hand around Simon's elbow. "It really isn't necessary."

He looked down at her, thinking of what she'd said. This *was* going to be different from the last time, and if that meant buying her an iron wedding band, then that was what he was going to do. Plus, he wanted this to be special for her in some way.

"I insist," he said quietly, looking into her eyes.

Mrs. Elliott returned with a ring and gave it to Simon. "The prettiest one we have."

It was rather slender, with a flower and a vine etched around the circumference. It was perfect. "Exactly what I had in mind, thank you."

He turned to Diana and took her hand. Taking a deep breath, he stared into her eyes. "I promise to protect you and keep you for all the days of my life." He then recited the part of the marriage vows he remembered most, the ones he felt Diana ought to hear from her husband. He slipped the ring onto her finger. Remarkably, it fit. "With this ring, I thee wed." He lifted her hand to his lips and kissed the soft flesh on the back. "With my body, I thee worship." He took her other hand so that he clasped them both, never breaking eye contact. "With all my worldly goods, I thee endow. In the name of the Father and of the Son and of the Holy Ghost, Amen." He leaned forward and brushed his lips across hers.

He felt her sigh against his mouth.

A loud sniff filled the room. "That was so romantic," Mrs. Elliott said, dabbing a handkerchief at her eye.

Simon turned to the anvil priest. "Thank you, Mr. Elliott." He bowed toward the anvil priest's wife. "Mrs. Elliott." He looked between them both. "Can you recommend a smaller inn where we might lodge?"

"The Dove will suit your needs," Mr. Elliott said.

Mrs. Elliott scoffed. "Pshaw. They said small, Robert." Her lips spread into a comely smile as she turned to Simon and Diana. "The Bell and Broomstick is what you need. Just to the west a bit off the main road."

"Thank you, Mrs. Elliott."

The boy brought their cloaks and hats and gloves.

"Your Grace?"

Simon had been busy drawing on his gloves, but he looked over and saw that the boy was addressing Diana. She was staring at her ring, and the boy still held her things.

Edging closer to her, Simon nudged her elbow softly.

She blinked up at him, saw him dart his eyes toward the boy, and gave the lad her attention.

"Your Grace?" he repeated.

A pale blush rose in Diana's cheeks. "Oh yes, thank you." She accepted her hat and gloves while Simon took her cloak and waited to help her put it on.

"Congratulations to you," Mrs. Elliott said, looking between them. "May you enjoy a happy and fruitful life together." She led them to the exterior door where the other couple had departed earlier.

Outside, Simon blinked up at the darkening sky.

"It's going to be dark soon," Verity said.

"And it's going to rain. Let's find The Bell and Broomstick, shall we?" He led them back to the yard, where Paddon waited with the horses. A few minutes later, they were on their way, and it didn't take them long to find the inn Mrs. Elliott had recommended.

The Bell and Broomstick was a smaller establishment, but still qualified as a coaching inn. But then Gretna was a main stop on the road between London and Edinburgh, so Simon presumed all the inns were of the coaching variety.

Again, he helped Diana from the horse. As he set her on the ground, he murmured, "Duchess."

She blushed again. "That's going to take some getting used to."

"Shall I call you that until you're comfortable with it?"

"No. I prefer you call me Diana." There was a saucy tilt to her chin and a mischievous sparkle in her eye that elicited a flash of desire.

She was his wife.

He froze for a moment, torn between elation and distress. Miriam hovered at the back of his mind. He pushed her away but felt horrible for it.

A fat drop of rain landed on his arm. "Let's get inside."

Simon took two rooms—one for Verity and one for him and Diana— for two nights. Tomorrow, they would rest. Uncharitably, he thought it was too bad Verity was with them for if they'd been alone, he could have looked forward to spending the entire day in bed with his bride.

Since they were ravenous, they decided to eat immediately. They sat in the common room, and Simon noticed that Diana kept looking at the ring on her finger. He hoped it was because it was new and not because she didn't like it. Not that it mattered. It was temporary—he'd buy her a new, fancier ring in London or Bath, maybe something with a sapphire. He'd wanted a symbol and for her to have that small part of the traditional ceremony. It had also been important to him that he pledge himself to her. Maybe this time, he'd do a better job of it.

"I think I'll see if I can do some shopping tomorrow," Verity said. "I'd like to find a present for Beau for Christmas."

Christmas. Miriam had loved the holiday. She'd wanted to get a tree and light it with candles like Queen Charlotte had done. They'd planned to do it for their very next Christmas, but of course, it had never come. He doubted he and Diana would reach Lyndhurst before the holiday and decided he'd rather not.

"Perhaps we should return to Beaumont Tower with you. For Christmas," Simon said, spearing the last of his mutton on his fork. "Diana, you'd like that, wouldn't you?" During their journey to Gretna, she and Verity had recollected the Christmas they'd spent together there two years ago. It had seemed a very happy time for Diana in particular since she'd come without her parents.

Before Diana could answer, Verity asked, "What if her father is there? That won't be enjoyable at all."

Simon gripped his fork more tightly. "I'll ensure he isn't a problem."

Verity smiled calmly. "I'm sure you will. However, I think you'd do better to face him at your own home, where you reign supreme."

Those little lines that had shown less and less in recent days appeared between Diana's eyes. "I keep thinking we'll pass him along the road at some point. He won't recognize our coach, of course."

And if they did see him, Simon had no intention of stopping. He understood Verity's point about facing Sir Barnard at Lyndhurst. What would the man do when he visited his daughter—who was now a duchess—at her new home? He'd bloody well behave, that's what he'd do.

Simon finished his mutton, then sat back with his cup of tea. At the end of the meal, they walked upstairs together. Verity's room was accessible directly from the landing. She bid them good night, then pulled Diana into a tight hug. Simon was aware she was whispering something in Diana's ear and wondered if she was giving Diana a brief description of what to expect.

Diana kissed her cousin on the cheek, then joined Simon as they continued along the corridor until they reached their room. The innkeeper had said it was the last door on the left and that it was their largest and finest room.

Simon opened the door and swept Diana inside. It was indeed spacious, definitely the largest lodging they'd encountered. The fire had been stoked so that happy yellow flames warmed the room. Two wing-backed chairs flanked the fireplace to their right, and a small table stood against the opposite wall.

But it was the four-poster bed, situated between two windows, that commanded the room.

"Oh, this is lovely," Diana said, moving inside. Their things had been brought up already, and the innkeeper's wife had laid out their nightclothes. Their cloaks and hats were hung on hooks next to the door, and their gloves lay atop a small dresser across from the bed.

Simon closed the door and followed Diana, letting her lead him. She went directly to the bed, moving to the side closest to the fire.

He stood at the foot and watched as she ran her fingers over the quilted coverlet. "There's a bed warmer," she observed with delight.

"Mrs. Insley thought of everything." Simon walked toward the fire and sat down to remove his boots. The warmth felt good, and he realized he was exhausted. But not too exhausted. Perhaps she was, however.

She sat in the chair opposite him and took off her half boots. She wiggled her stockinged toes in front of the fire and let out a soft sigh. "That feels wonderful. I will wear nothing but slippers for at least a week when we reach Lyndhurst." She looked over at him. "How long will it take?"

"It will depend on the weather, of course, but I should think somewhere between seven and ten days. It also depends on how quickly we wish to travel. Is it important to you to arrive before Christmas?"

"Not particularly, but don't you have traditions that you need to keep?"

He thought of the dinner he had for the retainers on Boxing Day. He ought to send word that he was on his way home. He'd done a dreadful job of communicating with them since he'd left. He'd rectify that tomorrow.

"I'll send word to my steward tomorrow, informing him we may not arrive until after Boxing Day."

They fell quiet, both of them staring into the fire. She yawned, and he wondered if she was in fact tired. "Should we go to bed?" he finally asked.

She looked over at him, her gaze tentative. "I suppose we should."

"Diana, we can go to sleep. It's been an exhausting trip."

She narrowed her eyes at him. "You make me wait until we're wed to engage in intercourse, and now you want to go to sleep?"

Simon should have known better. He knew *her* better than to think she wouldn't want a traditional wedding night. What's more, she deserved one.

He thought of his wedding night with Miriam, of her shyness. What the bloody hell was he doing? He couldn't keep thinking of her. He didn't *want* to keep thinking of her. And yet there she was, like a ghost haunting him, and truly, he deserved nothing less. He certainly didn't deserve this beautiful, charming, thoughtful woman who'd just become his duchess.

He stared at her, wondering what in the hell he'd done to win her? Nothing. He'd been in the right place at the right time. She'd needed rescuing, and he'd saved her. Was there any chance he could save himself in the process?

Before he could answer that question—and he doubted if he really could—she rose from the chair, her lips curling in a thoroughly seductive manner. "Are you going to help me undress? This time, you don't have to go quickly. Nor do you have to try to avoid touching me."

And just like that, the demons invading his mind faded to the background. He stood and shrugged out of his coat, letting it fall back onto the chair. He took the two steps necessary to stand before her and stared down at her pink, parted lips. "Turn."

She did, and Simon's mouth went dry as he allowed himself to contemplate disrobing her in the way he'd tried very hard not to think about during their long journey north. He plucked at the laces of her gown as he'd done so many times. This time, however, he went slowly, and he took no care to avoid touching her too much.

When the gown was loose, he pulled up the skirt and drew it over her head. Reaching around her, he draped it rather carelessly across her chair. Next was her petticoat. She tugged it up, and he helped remove it in the same fashion as her dress. It also followed the gown onto the chair.

Now the corset. He pulled at the laces, allowing his knuckles to graze her back, feeling her warmth beneath the thin linen of her chemise. Bit by bit, the garment came open and when it was loose enough, he helped her take it over her head. She clasped it and threw it to the chair as she turned to face him.

He shook his head. "Turn."

She gave him a quizzical look before presenting her back once more.

"I want to take your hair down," he said, aching to touch her dark, silken locks. He found the pins and one by one deposited them on the mantel until her hair fell about her shoulders. It reached to the middle of her back, hanging in soft, loose waves. "Please don't braid it."

She turned her head to look at him over her shoulder, her blue eyes glowing in the firelight. "I won't."

He touched her hair, gently sifting it through his fingers, then moving it to the side so he could bare the back of her neck. He bent his head and kissed her flesh, eliciting a shiver along her nape.

She edged backward the slightest amount, and a soft sigh—similar to the sound she'd made when she'd removed her shoes and yet wholly different—escaped her. He moved his lips along her neck, holding her hair to the side and trailing his fingertips along her left arm.

When his lips found her ear and he suckled her flesh, she cast her head back. He swept his hand beneath her arm and skimmed his palm up to her breast. She was soft and round and her nipple came to immediate attention the second he touched it. He let go of her hair and brought his right hand around to her other breast. Cupping her in both hands, he massaged her gently and trailed his lips down her neck.

She arched her back, her head falling against his shoulder. He closed his fingertips over her nipples and lightly pressed, then tugged. She cried out, and the sound spurred his desire. As he worked and fondled her breasts, her hips began to move. Her backside grazed his cock. He envisioned bending her over the chair and coming into her from behind. Not tonight, but perhaps some day.

He moved his hand down over her abdomen and pressed it between her legs. She moved her thighs apart for him, giving him better access. He cupped her mound and fingered her through the fabric of her chemise.

She moaned softly, her pelvis rotating. Then she lifted her hem, silently urging him to touch her with no barrier. He meant to do that and more. When she was bare to him, he found her clitoris and stroked her incessantly. She moaned again and strained back against him. He withdrew his hand, and she let out a quiet whimper.

"To the bed," he rasped.

She turned to face him, her eyes dark and sultry with lust. "You have too many clothes on."

"I do indeed." He quickly unbuttoned his waistcoat, and she barely waited for him to finish before she pushed it from his shoulders. Her hands found his waistband first and pulled the hem of his shirt free. He whisked it over his head and let it fall to the floor. Her fingers were already dancing across his chest, and while he appreciated her zeal, if he didn't taste her soon, he was going to go mad.

Pulling her against him, he kissed her, openmouthed and hungry. She met him, and her teeth grazed his lip. The contact was more fuel on the fire of his lust. He drove his tongue into her mouth, and she did the same to him, giving and taking with a demand that matched his own.

He was consumed with kissing her. He slowed, teasing her with long, lush strokes of his tongue. He pulled away to kiss her jaw, her cheek, her neck. Then he returned to her mouth to begin his assault anew. She clutched at him through it all, her fingertips digging into his shoulders and neck, his back. And then her hands were on his backside, cupping him and holding him as she pressed her pelvis to his. The contact of her heat against his erection roused a groan from deep within his throat.

They'd never make it to the damned bed.

He picked her up, and she let out a small, feminine squeal of surprise that made him smile. In three quick strides, he was at the bed, and he set her down near the top. "Where's the bed warmer?" He didn't want that getting in their way.

She reached for the coverlet and started to peel it back. "I'll take care of it while you take off the rest of your clothes."

He leaned against the mattress to remove his stockings. "I hope that means you're getting rid of your chemise."

She stopped what she was doing and made a show of lifting the garment over her head. As she put her arms up, her abdomen stretched, drawing his attention right to her breasts. He longed to put his mouth on her. She tossed the chemise from the bed and gave him a sultry stare before removing the bed warmer and taking it to the hearth.

Moving faster, Simon finished undressing. As she came back, he reached for her, wrapping his arm around her waist and drawing her forward. He kissed her again, nibbling at her lower lip, then licking it before sliding his tongue inside. She pressed up against him, and he cupped the back of her head, twining his fingers into her hair and gripping her tight. He pulled her head back, and she arched for him, extending her neck as if it were a delicious feast for his eyes and mouth. He kissed and licked her flesh, unable to get enough of her.

She clasped his head, sighing and moaning until his mouth trailed to her breast. Then she sucked in air—a sharp sound of surprise.

He closed over her nipple and brought his left hand beneath to cup her, holding her captive to his mouth and tongue. He teased her flesh, licking and sucking, pushing her to the edge.

She said his name over and over. He lifted her onto the bed again, laying her down and then continuing to lavish attention on her breasts. She held his head to her as her body writhed and arched, seeking his touch.

He skimmed his fingers along her abdomen and found the curls between her legs. She was warm and wet, and she cried out when he touched her folds. He lifted his head and looked at her face. Her eyes were closed, her lips parted, her neck extended. She was the embodiment of rapture. Desire personified.

"Diana, open your eyes."

Her lashes fluttered before her lids rose and revealed the deep blue of her eyes.

"I didn't want to shock you. I'm going to put my mouth on you here." He stroked her sex and slipped his finger into her silken sheath.

Her eyes widened briefly. "Like I did with you."

"Similar, but not quite the same, of course." He couldn't help but smile.

"Thank you for telling me. That would have been quite shocking."

Her hips moved up, encouraging the thrust of his finger. He was happy to accommodate her and used two to fill her. Her fingers dug into the bedclothes on either side of her, and she gasped.

He bent and suckled her clitoris while continuing to tantalize her with his hand. He withdrew his fingers and replaced them with his tongue, sliding into her and tasting her sweetness. She moaned, then cried his name, one hand burrowing into his hair.

He lifted his head briefly. "This orgasm may be more powerful than the others you've experienced. At least I will do my best to make it that way."

"*Simon.*" She urged his head back down, and he grinned before climbing onto the bed and settling himself between her legs. Time to make her senseless.

He draped her thighs over his shoulders and buried himself in her sex, licking, sucking, kissing. She thrashed against the bed as he continued relentlessly, driving her ever closer to the precipice. She cried out over and over, her voice rising higher and higher. He filled her with his fingers again, pumping until he felt her muscles clench around him. Using his mouth once more, he sent her into oblivion, not ceasing until the shudders in her body settled.

He wiped his mouth and sat back, staring at the pale beauty of her body bathed in firelight. Her breasts were taut, the nipples forming hard, pink peaks. Her chest rose and fell rapidly as she regained her breath.

He leaned forward and kissed the flesh above her mound, trailing his tongue up past her navel and farther still until he met the underside of her breast. Gently, he stroked his fingers over her skin, grazing her nipple as he licked his way to the tip. Then he sucked it into his mouth and cupped her. He withdrew, then blew on her flesh before sucking it once more. He repeated this several times before moving to her other breast and performing the same ministrations. All the while, her chest continued its rhythm, deep but slightly rapid breaths as her excitement began to build once more.

His was barely in check. His cock raged with the need to sink inside her. Soon. He didn't want to go too fast. Not this first time. In fact, he wondered if she'd had enough. "Should we continue? I don't want to overwhelm you."

She opened her eyes and narrowed them at him. "I'll repeat what I said earlier. You made me wait until we were wed. We are wed. I am not waiting any longer."

"This first time may not be as pleasant as everything that has come before," he said. He had precisely one experience with a virgin—Miriam. He didn't want to think of her just now, but it was damn near impossible not to. Their wedding night had been rather disastrous.

Diana reached up and stroked her fingers over his chest. "Why? You told me my mother lied, that it wasn't unpleasant."

"It isn't. At least not after the first time and not if you're with a man who knows how to ensure you enjoy yourself. Many men don't."

"Well then, I'm doubly glad I married you."

He was too. More than he'd ever thought possible. But how did he explain this to her? "The first time can be…uncomfortable for a woman because her flesh isn't used to being, er, invaded." He winced, disliking the way that had come out.

"Will it hurt?"

He thought of Miriam, who'd experienced some pain, but kept his features blank. "It could. But it should fade relatively quickly."

"You know this from experience."

It wasn't a question, so he didn't feel the need to answer. He gave her an infinitesimal nod.

She splayed her palm over his flesh and ran her hand up to cup the back of his neck. She pulled him down. "I appreciate your concern and all you've done to prepare me—and to pleasure me. I've no doubt you will take every care, and I can think of no man I'd rather share this moment with. Now show me what to do before I toss you over and make it up as I go along."

He laughed. "Like you did at Beaumont Tower? If that's the case, then I gladly give myself over to you." He narrowed his eyes and kissed her fast but deep. "But not tonight. Tonight you're mine, and I'm going to show you how much."

Chapter Thirteen
❧

DIANA SHIVERED AT the promise in his seductive gaze. He'd made her a bit nervous a moment before. After everything she'd been raised to believe about sex, it was easy to succumb to apprehension. But all he'd taught her so far had been so wonderful, each experience better than the one before. She had to believe this wouldn't be any different.

And if it was, well, she'd come too far to turn back now.

Simon kissed her again and any potential discomfort or disappointment fled her mind. She didn't think she'd ever grow tired of kissing him. Each one was different. Soft and sweet. Hard and demanding. Lush and provocative. This one was a combination of everything, his tongue delving deep into her mouth as his lips played over hers.

His fingers stroked her sex, reawakening the pulsing desire she'd vanquished just a short time ago. She loved the feel of him on top of her, their flesh pressed together, as intimate as two people could be.

His cock nudged between her thighs.

Perhaps not *quite* as intimate as two people could be.

He pulled his mouth from hers. "You can touch me, if you like."

Yes, she liked. She ran her hands over his shoulders and back, loving the feel of his smooth skin, then moved lower, caressing the curve of his backside. It seemed an outrageous thing to do, forbidden almost, but it was tame, really, when she thought of the other things she'd already done.

"I meant my cock." His hips pressed against hers, settling his erection firmly along her sex. The sensation of him there sparked a desperate need, not just the release of an orgasm, but the sensation of being filled. As he'd done with his fingers.

She slid her hand around his hip and reached between them until she found his shaft. Closing her hand around the base, she looked up into his eyes. His face was taut, his eyes dark as sin. "Like this?" she asked.

"Just like that." His voice was hard and raspy, arousing all on its own, which seemed ridiculous.

She stroked him once, slowly, then again and again. He moaned before kissing her once more. Then his hand was around hers, guiding his cock to her opening.

"Open your thighs a bit more," he whispered against her lips.

She did as he bade and felt him slide slowly into her. He hesitated, raising his mouth from hers. "Please tell me if anything hurts or if you want me to stop."

She couldn't imagine either of those things happening. It felt as though she were being stretched, but not unpleasantly so. Then his thumb pressed against her clitoris, and ecstasy began to build.

He slid farther inside and that sensation of being filled, of wanting more took over. Instinctively she raised her hips then lifted her legs and wrapped them around his thighs.

"God, Diana. How do you…" He didn't finish his question as he sank himself deep inside. It wasn't painful, but yes, there was a bit of discomfort—the feeling of being stretched intensified as her body worked to become accustomed to him.

"Are you all right?" His voice was strained, as if *he* were in pain.

"Yes, are you?"

A short, sharp laugh escaped his mouth. "Yes. I'm going to move now, Diana. I need to. I'm going to try to go slow, but God, you feel so good. I don't know if I'll be able to help myself."

"From doing what?"

"Fucking you senseless." He kissed her again. "My apologies, that was rather crude. But when a man is buried inside his wife and she's as stunning and seductive as you, there is nothing he wants to do more than lose himself in sexual bliss."

"Then by all means, do so." She squeezed his backside and ran her tongue along his lower lip. "Come for me, Simon. *Come* for me."

He cupped her neck and kissed her, his tongue spearing into her mouth as his cock did the same to her sex. He began to move his hips, thrusting in and out. The discomfort began to fade, and once more, the pleasure began to grow.

He broke the kiss. "Move your legs higher. To my waist."

She did and was rewarded with him driving even deeper into her. The discomfort returned for a few strokes, but again she grew used to the sensation, and again the pleasure returned.

"Diana. My God." His groans filled the room, and his movements sharpened, his cock filling her with delicious precision.

She rose to meet him, wanting the pressure of him against her and inside her. It was the most astonishing feeling as she reached for another climax to carry her away.

He stiffened, then cried out. Had he come? No, he continued to thrust. She was so close herself… But then he began to slow. His breath was hard and ragged. He kissed her forehead, her cheek, her lips.

"Are you done?" she asked.

He took a moment to answer. "Hell, you didn't have another orgasm, did you?"

She shook her head as disappointment settled into her. The need pulsing in her sex had diminished slightly, but it was still there, reminding her of how close she'd been. "I thought I was going to, but I didn't."

"I'll get to know your body better, and this won't happen." He slipped from her body and put his hand on her, doing what he'd done to her at Beaumont Tower—briskly massaging her clitoris and then putting his fingers in her.

She felt another bit of discomfort, but then he focused on her clitoris again, and the pleasure came rolling back. Ecstasy built as she rose up off the bed to meet his hand. He moved faster, driving her to the brink. Then she let go completely.

White light flashed behind her eyelids as she cried and whimpered her release. He stayed with her, guiding her back, then kissed her softly. "Better?" he murmured.

"So much. Thank you."

When she was still, he pulled the coverlet up and gathered her into his arms. "Sleep now, wife. And if you're not too sore and can still stand the sight of me in the morning, we can do this again."

"I'd like that." They were quiet for several minutes, their breathing returning to normal, and she wondered if he was drifting to sleep.

She yawned, as sleep tried to overtake her. But she wasn't quite ready to succumb. She wanted to bask in this moment he'd given her. She'd never felt so cared for, so treasured, so wanted.

She kissed him softly on the mouth. "Good night, husband."

She looked at the iron band on her finger. It felt only slightly less foreign than it had earlier. Wonder spread through her as she listened to his deep, even breathing. She'd resigned herself to getting married. But she hadn't expected it to be to this man. Nor had she expected to want it. To want *him*.

Yet there was still so much she didn't know about him—his family, his past, and, of course, his wife. His *first* wife. She knew there was much more to the tragedy and hoped that he would come to trust her enough to share it.

Will you trust him enough to reveal your secrets?

She shivered at the unspoken question from the recesses of her mind and snuggled against him. His arms tightened around her, and she welcomed the feeling of security she was now coming to know.

Yes, maybe she could trust him with all she'd worked to hide. And maybe—just maybe—she'd even be able to trust him with her heart.

◆€•3◆

THE JOURNEY SOUTH to Lyndhurst was the happiest fortnight Simon could remember. They'd stopped in Oxford for Christmas, where they'd spent several days shopping for new clothing for Diana, buying gifts for his staff, and, of course, exploring each other in bed. Her courses had come two days after the wedding, so when they'd reached Oxford, they'd been more than eager to resume their marital entertainments.

But now that Lyndhurst was on the horizon, Simon's stomach began to churn. In truth, his apprehension had started the night before. He'd known it was the last time he'd have Diana to himself and that the next day, he had to escort her into a home he despised.

The coach turned into the drive lined with oak trees, their bare limbs arching overhead. It was almost like driving through a skeleton. If one had a morbid mind. And apparently, Simon did just now.

He took a deep breath as they approached the turn that led to the front of the house. Diana touched his arm, and he turned his head to see her eyes glowing with warm enthusiasm.

"I'm looking forward to seeing your home."

They'd talked about it over the past few days, but not in depth. Every time the subject arose, he fought to maintain his equilibrium and invariably found a way to change the topic. But now they were here, and he couldn't avoid the past. It was about to hit him in the face.

He turned toward her. "Diana, this may be difficult for me—"

She pressed her lips to his and whispered, "Shhh. You don't have to say anything. Not now. Just know that I'm here with you." She kissed him again, and he was eternally grateful for her presence.

The coach stopped, and the door opened quickly—too quickly for Simon's taste. Tinley put down the step, and Simon clambered down. The familiar façade greeted him, with its stately Jacobean exterior. Beneath the portico, he could see his butler, Lowell, standing in front of the open door.

A sharp wind threatened Simon's hat as he turned to help Diana from the coach. The breeze whipped the ribbons beneath her chin, and she brushed them away from her face.

She looked up in appreciation. "Lyndhurst is beautiful. And large."

The original structure had been built in the early seventeenth century. Simon's grandfather had enlarged it and undertaken considerable repair and restoration.

Simon tucked her hand over his arm and led her into the shade of the portico. Lowell, a tall man in his late twenties—quite young for a butler—

with thick brown hair and a serious demeanor, bowed deeply. "Welcome home, Your Grace." He performed a second bow to Diana. "We are pleased to welcome you, Your Grace." Simon had sent word ahead that he'd married. He wondered what his staff thought but decided it didn't really matter. What was done was done. And he had no regrets. At least about that.

"Thank you, Lowell." Diana smiled warmly. In Oxford, when they'd shopped for gifts for the staff, Diana had taken care to ask after everyone—and not just those in the highest positions. She'd wanted to know how many maids worked in the scullery. Simon hadn't the faintest idea.

As they moved toward the threshold, Simon's steward, Nevis, greeted them. An affable man with a keen intelligence, he'd served as steward longer than Simon had drawn breath and had been a close and trusted friend of his father's. "Welcome home, Your Grace. The staff is assembled."

"Thank you, Nevis. Diana, this is my steward. Nevis, Her Grace, the Duchess of Romsey." He'd introduced her several times since Gretna, but the title still felt strange on his tongue. He'd known two Duchesses of Romsey—his mother and Miriam. It was a bit of an adjustment to realize there was a third and that it was Diana. He almost wished he could go back to calling her Kitty Byrd.

That thought served to lighten the weight in his chest. At least for a moment.

Then he stepped into the great hall with its gleaming marble floors and impressive collection of paintings filling the walls, and his breath caught. The staff was lined up before him, but his gaze couldn't help but stray to the right where the grand staircase led up to the first floor. God, he hated this room.

The door snapped closed behind them, and Lowell moved past them into the hall. He addressed the staff. "May I present Her Grace, the Duchess of Romsey."

They were arranged from the housekeeper to the footmen to the scullery maids—he counted two. This was just the inside staff, of course. Every single one of them bowed and curtsied toward Diana.

She walked forward, starting at the top of the line, and took the time to meet each retainer, spending a moment speaking with them one by one. Simon oversaw the arrival of the gifts they'd brought, which Tinley handled with the help of one of the grooms.

After Diana had greeted everyone, she gestured to the pile of gifts on a table that had been set up in the corner. "We were sorry to miss Boxing

Day, but we brought gifts to make up for it. Please know how much we value your service."

It was as if she'd been a duchess for years, not days. But then he knew she'd been trained for this and nothing else. Her father would be very proud, the prick.

Diana removed her hat and gloves and handed them to one of the maids, then supervised the distribution of gifts with the housekeeper, Mrs. Marley.

Lowell approached Simon and took his hat and gloves. "Your letter indicated that Her Grace would require a lady's maid. Two of the maids applied for the position, and I selected Miss Banford. Does that meet with your approval?"

Simon couldn't say. Most of the staff was new within the last two years, and he hadn't bothered to learn their names. The staff was new because many of the existing retainers had left following Miriam's death. Except for a precious few, they'd preferred to take new positions than stay and taint themselves with the scandal. Lowell was one of those few, having been the head footman when the former butler had departed. Nevis had promoted him with Simon's consent. Consent? Simon had barely known what day it was following Miriam's death. He'd given Nevis carte blanche to manage things as necessary.

Simon didn't even know which of the women in the line was Banford. "I'm sure she's more than satisfactory. The Duchess is not demanding."

Lowell inclined his head. "I wonder if we might schedule a meeting for tomorrow, sir. I'd like to bring a few things to your attention."

"Is anything amiss?"

"Not at all, sir. You've just been gone for some time, and I thought you might like to be informed of staffing changes and how the household is running."

Of course he should. Damn, he was a terrible duke. His gaze strayed to Diana as she moved along the line. She, however, was already an excellent duchess. Perhaps she ought to meet with Lowell. "Should the Duchess join us?" Simon asked.

"She could if you wish; however, I suspect she will be meeting with Mrs. Marley. I know it was the housekeeper's intent to give her a proper introduction to Lyndhurst as soon as Her Grace wanted."

That made perfect sense. "Thank you, Lowell."

The butler bowed and went to help with the gifts.

Simon had pivoted so that his back was to the staircase. If he couldn't see it, perhaps his tension would ease. Yes, and perhaps Society would welcome him with flowers and fanfare when he and Diana went to

London. He swallowed a derisive laugh at the likelihood of either of those things happening.

Diana came toward him. The lines were back between her eyes.

"You were meant to be a duchess," he said, hoping to ease the worry etched in her face.

"My parents certainly educated me for it," she said wryly. "Your staff seems well organized and superbly trained. I'm to meet with Mrs. Marley tomorrow—unless you have other plans?"

Such as leaving? He'd only just arrived, and he was ready to flee. How many days had he spent here since Miriam's death? If he tried, he could surely count them with ease.

The lines between her eyes deepened, and her mouth turned down. "Simon, your color's a bit off." She touched his cheek. "Are you feeling well?"

No, he felt like hell. "Fine."

Her gaze moved past him, and he knew she was looking at the staircase. Or perhaps just the floor at the bottom of it. "This can't be easy for you—bringing me here."

He turned his head slightly, following her line of sight. "It's never easy coming back here. That's why I seldom do it. Your presence neither improves nor worsens the occasion."

"I'm not sure whether to be relieved or insulted," she murmured.

He swung his gaze to hers. "What did I say?"

She touched his arm. "It doesn't matter. I was trying to bring a bit of humor, but that wasn't well done of me."

He appreciated her concern so much. He still didn't know what he'd done to deserve her. "I will also choose humor over depression. However, sometimes it's difficult." That was more than he'd ever admitted to anyone.

She rubbed his forearm reassuringly. "I know you meant to have me tour the house when we arrived, but I think I'd rather go directly to our apartments to rest. Will that be all right?"

Once again, she'd anticipated what he wanted. "How do you do that?" he asked softly.

"Do what?" The question seemed guileless, but surely, she knew.

"Know what I need, sometimes even before I do?"

She lifted a shoulder. "I've come to know you. We've spent a great deal of time together."

Yes, they had. And he was grateful for every moment.

Simon signaled for Lowell to come back over and informed the butler of their plans. He asked that they not be disturbed and that dinner should be ready at seven.

Then he turned toward the stairs and faltered. His mouth went dry as he stared at the place where Miriam had fallen. All he could see was the blood on the floor—long gone now—trickling from the wound on her head. He didn't remember the fall and was glad for it. He could well imagine the horrible sound she would have made, and having the actual memory in his mind would be another torture.

Diana took his arm and gave him a gentle squeeze. Then she started walking.

Simon focused on the stairs in front of him and wiped his mind blank. He moved quickly, probably climbing too quickly for her, but he couldn't help it. He rounded the corner at the landing and practically ran up the last set of steps.

When they reached the top, he slowed, but she was also tugging on his arm. "I can't go that fast. I might trip."

He froze for a moment, an ice-cold terror gripping him as he glanced back toward the stairs. He pulled her forward, away from the top step, and led her to the left around the railing that looked down over the stairs. He stared at her a long moment, torn between wanting to crush her against his chest and running away from her before he caused another tragedy.

She cupped his face. "Breathe with me, Simon. I'm fine. You're fine. They are stairs. We will need to use them every day. Unless you'd like to undertake some refurbishments and move our bedchamber downstairs. I would be happy to support that."

She would? Of course she would. She'd been nothing but thoughtful when it came to his despair—from seeing his reaction to the Taft children in Brereton to understanding his fear of his own bloody staircase.

"Which way is our room?" she asked softly.

Simon shook himself from the darkness of his mind and gestured to the right. "In the back corner." He took her hand, needing the warmth and pressure of her touch.

He led her into the apartments. "This is the sitting room," he said rather unnecessarily. "I usually take breakfast in here." He tried not to think of the breakfasts he'd shared with Miriam. He could picture her sitting at the desk in front of the window, writing a letter to her mother.

Blinking rapidly, he went into the bedchamber. It was completely different from the last time he'd seen it. He'd instructed Nevis to oversee its refurbishment. Everything was new—from the paint to the bed to the carpet. Before, it had been blue. Now it was green. In fact, the bed hangings reminded him of Shakespeare's room at Beaumont Tower. Good, that was a far better memory.

He didn't know how long he stood there staring at the changes, but he didn't stir until Diana touched his back. "Simon?"

He turned his head. "Mmm?"

"Is this all right? My being here?"

"Where else should you be?"

She shrugged. "I don't know. I could take another bedroom."

He shook his head. "No. Unless that's what you want."

"I've been sharing a bed with you for weeks now. Those few days we slept apart from Beaumont Tower to Gretna were rather vexing." She gave him a captivating look, her eyes sparkling and her lips just barely curving up at the corners.

He relaxed slightly, appreciating her efforts to keep the darkness at bay. "This room will be fine. I asked Nevis—my steward—to oversee refurbishments to several rooms since…since Miriam died." It was, he realized, the first time he'd uttered her name to Diana.

"I see. I like the green. It reminds me of your chamber at my cousin's."

He smiled. "I thought the same thing. And Lord knows I have pleasant memories of that room."

She blushed. "What else has been refurbished?"

"The stairs were first. The railings have been changed. They were gilt before. And all the artwork there and in the entry hall have been moved around—so that it looks different."

"A wise decision." She stepped toward him, her features tentative. "Simon, have you considered not living here?"

Every damn day. "One might argue that I don't. As you know, I've spent much of the last two years traveling. Or I'm in London for Parliament. I stayed here one night after I left the house party in October, and before that, I was here for just four or five nights in the summer."

She touched his hand, slipping her fingers between his. "We don't have to stay."

"We do—at least for a few days, maybe a week. A duke should probably see to his estate."

She moved closer so that their chests almost touched. "I don't want you to suffer."

He marveled at her empathy. "How can you be so kind? You know what happened here, what I did."

"Not entirely," she said. "I know your former wife fell and that you are blamed and that you don't remember what happened. It sounds like a terrible tragedy. Sometimes, no one is at fault."

Logically, he knew that was true, but that wasn't the case here. He'd apparently been arguing with Miriam, not that he could fathom why.

They'd never fought. While it was true no one could definitively say he'd caused her death, it certainly seemed as though he had. He ought to tell Diana all this, but the words froze on his tongue. She was so understanding, so generous with her faith—he wanted to bask in her light.

He realized this was what love felt like. He knew from loving Miriam. He'd wanted to spend every moment with her, to better himself by being in her orbit. But how could he love someone other than Miriam? He'd sworn he wouldn't. He could like and respect and admire Diana. He couldn't love her.

His chest ached with the unfairness of it.

Suddenly, he was tired of thinking, of hurting. He wanted to feel something good. And he wanted to forget. He clasped his hands around Diana's waist and pulled her flush to his chest. He lowered his mouth to hers and claimed her lips.

Again, she seemed to understand exactly what he needed. She pushed his coat from his shoulders, letting it fall to the floor, then tugged his cravat loose and slid the silk from his neck. When his shirt fell open, she slipped her hands inside the fabric and caressed his collarbones, curling her fingers around his nape.

Her tongue flashed into his mouth, seeking and claiming what he would freely offer. She'd been nothing short of adventurous and enticing in their marriage bed. He'd hoped to find a match like this once, but twice?

No, this wasn't the same as Miriam. It couldn't be.

And it wasn't. There was something fiercer about Diana—she was courage and fire and beauty all wrapped into a petite and astonishing package. She was, as he'd told her on several occasions, incomparable.

The familiar guilt tugged at him, more strongly than in recent days, probably because of returning to Lyndhurst. But maybe with Diana—with this glorious physical connection between them—he could begin to banish the ghosts of his past.

She trailed her lips from his, moving along his jaw, then down his neck. Her fingers made quick work of the buttons on his waistcoat, unfastening them with deft alacrity. Then the garment slid from his shoulders to join the growing pile of his clothing on the floor.

"Duchess, are you seducing me?" he murmured.

She pulled the hem of his shirt from his waistband and skimmed her hand up under the fabric, stroking the hard plane of his abdomen. "Do you want me to stop?"

"Never." He curled his hand around her nape and dragged her mouth back to his. Unbidden, he whispered, "Make me forget." The plea was dark and ragged, like the edges of a heart that had been split in two.

But just maybe it could be repaired.

Chapter Fourteen

◆E·3◆

AFTER DINNER LAST night, Simon had given Diana a tour of Lyndhurst. Quite a few refurbishments had taken place over the past two years, and she wondered if all the work would be enough to make living here tolerable for him. She wasn't convinced.

She *could* see, however, that her new husband was really quite wealthy. That might be enough to mollify her father, but she doubted it. She wondered when and how he would deliver his anger upon her—for never in a moment did she think he'd simply congratulate her on her elopement and wish her well.

Shoving those unpleasant thoughts aside, Diana made her way from the sitting room where she'd enjoyed a lovely breakfast with Simon. After enjoying a rather lovely night with him too.

She still blushed thinking of their intimacy and how wonderful it had turned out to be. She now had to speculate whether her mother's experiences were really as awful as what she'd told Diana, or if she'd lied on purpose to dissuade Diana from allowing any bachelors to kiss her while she was on the marriage mart. Unfortunately, Diana was fairly certain it was the former. Her poor mother.

Perhaps I should write to her, Diana thought. While she'd always seen her mother as complicit in her father's cruelty, she also accepted that the woman really had no choice. And now that Diana was married to a man who valued and respected her, she found she had a wealth of sympathy for her mother.

Simon had already gone downstairs to meet with his steward and butler, and Diana had an appointment with the housekeeper, Mrs. Marley. They'd planned to meet in the housekeeper's office, which was situated near the kitchen attached to the main house. As she made her way toward the stairs leading down to the hall, it was impossible not to think of Simon and the former duchess. And since it pained *her* to imagine his wife tumbling down the stairs to her death, Diana knew just how torturous it was for Simon to be here. It was no wonder he spent so much time away.

She also understood why he moved through this particular space rather quickly. Now she didn't linger either.

She hastened into the small parlor, then through to the lobby that opened into the breakfast room and led to the corridor that funneled to the kitchens. Simon had pointed them out last night, but they hadn't gone to investigate.

She stepped into a vestibule that led to many rooms, the largest of which was the main kitchen in front of her. However, before she could move forward, Mrs. Marley approached from the left.

"Good morning, Your Grace." The housekeeper smiled warmly. She was young for her position—not much older than Diana—with dark red-brown hair and rich brown eyes. In fact, Diana had noticed that most of the staff was rather young, with the exception of the steward and the cook.

"Good morning, Mrs. Marley."

"My office is just this way." She led Diana through the vestibule to a door that opened to a small room. Not much larger than a closet, it held a writing desk and straight-backed chair set against one wall, with another chair on the opposite wall. There was also a dresser and a small hearth with a low fire burning in the grate. The flames and a lantern on the desk were the only sources of illumination, for there were no windows.

"Is this office sufficient for your duties?" Diana asked.

"Oh yes, ma'am. I don't spend much time here. There's far too much to oversee throughout a house of this size."

"I hope you don't mind my saying so, but you're very young to be in your position. You must be quite accomplished."

Mrs. Marley blushed slightly, but her spine was straight and her head high. "I've always worked very hard and have been fortunate to move up. Unfortunately, I was likely promoted far before my time due to the tragedy that happened here."

"Many of the staff left?"

Mrs. Marley nodded. "Rather than be marked by the scandal. I considered leaving, but I am far too fond of the family. I've never worked anywhere else."

Diana understood that kind of loyalty and was glad to hear of it. Simon needed all the support he could get. "How long have you worked here?"

"Over ten years, ma'am."

"And when the former housekeeper left two years ago, you were promoted." Diana assumed that was how the butler had also gained his position. She thought of the steward and cook and presumed they must have remained despite what happened. "You say many of the staff left, but how many remained?" Diana didn't want to gossip, but she needed to understand the household that was now in her care.

"One of the scullery maids, a single footman, and some of the outside staff. Plus Mr. Nevis and Mrs. Dodd." The steward and the cook, just as Diana had thought.

"I'm grateful to those of you who stayed, and I'm sure the Duke is as well." Not that he likely told them. He was never here. "Has it been…difficult since then?" The house seemed to be well organized and finely run, but again, in Simon's absence, how could they really know if they didn't ask?

"It's been different. His Grace is rarely here. We didn't replace all the staff who left. There hasn't been a need to do so."

That made sense. "Well, it sounds as if you're managing things adequately. The Duke and I deeply appreciate your service—and your loyalty."

"It is my distinct honor and privilege to serve him, and you, ma'am. We were all distraught over what happened with the previous duchess. We only want for His Grace to find happiness once more. Now he's wed again, and it seems God's grace has smiled upon him." She smiled, and her eyes sparked with cheer. "Upon all of us."

Diana couldn't argue with that sentiment. She was just so pleased to hear that the staff was behind Simon. "I'd like to see the kitchens if I may?"

"Of course. You met Mrs. Dodd yesterday. She is probably the best person to show you her domain." Mrs. Marley lowered her voice to a conspiratorial whisper. "She'd prefer that. I may outrank her, but the kitchens are her kingdom, and I wouldn't dare interfere." She winked, a glint of humor in her eye.

Diana laughed softly. "I see. Thank you for telling me." She recalled Mrs. Dodd's confident and perhaps slightly taciturn demeanor yesterday. She hadn't remained for the disbursement of the gifts, saying she and her staff had to return to the kitchens or there wouldn't be any dinner. Their gifts had been delivered here to be handed out later.

"I'll take you to her," Mrs. Marley offered, gesturing toward the door.

Diana turned and went back through the vestibule to the entrance to the main kitchen on the left. A long table stood in the center of the room, and on the other side was a wall of brick masonry featuring a massive hearth as well as a new iron range. Diana had heard about them but hadn't seen one.

Mrs. Dodd turned from supervising one of the maids, who was stirring something on the stovetop. She wiped her hands on her apron. "Good morning, Your Grace."

"Good morning, Mrs. Dodd. It smells wonderful in here."

"Don't go into the scullery." She nodded to her left. "The maids are gutting fish for dinner tonight. Doesn't smell too good in there just now." She tittered, and Diana thought the cook seemed far more comfortable here than she had in the hall yesterday. Probably because she was in her element, her *kingdom*, as Mrs. Marley had called it.

"I wondered if you might show me around your kitchens?" Diana asked, glancing about the busy main room. There were several doorways leading to the various parts of the kitchen, and she was eager to explore each one.

"Certainly," Mrs. Dodd said brusquely. She directed a look at the housekeeper, who excused herself and left the kitchen with alacrity. "That one's a fine housekeeper, but she's always rubbed me a little odd." Her generous mouth ticked up. "But then most people rub me a little odd."

Diana could think of nothing to say to that, so she didn't. "This is a very large kitchen."

"The best in Hampshire. Come, I'll show you." She guided Diana through the various rooms leading off the main kitchen. There was a pantry, a dry larder, a wet larder, a buttery, the scullery with its own storeroom, and a door to the outside that led to the ash bin and fuel bins as well as the kitchen garden.

"My husband is the head gardener," Mrs. Dodd said. "He oversees the kitchen garden for me."

Diana hadn't met the outside retainers yet. She didn't realize any of the staff were married. "Do you and Mr. Dodd live here in the house?"

"No, the former duke, God rest his blessed soul, gifted us a cottage. No one can say the Lyndhurst staff aren't well cared for."

And yet many of them had left rather than face the scandal of what had happened here two years ago. "Is anyone else on the staff married?"

"Not yet, but I hear Lowell is speaking to His Grace about that this morning. He and Mrs. Marley would like to wed."

"Oh, she isn't actually a missus then?" Diana recalled that housekeepers typically went by missus, whether they were wed or not. She wondered why the housekeeper hadn't said anything about marrying the butler, but perhaps Mrs. Marley preferred to wait for her intended to speak with Simon.

"It's past time. They've been sneaking around for a long while now—since before the Incident." She lowered her voice. "We don't talk about it."

Diana had no problem comprehending what the "Incident" was. She shouldn't talk about it either, but it nagged at the back of her mind. What she knew of it didn't paint a full picture, probably because Simon couldn't contribute any memory of it.

Mrs. Dodd continued. "I don't let my girls talk about anything like that—no gossip in my kitchen, I say." She cracked a small smile. "Except for me, of course. Can't let the housemaids have all the fun."

The staff at Lyndhurst was perhaps as hierarchical and complicated as Society. Diana went back to the topic at hand. "I'm sure the Duke will support their marriage." As soon as she said it, she wished she hadn't. It wasn't her place to say such things without Simon doing so first.

Except she knew he would. Because she knew *him*. The admonition had come from the part of her brain that was still under the influence of her parents. She'd been able to push them from her thoughts more and more, but now that she was fulfilling the role they'd always intended for her, it seemed the knowledge they'd drilled into her was harder to ignore. She didn't want to be the kind of duchess her mother and father had trained her to be. She wanted to be the kind of duchess who knew her staff well and supported their lives and loves.

Mrs. Dodd put her hand on her hip and yelled toward the stove. "Becky, you need to stir that faster or it will burn and be ruined!"

The maid increased her movements as directed.

The cook shook her head. "Have to watch these girls constantly. But they're a good lot. Hard workers to a one." She blinked her light blue eyes at Diana. "What was I saying? Ah yes, Lowell and Marley getting married. It's hard for me to be too happy for them." She lowered her voice to a stage whisper. "As I said, Mrs. Marley rubs me wrong. Always a bit big for her station, if you ask me."

"But you said she's a fine housekeeper." Diana didn't wish to encourage the servants' gossip, but she also wanted to understand the complicated relationships between them so she could better manage her duties.

"That she is." Mrs. Dodd waved her hand, motioning for Diana to move toward the other end of the table so they were out of earshot of the other maids—relatively. The cook pitched her voice to its lowest volume yet, which still wasn't *quite* a whisper. "I admit I don't particularly care for Mrs. Marley because of the role she played in the Incident."

This time, Diana couldn't resist probing for more information. "Whatever do you mean?" She confined her voice to a genuine whisper.

"Mrs. Marley is the one who saw what happened. She said His Grace and Her Grace argued on the stairs, and the next thing she knew, Her Grace had tumbled to the hall." Mrs. Dodd's eyes darkened with sadness. "Terrible tragedy. Her Grace was as kind as they come." She flicked a wary glance at Diana. "I'm sure you're just as kind."

"I shall hope to display such a quality," Diana murmured. This staff was apparently not only loyal to Simon, but also to his first duchess. And yet, they'd also been welcoming to her. So far.

She couldn't help but delve deeper into the Incident. "So Mrs. Marley saw the Duke push the duchess?"

"Not directly, but she saw him grab her arm. The story goes that she didn't want them to see her, so she turned to leave. That's when she heard the sound of Her Grace hitting the floor." Mrs. Dodd winced as she shook her head. "It was most distressing." Sadness darkened her words.

Diana's stomach turned, and she felt a bit queasy. Simon had grabbed Miriam's arm? Diana had never believed he could push his wife, whether angry or drunk—or both. Her father was capable of that kind of behavior, but not Simon. Yet, she recalled the way he'd grabbed her in Brereton, when he'd seen the Taft children. He'd been completely unaware of what he'd done, of the stress that had provoked him to squeeze her too tightly. Had he done something similar with his first wife? She could see how it was possible, especially since he'd been drunk. Her blood ran cold. For the first time, she considered that he might actually be guilty of what everyone accused him of. And that made her feel sick.

Diana recalled her conversation with the housekeeper and how supportive she'd been of Simon. "Despite seeing that, Mrs. Marley stayed?"

"Oh yes, she's always been a staunch ally to His Grace. She and Lowell both, but I guess that makes sense. You tend to share everything with your mate." Her eyes narrowed, and her voice, which had risen to a normal tone, dipped again. "What I've always wondered is why the stupid chit couldn't just lie and say she didn't see anything. Why torture His Grace with the knowledge that he may have caused her death?" Mrs. Dodd's gaze sharpened on the maid stirring at the stove. "That's too fast now, Becky!" She exhaled with a tinge of exasperation. "It's time for the next step." She gave Diana an apologetic look. "It's her first time with the sauce. Excuse me, ma'am."

Diana inclined her head and watched the cook bustle off to instruct the young maid. Curious to see the kitchen garden—briefly, because it had been frosty this morning and was likely still quite cold—Diana went into the scullery. A single maid, the young Rose who'd been at the end of the line at yesterday's introduction, was cleaning the tools she and the other scullery maid had used to gut the fish.

"You're Rose, is that right?" Diana asked with a smile. The girl had been shy yesterday, her gaze never quite meeting Diana's.

She flicked a glance toward Diana but kept her attention focused on her task. "Yes, Your Grace."

"I remember you from yesterday. You said you liked to draw." Diana had tried to learn something specific about each member of the staff, both to help her remember them more easily and because she genuinely wanted to know them as people and not just faceless servants.

"I do, ma'am." Her cheeks flushed a charming pink.

"I can see you're very good at your job," Diana said, thinking it must be difficult work. She'd no idea how to gut a fish. She'd caught a few, put them in a basket, and they'd magically shown up on the table for dinner later.

"I try, ma'am. Working here is an excellent opportunity for my family. Hopefully, my younger sister will be hired on this summer."

"I'm sure that's a distinct possibility if there's an opening in the scullery. Perhaps you'll be promoted to kitchen maid," Diana said.

Rose finished washing the last knife and put it on the drying rack, then wiped her hands on her apron. When she turned to Diana, her lips lifted into a cautious smile. "I would like that. Maybe some day, I'll even work myself up to housekeeper like Mrs. Marley."

"Did she start here as a scullery maid?" Diana asked, intrigued with the rapid rise of Mrs. Marley, who'd apparently gone from scullery maid to housekeeper in barely over a decade.

"When she was fifteen. The same age I am now."

"And how long have you been here, Rose?"

"Just over two years."

She'd started just before the prior duchess had died. "Did you meet the former duchess?"

Rose's color faded, and her gaze dropped again. "Yes, ma'am." Her voice was small and wispy in the dim scullery.

A sound from outside the door brought Rose's chin up. Her dark eyes were wide. "Cook is coming."

Diana understood. Mrs. Dodd wouldn't appreciate Rose dawdling, especially to gossip. Although, Diana *was* the duchess. She would surely allow that. Even so, Diana didn't want to cause any trouble for the girl. Offering a warm smile, she said, "I'll let you get back to work."

Diana turned and passed the cook as she left the scullery. "Your staff is excellent, Mrs. Dodd. You should be very proud." She wanted to make sure the cook knew Diana was impressed.

The cook's chest puffed up a bit. "Thank you, ma'am."

As Diana made her way back out through the kitchen, her thoughts teemed with all she'd learned, especially about the Incident and the fact that her mind was open to the notion that he'd accidentally killed his wife. It fairly broke her heart. But did it change how she felt?

And how is that exactly, a voice in her head asked. Did she love him?

She couldn't know. She had no experience with the emotion. Fear, however, was one she was quite well acquainted with. And when she thought of what Mrs. Dodd had told her of what Mrs. Marley had seen and of what she knew of Simon, she felt a wave of apprehension.

He's not like your father, that voice said.

Belatedly, she recalled that she wanted to explore the kitchen garden. Perhaps the fresh air, however cold it may be, would clear her mind of troublesome thoughts.

It was a temporary reprieve, for she knew the past was bound to catch up with them.

•℃•3•

"SO THE STAFF is functioning well?" Simon asked Nevis, who sat on the other side of his desk in his study.

The steward nodded. "I'd wondered if Lowell would be able to fulfill the duties of butler, but he's exceeded my expectations. He's quite intelligent. It's a shame he wasn't able to attend university. I think he would have acquitted himself well."

Simon was pleased to hear this. He'd left the promotion and hiring of staff entirely to Nevis, especially after Miriam's death. "Most excellent."

As their meeting was drawing to a close, the older man sat forward in his chair. "How long will you be staying at Lyndhurst? I thought we might tour the estate. It's been a while since you did so."

It was a gentle admonishment, delivered without heat and accompanied by the hint of a supportive smile. The entire staff had treated him with kid gloves since Miriam's death, and Nevis was no exception. It was, in this case, a tad bittersweet because he'd known Nevis for so long. There was a fatherly aspect to him that Simon couldn't ignore.

"I was thinking so too." Which was true, but just because he'd been thinking he should stay for longer than a few days and actually pay attention to his estate didn't mean he planned to. However, guilt—a too familiar and painful emotion—ate at him.

"We'll be here at least a week." Simon regretted the words as soon as he said them, but then quietly scolded himself. He could stay here for a bloody week. Especially with Diana at his side.

"Excellent. I'll arrange something with the tenants. They'll be delighted to see you."

Simon assumed they were finished, but Nevis didn't rise. Indeed, he seemed hesitant. "Is there something else?" Simon asked.

Nevis's forehead creased, and his gray brows angled toward the bridge of his nose. "I'm getting older," he began, and Simon suspected where this conversation was going. "I expect I'd like to retire in the next year or two. It might be wise to bring someone on this year so that I may train them for the position."

Simon leaned back in his chair and blew out a breath. "I should have seen this coming. Indeed, I should have talked with you about it. I'm afraid I've been too preoccupied with my own troubles."

Nevis nodded sympathetically. "Which is more than understandable. I've known you all your life—any man would buckle under the strain. Not that you've buckled. Indeed, you've shown far more aplomb than most. Mrs. Nevis and I pray for you nightly."

Simon appreciated the man's kindness more than he could say. "Thank you. And please thank Mrs. Nevis. You and she must join us for dinner tomorrow so she can meet the Duchess."

"That would be wonderful. Thank you, sir." Nevis rose and straightened his coat.

"Have you given any thought to your successor?"

Nevis cocked his head to the side. "I've actually considered Lowell. Though he's not formally educated, he's been studying math and reading about estate management. He knows Lyndhurst, and he's certainly dedicated to you and the estate."

"I'll keep that in mind," Simon said. Lowell was his next appointment, so perhaps he'd speak to him about it.

Nevis nodded. "Thank you, sir." He departed the study, and Simon turned his head to look out the window at the front drive.

A moment later, Simon saw Lowell approach the threshold from the corner of his eye. He gave the butler his attention and beckoned him forward. "Come in, Lowell. Was there anything specific you wished to discuss today, or did you just want to deliver a report?"

Lowell looked down at Simon from his vast height with a somewhat tense expression. "I did have a particular matter to discuss, but I'm happy to provide a report first."

Simon suspected it was the "particular matter" that was causing Lowell's discomfort. It was probably best to get that out of the way. "Why don't you sit so we can discuss your 'particular matter.'" Simon indicated the chair Nevis had vacated.

The butler lowered himself slowly, perching on the edge of the chair as if he were afraid he might break it. Or as if he were ready to flee. "Thank you, Your Grace." He cleared his throat, and his shoulders twitched. "May I start by saying how glad we are to have you back at Lyndhurst and with a new bride? Her Grace is already making quite an impression."

"A positive one, I hope."

Lowell looked slightly alarmed. "Most definitely. The care she took to meet everyone yesterday was most appreciated."

"She's a singular woman," Simon said softly. His admiration for her only continued to grow.

"It seems that marriage agrees with you." The butler's neck reddened. "I beg your pardon, sir. I didn't mean to speak out of turn."

Simon shifted in his chair. Of course his staff would notice if he were happy or not. Particularly since he usually was not. This had to be quite a change. It was for him too. "You're not out of line. Now, what's your point of discussion?"

"Yes, of course. I mentioned marriage because I hope to enter that estate myself soon. Mrs. Marley and I would like to wed, and I humbly ask your permission to do so."

"You want to marry the housekeeper?" Simon blinked, thinking he'd misheard. Given Lowell's demeanor, Simon had been expecting a much more dire issue—such as someone had been caught thieving or that someone was ill. He laughed. "What a joyous occasion. Why do you seem as if you're marching to the gallows?"

The red in Lowell's neck crept up into his face. "I'm not sure, sir."

"Are you certain you wish to marry?" Simon asked.

"Absolutely. I am in love with Edith—Mrs. Marley, I mean."

Simon felt a rush of kinship with the man. He knew what it was like to be in love. In fact, he had to wonder if he was currently in the throes of that emotion. It had been scarcely an hour, maybe two, since he'd seen Diana, and he missed her something fierce. All he could think was that he was desperate to see her smile, hear her laugh, touch her softness.

Love?

"Sir?" Lowell's hesitant query drew Simon back to their conversation.

He gave the butler a half smile. "My apologies for woolgathering. Of course you have my permission. Would you like to marry here in the chapel?"

Lowell's eyes widened briefly. "That's very generous of you, sir. Is that possible?"

"I'm sure I can arrange it with the vicar."

"We are humbled by your generosity, sir." Lowell bowed his head briefly. "Mrs. Marley will be thrilled."

"I'm pleased to have a happy occasion to celebrate here." It would be good for everyone. He'd talk to Diana about arranging a nice breakfast for the newlyweds. He'd also need to talk to Nevis about living arrangements for the couple. "Your chamber is out near the kitchen, is it not?" Simon asked.

"It is, sir."

"I can't imagine it's large enough for you and a wife. I'll speak with Nevis about finding new accommodation. Do you have a date for the wedding yet?"

"We don't, sir. I wanted to secure your permission first."

Of course. "Well, let's not dally. See that the banns are read this Sunday, and the Duchess and I will work on the other arrangements." Yes, this was a welcome distraction from the depression that hung over the house. He was eager to share it with Diana. He had every expectation she would ensure Lowell and Marley had a wedding they would all remember.

Lowell appeared a bit confounded. "Thank you, sir. Mrs. Marley will be overcome."

Just as Nevis had lingered and seemed to have something else to say, Lowell behaved in the same manner. Simon folded his hands on the top of his desk. "Will you be delivering a report now, or is there another matter?"

"There *is* one other matter." It didn't seem possible, but Lowell managed to look even more uncomfortable than he had a few minutes ago. Good heavens, but the man perhaps needed to work on his confidence. Which made no sense, because from everything Simon knew, Lowell managed the household in an adept and assured manner.

"Go on," Simon prodded gently.

"I know Mr. Nevis will retire at some point, and I wanted you to know that I've been studying estate management in the hope that I may qualify to replace him."

Perhaps confidence wasn't Lowell's issue, but humility. It took courage to come out and ask for a position that was above your education. And it seemed Lowell knew that, hence his reticence. "Mr. Nevis told me of your aptitude and your intelligence. He seems to think you may be up to the task."

The flush came back to Lowell's face for a brief flash. "That's exceedingly complimentary, sir. I do endeavor to work hard."

"I appreciate you speaking with me about this. It demonstrates your determination and commitment. I would urge you to continue your studies."

Lowell stood. "Thank you, sir. I will. And thank you again for the wedding. I will talk to Mrs. Marley later this evening."

Simon rolled his eyes. "Oh bollocks—sorry. Go and speak with her now. If you aren't beside yourself to do so, then you may want to rethink the whole thing."

Lowell's mouth split into a wide smile that was completely at odds with his austere demeanor. "I'll do that, sir." He bowed and took his leave.

Simon realized he was feeling precisely the same—he wanted to see his wife. He got up and rounded his desk just as she appeared in the doorway. He smiled, absurdly pleased to see her. She was stunning in a new day gown they'd purchased in Oxford. It was the color of fresh cream with dainty flowers of gold and crimson. A gold sash encircled her rib cage, and he suddenly wanted his hands to do the same.

"I was just coming to find you, wife."

"Were you? I'm not interrupting, am I?" she asked, stepping over the threshold and looking around his study.

"Not at all. I just finished with Lowell, and he had the most extraordinary news."

"He wishes to marry Mrs. Marley."

Simon's shoulders drooped slightly. "You already know."

She went to the fireplace and looked at the miniatures of his parents that sat atop the mantelpiece. "Mrs. Dodd told me. She is a veritable fount of information."

Simon followed her, wanting to increase their proximity. "Is she?"

Diana turned and just a foot or so separated them. "Yes—and don't be angry—she told me about what happened two years ago. The 'Incident.'"

"The 'Incident'?" They had a fucking name for it? Fury curled in his gut. "It wasn't an 'Incident,' it was a bloody tragedy."

She winced. "Of course it was. I shouldn't have used that word."

"It wasn't your word, was it? That's what they call it?" Of course the staff talked about it. The event had been a massive scandal—one that followed him to this day and likely always would. As it should. Not because it was a scandal, but because it was a goddamn *tragedy*.

"Simon, I asked you not to get angry."

He turned from her and walked to the windows facing the drive. "Forgive me if I can't help myself."

The room fell quiet for a few moments, during which he regained his equilibrium. He shouldn't get angry. Servants would talk, and they meant him no harm. They'd all stayed here despite the potential damage to their reputations, hadn't they?

Before he could apologize, Diana said, "I wanted to ask you why you allowed Mrs. Marley to stay after what she said."

Simon turned. Diana was watching him warily but with empathy in the depths of her gaze. "What was I to do, cast out a loyal retainer for telling the truth?"

"No, but no one would blame you for not wanting her here. She's a reminder of what happened."

He lifted his hands and dropped them sharply to his sides. "*All* of it is a reminder of what happened." He put his hand on the back of his neck, anxiously massaging the flesh as emotion raged within him. "But I can't turn someone out because they told the truth. Especially not when they demonstrated extreme remorse. Did you know she offered to leave, out of guilt, but Nevis convinced her to stay?" Simon had learned that about a year ago.

Diana came toward him and took his hands. "Simon, if it's too much, we can leave. Why don't we just go to London?"

God, her understanding and compassion nearly undid him. "I told Nevis we'd stay at least a week. I haven't toured the estate in…" He shook his head. "I don't know how long."

"But I can't stand watching you tortured."

"Why are you so forgiving?" They were all so forgiving—the staff who'd remained and demonstrated fierce loyalty, Nick who never failed to bolster his spirits, and now Diana, who stood by him even in the face of his inability to forgive himself. "Did Mrs. Dodd tell you exactly what happened, the specifics?"

She nodded slowly. "Yes."

"Tell me." To hear Diana recite his crimes was like putting himself on the rack, but he deserved nothing less.

Diana swallowed. Her eyes were dark and unflinching. "She said you and…the duchess argued, that you grabbed her. Marley turned then and didn't see exactly what transpired."

Though she held his hands, he felt cold. "So you see how it happened. How it was my fault."

"I've decided fault doesn't matter. As you said, it was a tragedy. Whatever happened to cause it, the damage can't be undone."

His throat tightened, and he clasped her hands as if she could save him from drowning in the sea of his emotion. He would never know what he'd done to deserve her. "I will thank God every day for you."

She smiled and let go of one of his hands to touch his cheek before pressing her lips against his. Her kiss was soft and sweet and gave him the strength to let the pain go—at least for now. "It seems we are a gift to each other, just when we needed it most."

He kissed her again, slipping his tongue into her mouth. She speared her fingers into the hair at his nape and held him tight, kissing him back with a heat that made him weak.

When she pulled back, her lips were still smiling. "Now about this wedding. When is it to take place?"

Grateful for the distraction—no, he was grateful for *her*—he launched into the plans he'd discussed with Lowell. As expected, she was quite thrilled to take part.

Then he realized they should be here for the nuptials. And since they needed three consecutive Sundays for the banns to be read, that meant staying here for a month.

He wasn't sure he could do it. The week he'd promised stretched long and harrowing before him. But perhaps with Diana at his side, he could muster the strength to put the past where it belonged: in the past.

If not, he'd do what he did best. He'd flee.

Chapter Fifteen
❧·❧

SIMON STRODE INTO his office four days later and mentally checked off another night in his quest to see how long he could stand to be here. So far, he was managing all right—thanks to Diana. She brightened his days and seduced his nights. It was a bittersweet relief as he grappled with being here with her while still trying to hold on to the promise of remembering and loving Miriam.

That latter part was growing harder every day, and the strain of guilt was wearing on him. Well, more than it usually did.

Activity on the drive drew his eye. A carriage had just pulled up to the portico. He craned his neck to see who climbed out. Hell, it was his mother.

He turned on his heel and stalked to the entry hall, working to ignore the pricks of unease that always stabbed at him in that space. A footman was already opening the door to the portico, and a moment later, his mother breezed inside, her small spaniel following at her heels.

"I hear congratulations are in order," she said without preamble as she removed her gloves and handed them to the footman.

"Welcome, Mother." He'd sent her a letter from Oxford informing her of his marriage. But he hadn't invited her here. She hadn't come since Miriam's funeral.

She tugged at the ribbons of her hat, and the footman came forward to take the accessory from her after she pulled it from her head. She patted at the back of her gray hair. "Where is your new duchess?"

"I'll have her join us for tea in the drawing room," Simon offered in a genial tone he didn't particularly feel. The woman in front of him had turned her back when Miriam had died, and now she showed up as if they weren't estranged?

"Wonderful." She turned to the butler. "Good to see you, Lowell. Please have my things taken up to the Queen's Bedroom."

It was their finest guest room, and he wasn't surprised that was where she chose to stay. Nor was he surprised that she acted as though she were still the duchess. She'd done the same when Miriam had been alive.

The dowager started toward what used to be the Red Drawing Room, snapping her fingers so the dog trailed her. Simon fell into step behind them, wondering if the pup felt as disgruntled as he did.

"To what do I owe the pleasure of this visit?" Simon asked as they entered the drawing room. It was, as his mother had just become aware, no longer red.

"What did you do?" The high pitch of her voice made her dog whimper. She looked down and clucked her tongue. "Quiet, boy." She directed her gaze to Simon. "Not you. You explain. What did you do to my Red Drawing Room?"

"I refurbished it." The red wallpaper was gone and replaced with a pale yellow. The dark, rich furnishings in shades of garnet and cherry had been removed and in their place were blues and golds. "The painting over the mantel is the same," he said helpfully.

She sniffed. "I loved this room. The entry hall was different too. Have you changed everything?"

"Not yet."

"That sounds as though you plan to."

At that moment, Diana strolled in, her face a mask of serene beauty. She went straight to Simon's side and offered a curtsey to his mother. "I'm pleased to make your acquaintance, Duchess. To answer your question, though I suppose it wasn't really a question, we do plan to refurbish the entire house. It's important for Lyndhurst to become our home. I'm sure you understand why that would be necessary for your son." She stepped closer to him and briefly clasped his hand.

Oh my God, how he loved this woman. Her fierce protection and quick wit astounded him. He was continually humbled by the grace she showed him. Yes, he loved her. Beyond all odds, beyond every expectation, he loved her.

He squeezed her hand. "Mother, may I present my wife, Her Grace the Duchess of Romsey."

His mother showed her respect in a rather shallow curtsey, but he didn't take offense. He knew her knees were creaky. "You were formerly Miss Diana Kingman, is that right?"

"Yes, ma'am."

"I shan't be ma'am to you. You'll call me Mother, of course." The dowager looked around at the furniture. "Where shall I sit? You got rid of my favorite chair."

"Actually, I had it moved to the dower house," Simon said. He'd sent many of the things he'd removed from the main house to the smaller dwelling that sat two miles west and that his mother hadn't visited since Miriam had died. "If you ever care to stay there again, you'll likely find what you're missing. In the meantime, you might like that gold chair." He indicated an overstuffed chair of particular comfort angled near a light blue settee.

"Well, that was thoughtful of you." She went to the chair and settled her narrow frame onto the cushion. Her dog jumped up next to her and immediately snuggled between her thigh and the arm of the chair. "There's even room for Humphrey, just as there was in my old chair." She gave Simon a wary look, as if she wasn't quite ready to admit defeat. Not that he knew what she was even battling. Him, he supposed, though he wasn't sure why.

She looked up at Simon and Diana. "Are you going to sit?"

Diana gently tugged him toward the settee. They sat down together, and, regrettably, she let go of his hand. "How kind of you to pay us a visit," Diana said. "Are you staying here or at the dower house?"

"Here, but only for a few days. I had to come meet my new daughter-in-law. Weren't you betrothed to the Duke of Kilve?" The dowager gave Simon an accusatory look. "Your friend. Or so I thought."

Ah, this was the problem. She thought there was a scandal, and he supposed there was, albeit a minor one. Or so it seemed to him. How did a broken engagement and two subsequent marriages—he assumed Nick and Violet had married, but hadn't yet corresponded with them—that had pleased all parties compare to the tragic death of one's wife? Hell, none of it should be a scandal. What it should be was no one's bloody business.

"The duke and I decided we wouldn't suit," Diana said. "As it happens, he was enamored of Lady Pendleton, whom he will shortly wed, if he hasn't already. And I preferred to wed your son."

Couldn't she have been enamored too? Love fairly burst forth from his chest, but did she feel the same? He knew she cared for him, but he also knew she was reticent where that emotion was concerned. And given what he knew of her upbringing, he understood. Whereas he'd been raised with plenty of that emotion, even if his mother wasn't necessarily showing it just now.

His mother looked between them, her gaze skeptical. "How…convenient. You couldn't have had a normal wedding? Or was there a reason you had to run off to Gretna?" Her meaning was clear as her gaze dipped to Diana's abdomen.

"There was no such reason, Mother," he said coolly, taking Diana's hand in his. "We simply wished to be wed with haste."

Mother shook her head and waved her hand. "You could've gotten a special license. Or perhaps not. It may not have been granted in your case." Because of the stain of his wife's suspicious death. Simon hadn't considered that, but that was because a special license hadn't ever entered into their deliberations. Not that he planned to disclose that.

"In any case, we're quite happy to be married and to welcome you to Lyndhurst," Diana said brightly, as if she hadn't just had to defend her decision to marry him. She'd been denied choice her whole life, and to have this most important one questioned had to upset her. Yet she didn't show it. She was the consummate hostess and duchess. Her parents, damn them, would be pleased.

"That's excellent to hear," Mother said. "Perhaps it will improve my son's reputation. He's in need of good favor."

"Not from me," Diana said quietly. She looked at him as he turned to look at her, and their eyes connected for a long, beautiful moment, their hands still clasped. When they finally broke the contact and directed their attention back at the dowager, she was scrutinizing Diana.

"Do you know the truth of what happened here?"

"*Mother.*" Simon practically growled the word. He'd put up with quite a bit—hell, he'd put up with everything Society had thrown at him, both to his face and behind his back—but he wouldn't tolerate his mother insulting his wife in her own bloody drawing room.

"Yes." Diana's answer was firm.

"You're aware they argued, that he grabbed her?"

Diana's grip tightened. "Yes."

"And do you know why they argued?"

Simon didn't even know why they'd argued. He'd never been able to reconcile it. He and Miriam hadn't ever quarreled. His insides churned. "Mother, how can you know that?"

"Because I do, and it's perhaps time you do too since you can't remember." Despite her obnoxious line of questioning, her tone had carried a thread of warmth and care. Until the last, which she'd delivered with a healthy dose of disdain. She'd despised his drinking. It was a remnant of his rakish ways, which she'd loathed.

"W-why do you think it's your place to do this?" Diana's voice trembled slightly, and Simon caught the stutter. He refused to allow her to be upset.

"Watch yourself, Mother," he warned.

"The rumor amongst the staff was that Miriam had been unfaithful, that the babe wasn't Simon's."

Simon felt as though the world had disappeared beneath him. He was floating, untethered and adrift in a void. He felt nothing.

Until he felt the grip of her hand on his. Suddenly, he had something to hold on to. Some*one.*

And just when he thought nothing could get worse, Lowell stepped over the threshold and announced, "Sir Barnard and Lady Kingman."

Diana's hand went slack in his, and all the color left her face. Simon leapt to his feet, intending to physically vanquish her father if necessary. Dammit, he'd wanted to manage this meeting on his own terms. On *Diana's* terms.

The baronet was a tall, broad-shouldered man with dark hair salted liberally with gray. His dark brows pitched low over his eyes, which he'd targeted on Diana. "Found you at last."

"Found her? Did you misplace her?" Simon's mother asked.

Sir Barnard ignored her, his furious gaze never leaving Diana. "You've caused me a great deal of trouble." He tipped his head up to look at Simon. "But not as much as you. Kidnapping my daughter and forcing her to marry you… You're despicable."

His mother's high-pitched squeal caused Humphrey to bark. "Kidnapping? You kidnapped her?"

Simon scowled at the room at large. "No."

Diana rose slowly. "He d-did not k-kidnap m-me."

There went her stutter again. Simon was going to throttle her father.

"You went of your own accord?" her father snapped. "Why accept one duke only to throw him over for another? Did we teach you nothing?"

"I'm a d-duch-duchess. Wh-what does it m-matter wh-who the gr-groom is?"

The baronet shook his head in disgust. "Listen to you." He curled his lip toward Simon. "Do you hear her? I can't imagine you were aware of her defect when you decided to wed her. But the jest is on you, because you're stuck with her now." He looked back to Diana. "At least you *are* a duchess, even if your husband is a pariah."

Throughout this exchange, Diana's mother simply stood there and watched, her face a mask of calm. In fact, she reflected no emotion whatsoever, as if she couldn't hear the vitriol pouring from her husband's mouth.

Diana lifted her chin and stared her father in the eye. "Yes, I-I am a d-duchess. You owe m-me r-respect."

"I owe you nothing. You're a duchess because *I* made you one, not him. All he made you was a whore."

Three sharp inhalations filled the room as all three women gaped at the baronet. Meanwhile, Simon's hand curled into a fist. He wasn't fond of violence, particularly after what he'd done—the revelation from his mother stole through his brain, momentarily distracting him. It was enough for Diana to flee the room before he could stop her.

Torn between wanting to thrash her father and chasing his wife, he chose the only path he could. He ran out after her.

❦

DIANA NEARLY STUMBLED as she reached the landing of the stairs. She grasped the railing hard and forced herself to take a breath. But she didn't stop. She tore up the last few steps and raced to their bedchamber, throwing the door closed as she ran inside.

Her chest heaved, and her eyes were wet. She shook horribly as rage and sadness ripped through her.

"Diana."

She couldn't bear to turn and look at Simon. That he'd seen that horrid side of her father filled her with shame.

"G-go away."

He came up behind her and slipped his arms around her waist. "Not a chance."

She lurched forward and moved quickly to the other side of their bed, putting it between them. "D-don't t-touch m-me." She couldn't bear it just then. Not with the memories pouring in on her, threatening to drown her in their weight.

"Please, Diana. Don't let him do this to you. You're safe now. I'm going to toss him out when I go back downstairs, and he'll never be able to hurt you again."

An anguished sob escaped her mouth. "You think it's over?" The question was a ragged whisper she had to force from her lips. "I c-can't f-for-forget wh-what he d-did. It's al-always with me. And ev-every t-time I f-fal-falter, ev-every t-time this w-weak-weakness c-comes o-over m-me, I'm r-re-reminded of my in-inad-inadequa—" She swore violently before shouting, "*inadequacy.*"

It took every bit of self-control she'd learned to get that word out. Self-loathing filled her.

"What did he do to you?" The question was low, and his gaze intense. "I'll listen—and there's no shame. How can I possibly think less of you after what I've done?"

She hated the self-derision in his tone—it was too close to how she felt. They were a disaster, she realized. But no, he wasn't. Not really. "Y-you're a g-good m-man, S-Simon. Y-you j-just m-made a m-mis-mistake. Y-you w-were a-ang-angry."

"You really think I pushed her." He sounded surprised, devastated. "After all this time telling me I wasn't a murderer, now you believe it." He shook his head. "I just realized that *I* didn't really believe it." He wrapped his hand around the bedpost. "I'd thought it was an accident and that you thought so too."

"I d-did. B-but kn-knowing what w-we know n-now… I-I've s-seen you wh-when you're up-upset. Like n-now. L-look at your h-hand, Simon."

His head turned, and she watched the color drain from his face as he saw how white his knuckles were, how hard his hand gripped the wood, as if he could choke it.

"Y-you gr-grabbed me l-like that in Br-Brereton, wh-when y-you m-met the Tafts. It hurt, and y-you h-had n-no idea."

He gasped, then dropped his hand and shook it out.

His gaze was unfocused, his face pale. "I don't remember arguing with her. I don't remember that…rumor." He turned from her, and then he went down, sliding to the floor against the other side of the bed.

Diana rushed around and knelt beside him. His eyes were open, glazed, as they stared off into nothing. His breathing was shallow, his lips parted. Her heart was racing as she tried to reason what to do. He hadn't fainted, but neither was he entirely there.

She gently touched his arm, then his shoulder. Then she caressed his neck and murmured his name. It took another moment, but he finally blinked. He turned his head and squinted briefly.

"The lines are back between your eyes." He reached out and smoothed his thumb over her flesh. The touch was light and abrupt. His arm dropped back down to his side, and he looked away from her. "I loved her very much. I felt so lucky to have found that, to have found *her*. And then she was gone, and I thought I'd never be whole again."

The words poured from him like a confession. And they seared her soul. She'd known he loved her, but to hear it from his lips, and to witness the depth of the emotion he'd felt tore at her insides. How could she possibly fill the void Miriam had left?

"I don't remember that…what my mother said." He shuddered. "I certainly don't remember grabbing her, but then I don't remember grabbing you either. I do *now*, but at the time, I had no idea." He turned his head toward her again and blinked. "Am I a monster?"

She shook her head fiercely, unable to speak. She was working so hard to control her speech, but emotion was playing merry hell with her efforts.

He blinked again, and she realized there were tears in his eyes. "When I think of her carrying someone else's child, and I loved her so much… Maybe I am capable of murder."

She didn't know what to say. Love was such a foreign emotion. She knew hate could drive someone to do terrible things. Just look at her father. He hated her and her affliction.

Simon went on. "It always bothered me that people said we'd argued. Our marriage was perfectly harmonious. There were no disagreements, no quarrels." He looked up at the ceiling and squinted briefly, his head tipping to the side. "In truth, sometimes we fought over the last cake."

Miraculously, Diana felt the urge to laugh, but she didn't. Leave it to Simon to find a bead of humor, even in this agonizing moment.

"It never made sense to me." He dropped his gaze to hers. "Not until now."

"And yet you never defended yourself. Why?" She'd long wanted to understand that. She'd certainly never believed him capable of pushing her, and she still didn't think that was what he'd done.

The look in his eyes turned bleak. "Does it matter? The truth is that I *am* as horrible as everyone believes."

"It was guilt." At last she understood. "Allowing everyone to think the worst of you was the punishment you gave yourself." She cupped his face with both of her hands. "Well, now you will stop. You've tortured yourself long enough, and it's time for it to end."

"How? Now that we know the truth—"

She put her fingers over his lips. "It changes nothing. Now you know why you fought, why you grabbed her arm. No one knows what happened after that, and while you may have a strength you don't always realize, you wouldn't push her." She moved her hand to the back of his neck, cupping her fingers around his nape. "How angry were you with my f-father d-down-downstairs?" Damn, she'd just gotten herself under control, and the mere mention of him was sending her back into a dither.

"Furious."

"Enough to thrash him, I'm sure. And yet you didn't. You are not a violent man, Simon."

"You don't know what happened, and neither do I. Because I was stinking drunk." He spat the last, his eyes narrowing with self-disgust.

"You drank often and to excess before you married, did you not?" At his nod, she continued. "Did you ever get into a fight or find yourself in a violent situation?"

"No."

She wasn't surprised. "I know enough of your reputation to think you had the opportunity. You were a consummate rake, if rumors are to be believed—gaming hells and brothels."

"Once again, you're employing logic. With wondrous results."

"And you're employing humor to avoid the matter at hand." She exhaled sharply. "Am I getting through to you?"

He clasped her waist. "Yes. But to be clear, there were no brothels. I had a mistress."

"Whom I don't want to hear about. *Ever.*"

"Don't be jealous, my love. You are the only woman I want. Now and forever."

His words enflamed her, taking the anguish clawing at her insides and turning it into something wholly different. "Show me."

His eyes widened. "Now? Despite everything that just happened?"

"*Because* of everything that just happened. I need to feel you, to know that I'm not alone in this world, that I'm safe."

Chapter Sixteen

◆€•3◆

HIS BRAIN DIDN'T have time to catch up with his body. Simon brought her to him, pulling her against his chest. He pressed his mouth to hers, his lips already parted and hungry for her kiss.

She didn't make him wait, twining her arms around his neck and licking into the recesses of his mouth with long, lush, eager strokes of her tongue. She threw her leg over his hips and straddled him. Her pelvis pressed down, but her skirts were bunched between them.

With a strangled cry, she pushed them out of the way. He aided her cause, pooling the fabric around them so that when she came down again, her bare sex pressed wantonly against his breeches.

His cock jerked, desperate for her. But this was an unfortunately awkward position, with his legs sprawled out in front of him. He wanted to drive into her, to feel her muscles squeeze around him.

Lifting her skirts, he slipped his hand between her thighs. She was unbelievably wet. The moment his fingers stroked her flesh, she moaned deep into his mouth. He kissed her hard and rubbed her clitoris until she moaned again.

Her hips thrust against him, and she pulled her lips from his. "I need you now." She brought her hand down from his neck and unbuttoned his fall. A moment later, her fingers encircled his cock, tugging impatiently on his flesh. As good as she'd been that first time, she'd learned much more. Her slightest touch stirred his lust and made him mindless with need.

"I have to get up," he rasped.

"No, I can ride you here." She rotated her hips, grazing her sex along the length of his cock.

"I can't move. *I have to move.* If I can't drive into you, I might die."

"Well, we wouldn't want that," she murmured, sliding off him. "Hurry."

He rose against the bed and clasped her hips, lifting her with him. Turning, he set her on the edge of the mattress and spread her legs so he could stand between them. He pushed her skirts to her waist, exposing her sex and the pale silk of her thighs. He wanted to kiss her, to lick her, to stoke her desire until she panted his name.

She freed his cock from his garments and pulled at his flesh, urging him toward her. "Now, Simon. I need you inside me."

He traced his fingers over her folds as he thrust forward. She guided him into her slick channel and claimed his mouth once more. The kiss was wild and reckless, their tongues tangling as he drove deep into her body. She welcomed him, her legs curling around his hips, squeezing him as her hands clutched at his back.

He wanted to watch her face, to revel in the joy and wonder of her orgasm when he led her over the edge. He tore his mouth from hers and pushed her back on the bed. Halfway down, she clutched at his shirt, her fingers snagging in his cravat. The silk came loose, and she pulled it free. After she tossed it aside, he clasped her hands and leaned forward, pressing her backward until she was flush against the mattress. He pinned her hands on either side of her head and stared into her slitted eyes. Her gaze was dark and seductive.

Never taking his eyes from hers, he held her down as he pulled almost completely out of her sheath, then plunged forward again, filling her to the base of his cock. She cried out and tightened her legs around him, her heels digging into his backside.

He repeated his thrust, moving a bit faster, but taking care to give her his entire length. "Yes," she moaned, over and over, reminding him of that night in Coventry when Mrs. Ogden had done the same thing. He'd never imagined that night would spark an attraction between him and Diana that would only grow and flourish and become an intrinsic part of him.

Her eyes opened a bit wider as she focused on him. "Harder," she demanded. "Faster. Please, Simon," she purred. "I need you to let go. Show me why I'm the only woman for you."

White-hot desire pulsed through him, and he relinquished his restraint. He thrust into her, over and over, and felt her muscles tense. She was so close. He let go of her hand and stroked her clitoris, stoking her orgasm. Her sheath squeezed him mercilessly as she came. "Don't stop, don't stop." She repeated the plea until he clasped her hips and brought her up off the bed. Tilting her to the perfect angle, he drove into her as his pleasure built. He felt her tense again and knew she was on the precipice once more.

Her heels pressed into his backside, and her thighs squeezed as her muscles contracted around him. He shouted her name and poured his seed into her, giving himself completely over to rapture.

He continued to move for another moment as her body took everything he had to give. Then he fell forward carefully, putting his weight off to her side but managing to stay inside her. He wasn't ready to leave. Not yet.

She ran her fingers through his hair and kissed his forehead, then his temple.

He tilted his head back and looked up at her. "I need to go back downstairs and throw your father out. You don't need to come with me."

"I d-don't w-want to."

"Have you always done that?" he asked softly. "The stutter."

She nodded, her gaze suddenly shy. She looked up at the ceiling. "It grew worse as I got older. By the time I was to make my d-debut, it was quite awful, much to my f-father's cha-chagrin. So it was delayed until I was able to master the problem. And my father insisted I pretend to be younger than I am rather than be judged a spinster." Her gaze dropped to his. "I'm twenty-four, not twenty."

Simon stared at her. "Well, that makes sense. You've always seemed much more mature than most young ladies."

She laughed. "Is that right?"

"Absolutely." He grasped her hand and brought it to his mouth, pressing kisses along her palm and wrist.

"I had to be," she said soberly, her gaze returning to the ceiling. "My father insisted upon it."

"How did you do it? Stop stuttering, I mean."

She didn't immediately respond, and he almost told her to ignore the question. He didn't want to press her. "I wasn't given a choice. Every time I stuttered, he forced me to do speech exercises. And if I failed at those, which I often did, he put me in a closet for an allotment of time—one hour, two hours, three hours. I had to sit on a stool and balance a book on my head." Her gaze drifted to his briefly, and he saw the anger and suffering in their depths. "Do you know how difficult that is? My back would ache relentlessly, and if the book fell, I had to start over. All the while, I had to recite the speech exercises while my governess supervised me." She paused to swallow. "I went through four governesses because they would all eventually leave. They couldn't bear my father's cruelty any more than I could. But I didn't have their luxury of leaving." She turned her head toward him, and her features softened. "Until you."

Her blue eyes sparked with gratitude. "You took me away. You saved me."

He slid from her body and rose up and took her mouth in a fast, possessive kiss. "We saved each other, and I would do it again. In fact, I'm about to." He reluctantly stood, thinking he'd much rather stay in bed with her and let the villains downstairs rot.

He fastened his breeches as she pushed herself up to a sitting position. "What are you going to do?"

"Throw the baronet out and forbid him from returning. You can choose to see him when you feel like it. *If* you feel like it. Or not. The choice is yours." He reached for his cravat and then decided he didn't want to bother. Instead, he cupped her face. "The choice will always be yours as long as I draw breath."

She nuzzled his hand with her cheek. "I never thought I was worthy."

"You are a magnificent woman, Diana. Any man would be lucky to have you. But I'm the one who gets to claim you." Pride soared in his chest, and he was nearly overcome with the joy of his fortune. He leaned forward and kissed her again. "I'll be back soon."

She nodded and smiled at him before he turned and left.

Before he reached the stairs, he stopped to adjust his clothing. Minus the cravat, he supposed he would pass muster. Not that he cared. He didn't give a fig what Diana's parents thought of him, and right now he wasn't sure if he was going to toss his own mother out as well.

He rushed down the stairs and when he reached the bottom, an odd sensation stole over him. That was the first time he'd come down without hesitating, without feeling a cold rush of guilt.

Not wanting to contemplate that too deeply, he stalked toward the drawing room. He was shocked to find his mother taking tea with his in-laws. It looked far too…pleasant.

He surveyed the room and its inhabitants with a frown. "I'm glad to see you've enjoyed some refreshments. Now get out."

His mother looked aghast, particularly when her gaze dipped to Simon's lack of a cravat, but it was Sir Barnard who responded. He stood from the settee and glowered at Simon. "I should have left that house party the minute you arrived. You poison everything you touch."

Simon rounded on the man and gave full rein to his ire. "Actually, I think that's probably a better description for you. Just look at your wife. She would clearly prefer to be anywhere other than here. Every time you speak, she flinches." Simon turned his attention to the woman, whose eyes were wide with shock and perhaps a bit of fear. "If you ever require a place to stay, you are welcome here." He hoped he wasn't making an offer Diana wouldn't support, but he had the sense her mother, while complicit with her husband's abuse, had suffered too.

Simon returned his icy gaze to the baronet. "You, however, are not welcome. You'll leave now and not return unless you are explicitly invited. If you try, I shall have you forcibly removed. Do I make myself clear?"

"You can't do that. My daughter won't allow it."

"She not only allows it, she endorses it. She is no longer your daughter. She is my *wife*. The duchess you always wanted her to be, and as such, she can decide whom she wants to see and when she wants to see them. You are not on that list. Now, do remove yourself, or I shall call my staff to assist you."

Lady Kingman stood slowly and lightly touched her husband's arm. He pulled away from her and sent her a nasty glare. She jerked away, giving Simon a sad look. "You'll take care of her. Thank you. Come, Barnard."

Sir Barnard's throat worked, and his eyes blazed. "I will not be pushed out."

Simon's mother jumped into the fray. "She married a duke. What more do you want? If it's to have the duke *like* you, I think you've missed that opportunity. Off with you, then." She waved him away as if he were an annoying insect.

When it appeared the baronet wasn't going to leave, Simon called for Lowell.

Sir Barnard looked as though his head might explode. Even his ears were red. "I'm going. For now."

"Forever," Simon corrected. The butler appeared in the doorway, and Simon inclined his head. "Please show Sir Barnard out. Permanently. If he tries to return, you may not admit him. Lady Kingman is welcome *if* she arrives alone."

"Yes, Your Grace." The butler escorted Diana's parents from the room, and when Simon heard the distant sound of the front door opening, he allowed his muscles to relax.

But only for a moment.

Then he turned to address his mother. Before he could speak, she said, "That was very well done. Your father would be proud."

Simon could've said a dozen things, but ended up blurting, "Whatever were you doing down here with them?"

His mother arched a sardonic brow. "Having tea. Wasn't it obvious? Don't think I was *nice* to them. For the most part, I ignored Sir Barnard, and he was content to simply sit and seethe. Lady Kingman is actually a decent sort—she clearly cares for her daughter. She apologized for her husband's behavior, which earned her a glare that would strike fear into the bravest of men, and said she was happy her daughter had made a love match. I'm happy too. You've been very lucky when it comes to love, my boy."

Lucky? Was she mad? "How can you say that after I lost my first wife?"

"Because I see you with your second wife. Ask yourself this, if you could turn back the hands of time and have Miriam, would you be willing to say good-bye to Diana? Could you?"

That was a bloody nonsensical choice. And he couldn't make it. But even as he thought that, he already had an answer. He simply couldn't imagine his life without Diana in it, whereas he'd *had* to move on without Miriam. "Thank you for making me feel horrible again."

She got up from her chair, causing Humphrey to stir from his nap. He stood up and stretched, turned in a circle, then settled himself in the center of the cushion where it was warm.

"I didn't mean to make you feel horrible. You know I speak plainly." She always had. "I was only trying to point out that you're a lucky man to have found love twice, especially after losing Miriam."

He eyed her skeptically. "You sound sympathetic. What happened to the woman who blamed me for her death, who turned her back on me after the funeral?"

"She realized life is too short and that she knows her son." She stepped toward him. "It was an accident. You wouldn't hurt her, even if she was carrying a bastard."

"Do you think she was?" The pain of that possibility was less now that it had been earlier. He didn't know why exactly, but he'd welcome the improvement.

She shrugged. "We'll never know. Mrs. Dodd confided the rumor to me, and I didn't tell you because you were in such bad shape."

"And yet you told me today."

"It's time to put it all to rest, don't you think?"

"I'd like to, but I don't know if it's possible." This was an improvement too. Before, he would have flatly said it was impossible, that he'd made a promise to Miriam never to let her memory fade. "Why did you abandon me?"

She exhaled, and he detected a note of self-recrimination. "I can't say I'm proud of it. I was angry at your behavior. Not because I thought you'd maliciously pushed her down the stairs, but because you couldn't remember. You know how much I hated your drinking."

Yes, he did. "You were right to hate it. I don't drink anymore."

"Ever?"

"Not a single drop. I've become quite a tea enthusiast."

"How remarkable." She blinked and glanced away for a moment, bringing her fingertip to the corner of her left eye.

"You were right to abandon me." Diana was right—he'd cultivated people's scorn and derision as a form of self-punishment. He'd accepted his mother's treatment as something he'd deserved. "I could barely live with myself. Why should anyone else?"

Her brow creased. "You needed care and support. I should have been there for you. Yes, it was a horrible thing—an accident. You must find a way to forgive yourself. But it seems you may be on that path. I wasn't there for you, but clearly Diana was. And is. I can see how much you care for her. It's similar to Miriam, but different too."

"I miss her, but I do care for Diana. More than I ever thought possible. How can there possibly be room for both of them in my heart? Already, Miriam is starting to fade a bit." His chest constricted as he recalled coming down the stairs just now and not even thinking of her until he was at the bottom.

Mother gave him a wan smile. "My dear boy, she will fade with time. Even your father has faded for me—and I haven't remarried. It doesn't mean I love or miss him any less. It only means I've found a way to continue, to move forward. And he would want me to do that. Miriam would want that for you too."

"But it's my fault she isn't here."

"Fault isn't important, Simon." She hadn't called him by his first name in a very long time. It made him feel like a boy again, and right now, that wasn't a bad thing. "Forgiveness is what matters. You've found the chance to be happy again. Do that. Look forward, not back. Your father would be proud of the duke you've become."

Forgive himself. Look forward instead of to the past. Let the past stay where it must—behind him. He had to find a way to live with what he'd done. This wasn't a revelation. He'd known he'd have to do that if he had any hope for a future. But he'd never had that hope. Not until Diana.

"Thank you," he said quietly, appreciating her words.

She came to him and patted his arm. It was as close to a hug as he might expect from her. She'd never been overly demonstrative. His father had been the one to wrap him in a tight embrace and drop a kiss on his head. Simon missed him so much. But he was also glad to have his mother here.

"You'll stay for a few days?" he asked.

She nodded. "Apparently, I need to investigate the dower house. I'm weary of my cottage in Kent, but it's nice to have so I can visit your sisters." They lived within about forty miles of each other. "They might like to see you and meet your new wife. If you wanted to invite them here."

Simon still wasn't sure he could stay here for a long period of time. He was going to try to last until Lowell and Marley's wedding, but he wasn't entirely convinced it was possible.

"I'll think about it."

"You do that. I'm going to have a rest before dinner." She started toward the door, and Humphrey jumped down from the chair to follow her.

Simon tried to sort through the outrageous events of the day. It hadn't been all bad—he felt even closer to Diana, and he'd reconciled with his mother. But learning the reason for his argument with Miriam had been a blow. It gave proof to a truth he'd secretly doubted, deep inside—that he *had* caused her death.

So he wasn't a *murderer*, but his wife had died because of him. Probably. He'd never know. And yes, he'd have to learn to live with that.

Chapter Seventeen

❦

DIANA SLEPT LATER than normal after the events of the previous day. They'd enjoyed a nice dinner with the dowager, opting to avoid discussing anything to do with Diana's parents or the revelation regarding Simon's first wife's death. Instead, his mother had regaled Diana with his youthful exploits on the estate—fishing in the pond, climbing trees, bringing creatures into the house and causing general mayhem, daily rides with his father. When the conversation turned to the previous duke, the love Simon and his mother felt for him was palpable. Diana realized Simon had lost two of the most important people in his life. That had to be difficult. Whereas Diana didn't even *have* important people in her life.

That acknowledgment came with a shadow of melancholy. Or maybe it had come with what Simon had said yesterday. About Miriam. Diana could see how much he'd loved her and how he'd suffered with her loss. There was a void inside him, and she doubted her ability to fill it.

How she wanted to.

The other thing she'd realized was that she loved him. She *had* to. She'd no idea what that emotion should feel like, but he was never far from her mind, she burned for his touch, and she ached to make him whole again. If that wasn't love, then perhaps she was simply incapable of the emotion.

While that was certainly possible, she refused to believe it was true. She *wanted* to love him. Furthermore, she wanted him to love her in return.

Yes, therein lay her melancholy.

As she made her way to the stairs, she saw Mrs. Marley talking with a maid. The maid nodded at whatever she said and departed along the gallery. Mrs. Marley turned and started down the stairs.

Making a quick decision, Diana increased her pace to catch up with the housekeeper and did so on the landing. "Mrs. Marley, may I speak with you a moment?"

The housekeeper turned, her brown eyes reflecting a slight surprise. "Oh, Your Grace, I didn't see you. Of course. How may I be of service? Or is this about the wedding?" Her lips curved into a small smile.

"It's not, actually, but the arrangements are coming along." After what Diana had learned yesterday, she wondered whether it was appropriate to host their wedding here at the chapel. While none of what happened was the housekeeper's fault, Diana couldn't help being bothered by her role.

She found herself thinking of what Mrs. Dodd had said—if only Mrs. Marley had kept what she'd seen to herself.

Except then she would've borne the burden of that secret, and Diana decided that would have been terrible. Mrs. Marley wasn't at fault; however, perhaps the housekeeper could help. "I hope you won't mind my asking, but I wanted to speak with you about the former duchess's death."

Mrs. Marley glanced toward the bottom of the stairs, and her face paled. "They were standing right here." She looked around at the landing before settling her somber gaze on Diana.

A shiver jolted up Diana's spine, and her skin turned to ice. "Would you tell me precisely what you remember?"

The housekeeper closed her eyes for a moment, her features tensing. When she opened her eyes again, there was anguish in their depths. "I've worked so hard to block it from my mind, ma'am, but I can try."

"I understand. And I appreciate you trying."

Mrs. Marley gave a small nod. "They were a happy couple at first. Which is why what happened was so awful. We were all shocked."

"Are you speaking of the accident?"

"And what happened before. *Why* it happened." The housekeeper looked away.

The rumored affair.

"Go on," Diana urged. She'd started this folly, and she meant to finish it.

"They were only married a few months before Her Grace got with child. I'm not sure where the rumor started, but it was soon whispered that the babe wasn't His Grace's." Mrs. Marley said this with considerable effort, her face reflecting her sorrow.

"And why was this suspected?" From everything Diana knew, it made no sense.

"There was a young footman who was clearly enamored of her. They were seen together on several occasions—close together."

"Someone saw them...kissing?"

"No, not that. They were very discreet." Mrs. Marley clasped her hands together nervously. "Or maybe there was nothing, and it was just a rumor. How can we ever know?"

That was unfortunately true. In fact, they'd never really know what happened here on the stairs. So why was Diana asking this poor woman about it? "We can't. Just as we can't know what happened after you turned from their disagreement in this very spot."

Tears formed in Mrs. Marley's eyes, but she blinked them away. "I was so distraught after it happened. Even now, I can't think about it without becoming upset. And to stand here discussing it..." Her voice trailed off, and she sucked in a sharp, quick breath.

Diana put an end to the torture. "Let us not speak of it." She touched the housekeeper's arm gently. "I'm sorry I brought it up, and I shan't do so again. The Duke is very fortunate to have your support—you mustn't blame yourself for telling the truth."

"Thank you, ma'am." Mrs. Marley bobbed her head. "You're too kind."

"Come, let us get off this landing." Diana forced a soft laugh, then led the housekeeper down to the hall where Lowell met them. He cast a concerned look at his betrothed but didn't say anything.

Mrs. Marley continued toward the kitchens.

"Your Grace," Lowell began. "The dowager is in the Blue and Gold Room and asked if you might join her."

"Thank you, Lowell." Diana made her way to the drawing room and found her mother-in-law ensconced in her new favorite chair, scratching Humphrey's head.

"Good afternoon, Diana," the dowager said. "I'm glad to see you've taken the time to rest after yesterday's trials, but may I say you still look a bit pale."

Diana had already learned that her mother-in-law didn't mince words. "I just had an encounter with Mrs. Marley on the stairs. I'm afraid I reopened the old wound and asked her about the accident."

The dowager nodded serenely. "You mustn't chastise yourself. It's natural to want to find answers. I did the same after it happened. I interrogated every member of the staff. She's the only one who saw anything, and even then, it wasn't enough to provide a full account."

Diana sat on the settee and surveyed the garden behind the house. Simon was out there somewhere on his vast estate, conducting the duties he felt he'd neglected for far too long. She missed him.

"What did she say?" the dowager asked, drawing Diana back to the conversation.

"She told me about the rumor." Diana cocked her head at Simon's mother. "How did you learn of it?"

"When I spoke with the staff afterward, Mrs. Dodd told me. No one else would have the courage to tell me, but Mrs. Dodd and I have a special relationship. I hired her as the cook when I became the duchess." The dowager smiled, the sharp angles of her face softening. "She was Miss Chambers then. She's the reason I'm here, actually. She wrote to tell me about your arrival, and I decided to come myself."

"Mrs. Marley said there was a footman who was presumably too close to the Duchess."

Simon's mother frowned. "Yes, I'd heard that, but I dismissed it as nonsense. That woman—Miriam—loved my son to the point of distraction. She could never quite believe that a duke had married her. She wasn't groomed for this life, not like you were."

Diana's chest ached. She loved Simon like that. Even now, her mind was drifting to where he was and what he was doing and counting the moments until he returned. But the pain came from knowing Simon had loved his first wife in precisely the same way. Diana knew he cared for her too, but doubted it could ever be the same. "Simon loved her too. It doesn't make sense that she would cuckold him."

"No, it never made sense to me either. But apparently Romsey considered it, because he confronted her."

"It may have been best to keep that from him," Diana suggested.

"Maybe, but he would've learned of it sooner or later. Things like that never stay quiet. Not forever. Much better that he hear it from me. And it's not as if it were actually *true*. I don't think anyone believes that."

Diana wasn't sure she agreed with the dowager's reasoning for telling him, but didn't see the point in debating her. She did, however, want to talk to Mrs. Dodd about this rumor. If no one *really* believed it, how had it started and why had it taken hold? She stood from the settee. "I'm going to the kitchens to discuss next week's menu with Mrs. Dodd."

"She's the best cook in all of Hampshire," the dowager said. "Maybe all of southern England. Have you had her trifle yet? That's the reason I hired her. She made a selection of dishes for my consideration, and that trifle won her the position. Would you be so kind to ask if she could make it for me before I leave?"

"Of course." Diana excused herself and went directly to the kitchens to find Mrs. Dodd. The main kitchen was surprisingly empty, so she went into the scullery, where Rose was scrubbing a pot. "Good afternoon, Rose."

The girl jumped, nearly dropping the pot. She lifted her wide-eyed gaze to Diana's.

"Please forgive me for startling you," Diana said. "I'm looking for Mrs. Dodd."

Rose's frame relaxed—as much as it ever did, for the girl seemed eternally tense to Diana, which was perhaps why she'd developed a special fondness for the young maid. Diana knew what it was like to feel constantly on edge.

Rose went back to scouring the pot. "Everyone's taking the midday meal."

"Why aren't you with them?"

"It's my job to watch after the kitchen. I'll eat when they're done."

"You never get to eat with them?" When Rose shook her head, Diana wondered why they couldn't rotate that responsibility so that Rose wasn't always isolated.

"I don't mind, Your Grace. I like to keep to myself. That's the best way to stay out of trouble. I learned that real fast."

Diana could imagine Mrs. Dodd instilling fear in Rose from the moment she arrived. The cook ran a tight kitchen and expected her maids to keep their hands clean. And yet Mrs. Dodd seemed to be the chief purveyor of gossip in the house. A thought struck Diana—perhaps Rose might flourish in another area.

"Rose, would you like to work in the house as a maid?"

Rose looked up from the pot in surprise. "Why?"

Diana wondered if the girl might be more comfortable away from Mrs. Dodd's somewhat autocratic ways. She shrugged, acting nonchalant. "I thought you might like to try something new."

Rose shook her head rather vehemently. "No, thank you, ma'am."

Taken aback by the girl's fervent refusal, Diana couldn't keep herself from asking why. "Is there a reason?"

Rose set the pot in the sink, where she poured water into the vessel and swirled it about to rinse it clean. After pouring the water down the drain, she set the pot on the drying rack and turned to Diana as she wiped her hands on her apron. "I'd rather not work in the house. Mrs. Dodd is not so bad as Mrs. Marley." Rose shuddered before crossing the scullery and entering the small storeroom. Inside, she began to rearrange the cookware on the shelves.

Diana blinked. The housekeeper seemed so lovely. And capable. She'd heard nothing to support her having a poor reputation amongst the staff. Diana joined Rose in the storeroom. "Why do you feel that way about Mrs. Marley?"

Rose hesitated, as she often did, and Diana sought to reassure her. "I hope you know that whatever you tell me is in the strictest confidence. I care about everyone on the staff, but for some reason, you are already special to me."

Though the storeroom was dim, with only the light from the high bank of windows on the opposite wall of the scullery to provide illumination, Diana could see the pink swathing Rose's round, youthful cheeks. "Thank you, ma'am. I've never cared for Mrs. Marley. She scares me. Because of the...Incident."

Diana had to strain to hear the last word. "The accident involving the previous duchess?" At Rose's nod, Diana tried to think of why Mrs. Marley's behavior would have frightened the girl. "Is it because she spoke out?"

Rose stopped organizing and turned to Diana, twisting her fingers in the front of her apron and shook her head. "No, because she lied. I saw everything what happened."

Diana's heart stopped for a second. Here was a witness. "Why didn't you tell anyone?"

Panic flashed in Rose's eyes as they grew as big as dinner plates. "I'd only worked here for a week, but I already knew that Mrs. Dodd didn't tolerate gossip from us unless we shared it with her and her alone. But seeing His Grace…" A tear slipped from Rose's eye, cracking Diana's heart.

"What did you see?" Diana was desperate to know.

"It was Mrs. Marley who argued with Her Grace on the stairs. Her Grace slipped and reached for Mrs. Marley, but Mrs. Marley drew back, and Her Grace fell." Rose squeezed her eyes shut. "It was horrible. Sometimes I wake up and see the terror on her face and hear the sound of her hitting the floor." Rose wrapped her arms around herself. "And then I see His Grace rushing from his study into the hall. I hear his cry of distress. Then I see him holding Her Grace, begging her not to die." Her eyes had taken on a glassy sheen. She blinked and refocused on Diana. "That was when I ran. I ran all the way up to my room in the attic, and I've never told a soul about it."

Tears fell unheeded from Diana's eyes. The image of Simon cradling his dead wife's body would've haunted her too. And maybe it would now that she knew the truth. He hadn't even been on the stairs. Marley had lied about it all to cover up her own misdeed. To think Simon's suffering could have been abated… None of this would bring Miriam back, but at least he wouldn't have blamed himself.

"Why didn't you tell Mrs. Dodd at least?" Diana tried not to sound accusatory. The girl had been thirteen and brand-new to the house. If she'd been in the same circumstance, Diana wasn't sure she could have found the courage to speak out either. "Never mind, I already know the answer. You were deathly afraid for many reasons, all of them valid." She wiped at her wet cheeks and summoned a smile of encouragement for the brave girl. "I'm so glad you told me the truth. This will help the Duke immeasurably."

Rose's eyes brightened. "Will it really?"

The door behind Diana slammed closed, followed by the sound of a bolt. Diana whipped around and tried to push the door open, but, as expected, it was locked.

She turned back to Rose, but they were now in total darkness. "D-did you see who cl-closed the door?" Diana asked as anxiety tripped through her. Why would someone lock them in the storeroom?

"Not clearly. But I saw a flash of skirt." The maid blanched. "I think it was Mrs. Marley."

The fear in Rose's tone echoed in Diana's chest. The darkness of the storeroom took her back to the countless times her father had shut her in a pitch-black closet where she'd been forced to spend the night and contemplate her deficiencies. Panic rose in her throat, and she simply couldn't make any words come out.

"What should we do?" Rose asked, her voice small and scared in the dark.

They should call for help, but Diana was frozen. Then a smell filtered beneath the door. Smoke.

"Someone will find us, won't they?" Rose asked fearfully.

Diana hoped so. They weren't very far—Mrs. Dodd and the others were just on the other side of the kitchen. But would they hear them if they yelled? It was a pointless question since Diana couldn't even speak. Hysteria bubbled in her chest as smoke began to filter beneath the door.

Rose pushed past her and pounded on the door, but quickly drew back. "It's hot."

Diana heard the faint crackle of flame. Dear God, the door was on fire. Very shortly the storeroom would become an oven. And she and Rose were going to be cooked inside.

Her mind went to Simon and the pain he would suffer if he lost her too. She prayed he wouldn't have to endure that again. Surely life wouldn't be so cruel.

Yet as the smoke increased, the heat grew, and Rose began to cough, Diana's hope faded. She was no stranger to cruelty, and it seemed that would be her end.

◆€◆3◆

AS SIMON RODE into the yard with Nevis, he saw the stable lads racing toward the kitchens. "What the devil is going on?"

Nevis squinted toward the kitchens. "Smoke. More than normal, it looks like. Could be a fire?" He slid from his horse.

Alarmed, Simon dismounted. Since it seemed he couldn't call for a stableboy to take the horses, he handed the reins to Nevis. "I'll send a lad back."

The steward nodded as Simon ran toward the kitchen. Smoke billowed from the scullery, and the door to the outside was thrown open as the staff worked to assemble a bucket line.

"What happened?" Simon asked Tinley, who was organizing the line.

"A fire in the storeroom." His face was grim. "There may be someone inside."

Terror gripped Simon's chest. He couldn't suffer another tragedy. He looked about for Diana. She would be here helping. He was sure of it.

He saw his mother hurrying toward him, Humphrey in her arms. "Where's Diana?" she asked sharply. "She went to the kitchens." Her eyes darted about frantically.

The fear in Simon's gut intensified, searing him until he nearly dropped to his knees. No, he couldn't survive losing her too…

He ran into the scullery and saw that the door to the storeroom was ablaze. Dashing back out, he shouted for an axe or some sort of tool to batter at the door.

Tinley ran to the woodpile and came back with an axe. "You need a cover for your face, for the smoke."

Simon didn't have time for that. He ran back inside and got as close to the door as he dared. Heat scorched his face and arms, then he felt water dousing him from behind, wetting him from head to toe and splashing against the door. The intensity of the heat diminished, and the flames fought to stay ablaze.

"Diana?" he yelled, his hands shaking. "Are you in there?"

"Help us, please, Your Grace." It wasn't Diana's voice, but her use of the word "us" told Simon all he needed to hear. His wife was in there. He was sure of it.

"Step as far back from the door as you can!" He sent the axe into the blazing wood as another bucket of water came to the end of the line. This one was tossed over the door, extinguishing some of the flames. "Keep the water coming!" He brought the axe back and slammed it into the door again, over and over until the wood splintered.

Another bucket arrived and was thrown on the door. The fire sputtered and managed to keep its hold near the bottom. Simon reached for the latch, but jerked his hand away as the still-hot metal burned his fingers. He went back to hacking at the door, battering it into bits until there was a hole large enough for him to see inside.

Curled against the shelves on the opposite wall was one of the scullery maids holding Diana, who was slumped on the girl's lap.

Despite the burns on his hands, he felt nothing but ice as his world seemed to stop. He couldn't move or breathe or think. She was gone.

Tinley nudged him as he pushed past with a large bucket. Water sluiced over the last of the fire, leaving a smoldering door with a blackened hole in the middle.

"Your Grace, we need to get them out," Tinley said. When Simon didn't move, the coachman took the axe from his slack hand and whacked a hole big enough for a person to get through.

Galvanized, Simon pushed past Tinley and stepped into the storeroom. He coughed as smoke filled his lungs, then he bent and picked Diana up. Holding her close to his chest, he slipped back out through the charred door. "Help the maid," he said as he carried Diana through the scullery past the kitchen into the servants' hall, where he laid her on a bench.

He knelt next to her on the hard stone floor. Her dark hair had come loose, and silky tendrils framed her unnaturally pale face.

"She's breathing." It was his mother's voice.

She *was* breathing, but Simon knew better than to hope. Miriam had been breathing too before she'd died in his arms.

He stroked Diana's face and bent forward to kiss her lips. His tears fell onto her cheeks. "Please, Diana, don't leave me. I can't bear to lose you. I won't survive it."

How could he go on with the knowledge that he hadn't been able to save two wives? Two women he loved more than he ever dreamed possible.

Laying his head on her chest, he listened to her shallow breaths as he stared up at her still features. "I love you. And if you could just stay with me, *please*, I'll show you how much."

Her breath caught in her chest, and he listened for it to start again. When it didn't, he clutched at her savagely, anguish tearing through him as he gave in to the grief that would torment him forever.

Chapter Eighteen

❧

DIANA GASPED AS she pulled air into her burning lungs. Her eyes fluttered open. There was something on her chest...

"Simon?" He'd been begging her not to die. "I'm not dying. I refuse to do that to you."

The weight came off her chest, and she saw his face over hers, his dark eyes wide with wonder. "Diana?"

She began to cough, deep, racking spasms that shook her body. He helped her to sit up and called for water. Tears streamed from her eyes, and someone pressed a tankard into her hand. She drank deeply, urging the cool liquid to soothe her sore throat. She heard him send someone to fetch the doctor in Romsey.

When she finished the water, Simon took the cup and handed it off to someone. She'd no idea who, because she couldn't take her eyes from his beloved face.

"Did you say you loved me?" she croaked.

"Shhh." He kissed her softly, reverently, his hands cupping her cheeks. "Yes. More than my life."

She reached for him, clutching at the lapels of his coat. "I love you too. Why are you wet?"

"We were frantic to put out the fire. But I was trying to get the door open. They doused me with water."

She turned her head and pressed a kiss to his palm, but he winced. Taking his hand, she looked at his reddened flesh. "You're burned."

"Just a bit. A small price to pay to have you back."

"I didn't go anywhere."

His gaze was so dark and intense, she shivered. "I thought I'd lost you." The words crackled from his lips.

Lost... The events preceding the fire came rushing back to her. She looked around and realized she was in the servants' hall, the remnants of their meal still on the table in front of her.

"Where is Mrs. Marley?"

Simon frowned. "What does that matter?"

Diana shook her head. "First, is Rose all right?"

"Who's Rose?"

Frustration threatened her patience as her mind whirled with what she now knew—and what Simon didn't. "The maid who was with me. Is she safe?" She grabbed his hand and, when he winced, let go with an apology. "Please find out for me. I need to know she's safe."

Simon stood and put his head around the corner. "Tinley!"

Diana pushed herself to her feet, holding the edge of the table for support, as she listened to their conversation.

"Where's the maid?" Simon asked.

"Mrs. Dodd is fussing over her. She'll be fine. How is Her Grace?"

Simon turned his head and, when he saw that she was standing, rushed to her side. "Not taking it easy, as she should."

Diana coughed again. "I'm fine. We need to find Mrs. Marley immediately. I'll explain shortly, but we need to find her." She took his arm, and they walked into the main kitchen. Smoke still clung to the ceiling as people worked to clear the scullery out.

"Lowell!" Simon barked for the butler, who stood near the door to the scullery. The servant turned, his brows climbing with surprise.

He came toward them. "Yes, Your Grace?"

"Where is Mrs. Marley?"

The butler glanced back toward the scullery. "I don't know. Shall I look for her?"

"That won't be necessary." The dowager came into the kitchen from the corridor leading to the house, her hand wrapped around Mrs. Marley's arm. "I caught her just as she was trying to leave. I thought to myself, why would the housekeeper leave at such a time?" She pursed her lips at Mrs. Marley in a thoroughly disgusted fashion.

Diana let go of Simon and walked toward the housekeeper. "You locked us in."

Simon rushed to her side. "The hell she did." He glared at Mrs. Marley. "Why would you do that?"

Her gaze found Lowell. "It's his fault! All of this is his fault. If not for his stupid plan, none of it would have happened." She began to cry, covering her face with her hands.

"She's lying," Lowell said coldly. "Any plan—and it *was* stupid—was hers."

Mrs. Marley dropped her hands as her eyes darkened with anger. "How can you say that? It was your idea to create a scandal that would encourage Andrews and Mrs. Harker to leave."

Simon looked between them. "Stop. Explain. What scandal, and why did you want my butler and housekeeper to leave?"

"So we could have their jobs," Mrs. Marley said. "Davis had it all planned out." Following her furious gaze, Diana realized Lowell must be

Davis.

Lowell sent his fiancée—likely former fiancée at this point—a look of pure loathing. "She lies, Your Grace. It was Mrs. Marley's idea to start the rumor that Her Grace was unfaithful and that the babe may not be yours."

The housekeeper jabbed her finger toward him. "Because you wanted to be promoted to butler! The plan was yours. I only came up with the particulars."

Lowell's eyes narrowed, and Diana recognized the glint in their depths for what it was—cruelty. "You're also the one who caused her to fall."

Simon staggered, and Diana reached out to put her arm around his waist, struggling to keep him upright. He blinked at Diana, his gaze glassy and unfocused. "What are they saying?"

"It wasn't your fault at all, my love. None of it. You weren't even on the stairs with her. She argued with Mrs. Marley, and she slipped."

"I tried to stop her," Mrs. Marley cried.

Diana surveyed her with a mixture of disgust and pity. "That's not the way Rose tells it, and she was there—which you know, since you apparently overheard us talking in the storeroom. Why else would you lock us in and set the door on fire?"

"You're a fool," Lowell whispered, his gaze spearing daggers at the woman he'd planned to marry.

She rushed forward and put her hands on his chest. "I did it for you! For us! I didn't know she saw what happened. When I heard her telling Her Grace, I panicked. I just knew they couldn't be allowed to tell anyone. You would have done the same thing!"

Lowell said nothing, just stared frigidly down at her. "You're pathetic. To think I loved you, and here you are trying to drag me into your tangle of deceit and murder."

"I didn't murder Her Grace! She fell, truly." Mrs. Marley swung her head around and looked from person to person, her eyes wild.

Besides the dowager and Tinley, Nevis had come into the kitchen along with Mrs. Dodd and Rose.

Mrs. Marley pointed a shaking finger at the scullery maid. "*She* made everything up! You'd believe her over me?"

"Since you tried to set her—and *me*—on fire, yes." Diana looked to Nevis and calmly instructed him to lock the housekeeper up somewhere.

"Happy to, Your Grace." Nevis took Mrs. Marley by the arm and led her outside.

Diana turned her attention to Lowell. "I'm not sure what crime we can accuse you of, but until I can think of one, you are hereby relieved of your duties. Remove yourself from Lyndhurst by nightfall or I'll have Nevis lock you up with your would-be bride."

The butler's jaw worked, and his eyes burned with fury. He turned to Simon. "Your Grace—"

Simon looked toward his coachman. "Tinley, please see Lowell out immediately." He turned a scathing glare on his former butler. "Someone will pack your things and have them delivered to the drive. Because I want you off my property as quickly as possible, Tinley will drive you to the village. I would encourage you to keep walking from there—straight out of Hampshire—because I will ensure that no one in this county will hire you, not even to muck their stalls or clean their chamber pots."

Tinley gestured for Lowell to precede him, his eyes glittering with revulsion. "Happy to escort you out with or without your help."

The butler lifted his chin and stalked out of the kitchen.

Diana coughed again as she worked to get the feeling of soot out of her lungs.

Simon turned and took her in his arms. "Are you all right? You should rest."

She glanced down at the angry patches of red on his hands. "And you should soak your hands. And get out of your wet clothes."

"The doctor will be here soon, I should think," the dowager said. "In the meantime, take yourselves upstairs, and I'll manage things here. Go on." She gestured toward the corridor that led to the house, wordlessly shooing them on their way.

Diana took Simon's arm, clinging to him as they went into the house. When they walked into the hall, he paused at the base of the stairs. "It's silly, but this feels different now. I'm still sad she's gone—I shall always miss her—but to know that I had no part in it gives me a small sense of relief."

"I know how much you love her. Don't think that I ever hope to take her place." She touched his chest with her fingers. "Is there room for me in there too?"

He slipped his arms around her and pulled her against his chest. "Plenty. I told you I thought I'd never be whole again. But now there's you. And I love you even more than I thought it possible to love another person. When I'm with you, I'm more than whole. It's you and me together. It feels as though we can do anything—overcome anything."

She stood on her toes and kissed him, loving the feel of his lips on hers and so thankful they'd found each other.

Later, after the doctor had tended to them and they were ensconced in their bed following a dinner his mother had insisted they take in their chamber, Diana smoothed her fingers over the bandages on his hands.

"Does it hurt?"

"Not much. The pain is *nothing* compared to the distress of the doctor telling me not to use them for a couple of days." He held them up and looked at them with frown. "How can I show you how much I love you without my hands?"

Diana pushed up from the pillows and straddled his hips, lifting her nightgown so she was bare against him. He still wore his shirt but had removed his breeches before they'd climbed into bed.

She wiggled her fingers. "I have hands." She used one to stroke his hardening cock.

"Mmm, so you do." He leaned his head back and closed his eyes as she coaxed him to a full erection. "It occurred to me that when you handled that situation this afternoon"—he opened his eyes and looked up at her—"with magnificent aplomb, I would add—you didn't stutter once."

He was right. And she'd been distraught and angry. "How s-strange." She shook her head. "Damn."

He laughed. "I'd ask that you *not* stop it. Your imperfections are perfect to me."

She stared at him, her hand stilling. Emotion threatened her speech, but regardless of what he said, she would get this out without faltering: "I love you so very much."

He smiled with contentment, but it quickly faded. "Please don't stop that either." His gaze dipped down to his pelvis. "Your hand, I mean." He narrowed his eyes seductively. "I'd help, but the doctor said—"

She released his cock and clasped his wrists, lifting them over his head. "Don't hurt yourself, my love. Let me take care of everything."

She reached back down between them, and that's precisely what she did.

Epilogue

◆€◆3◆

HE WAS STILL here, and he didn't hate it.

Simon marveled at the changes in his life over the past fortnight. He'd returned home the same broken man who couldn't bear to face his past, and now he was content and happily contemplating the future.

Even if his hands *were* a little worse for wear. Actually, they were much improved. He flexed his fingers to prove it to himself—as if he needed to. He'd used them to great benefit just that morning as he'd roused his beloved wife from sleep.

Movement outside the window caught his eye, and he stood from his desk. He walked into the small sitting room between his study and the hall, where Diana sat composing a letter to Verity.

Her left hand lay flat atop the desk above the paper, and the iron band on her finger caught his eye. He still meant to replace it.

Sensing his presence, she turned her head and smiled. "Simon. What are you looking at?" She followed his gaze with hers, landing on her hand.

He went to her side and slipped his fingers beneath hers. "You need a jewel."

"I need nothing but you."

He laughed softly. "While that is excellent to hear, my duchess deserves something better than this iron band to wear."

She gave him an obstinate but charming stare. "If you buy something else, I'll simply wear this on my other hand."

Love swelled in his chest. "You are a treasure greater than any jewel," he murmured as he bent to kiss her temple. He offered the reason he'd come to find her. "They're here."

She set the pen down and looked up at him. Taking a deep breath, she stood. "I'm ready."

They walked together into the hall as the new butler, Eddleston, opened the door. Lowell had evaded prosecution for any part he'd played in Miriam's death—the blame had fallen squarely on Mrs. Marley. She'd confessed to lying about everything and to setting fire to the scullery with the intention to kill Rose and Diana. The former housekeeper was to be transported any day now.

As the guests came in, Eddleston announced their arrival. As if Simon and Diana didn't know perfectly well who they were. "The Duke and

Duchess of Kilve."

Simon's gaze connected with Nick's, and they exchanged slight nods. Their wives, however, eyed each other warily for a moment. It was Violet, Nick's new duchess, who spoke first.

"I'm so sorry, Diana." She winced. Her hazel gaze was apologetic. "You must hate us."

"Why would I do that? If not for you, I'd be married to *him*," Diana said with a tinge of derision as she waved a hand at Nick, "instead of *him*." That word carried a warmth of love and desire. She curled her hand around Simon's arm and gave him a squeeze.

There was a long beat of silence followed by Simon letting out a howl of laughter. Nick immediately joined in, and soon after, Violet did as well. Diana merely smiled, her expression one of a cat who'd just caught every mouse in the barn and had no intention of sharing.

"Come in," Simon beckoned as he led them to the drawing room.

Violet left her husband and went to Diana. "You're truly not angry?"

"Not anymore. It all seemed meant to be." Diana took her hand from Simon and clasped Violet's hand. They'd become friends at the house party, and Simon was glad to see they apparently would still be. "Are you happy?"

"Never more." Violet looked to Nick, and the love between them was palpably strong. She returned her gaze to Diana. "Are you?"

"For the first time." She slid a glance at Simon, and her lips curved up. "Forever."

Heat spread through Simon. Impossibly, his love for her grew day by day.

"What a sickening lot," Nick said.

"We deserve it, don't you think?" Simon asked wryly. He and Nick had known each other since Oxford, and between them had spent more time battling sadness and despair than anyone ought.

"Of course you do," Violet said. "We all do."

Nick came forward and stood in front of Diana. "I owe you a sincere apology. I never meant to cause you distress—or scandal. I'm afraid I was an enormous ass."

"I made him stand in the snow for days before I would forgive him," Violet said. "I only relented because I feared he would freeze to death."

Diana put her hand over her mouth to stifle a giggle.

"Would've served him right," Simon muttered with a smile.

"Indeed, it would have," Nick agreed. "But fortune took pity on me, apparently."

"No, *I* took pity on you, and don't ever forget it." Violet narrowed her eyes at him playfully.

"Anyway, I'm the one that ended up causing a scandal," Simon said, putting his arm around Diana and drawing her close. "In trying to rescue the fair damsel, I delivered her right into the heart of disaster when we were recognized on the road to Gretna." Simon had explained all their travails when he'd written to Nick.

"I received a letter from Hannah," Violet said, glancing toward Simon and Diana. "Mrs. Linford—she hosted the house party where you met."

Simon briefly recollected that house party and the first time he'd kissed Diana. He'd gone in the hope of emerging from his grief, never imagining that it would so utterly change his life for the better. He itched to kiss her right now.

Violet continued, "Hannah asked if you two were going to duel. Since Simon stole Diana from Nick."

"What a brilliant idea," Simon said. "We'll organize it for the start of the Season and stage it in Hyde Park."

Diana's and Violet's eyes rounded. "You can't mean that," Diana said.

"I most certainly do. We wouldn't *actually* duel, of course. But what a laugh it would be at everyone's expense."

Nick joined Simon in laughter. "I like this idea. We'll need to explore its merit." Since they'd be staying for a week, they had plenty of time to do so.

"Excellent." Simon reached over and clasped his friend's hand. "It's good to have you here."

"It's good to be here, and thank you for cleaning up my mess."

"Your mess ended up being my miracle." Unable to hold himself back any longer, Simon kissed Diana briefly, his lips grazing hers. "And I shall thank you for all eternity."

The end

Thank You!

❧

Thank you so much for reading *The Duke of Ruin*. I hope you enjoyed Simon and Violet's romantic story! I loved writing them so much that I could truly write a series just about them. I was very sad to type the end. But never fear, they will appear in *The Duke of Lies*, so stay tuned!

Would you like to know when my next book is available? You can sign up for my newsletter, follow me on Twitter at @darcyburke, or like my Facebook page at http://facebook.com/DarcyBurkeFans.

The Duke of Ruin is the eighth book in The Untouchables series. The next book in the series is *The Duke of Lies*. Watch for more information! In the meantime, catch up with my other historical series: Secrets and Scandals and Legendary Rogues. If you like contemporary romance, I hope you'll check out my Ribbon Ridge series available from Avon Impulse and my latest series, which continues the lives and loves of Ribbon Ridge's denizens – So Hot.

I appreciate my readers so much. Thank you, thank you, *thank you*.

Books by Darcy Burke
❧ ❧

Historical Romance

The Untouchables

The Forbidden Duke
The Duke of Daring
The Duke of Deception
The Duke of Desire
The Duke of Defiance
The Duke of Danger
The Duke of Ice
The Duke of Ruin
The Duke of Lies
The Duke of Seduction
The Duke of Wishes
The Duke of Mischief

Secrets and Scandals

Her Wicked Ways
His Wicked Heart
To Seduce a Scoundrel
To Love a Thief (a novella)
Never Love a Scoundrel
Scoundrel Ever After

Legendary Rogues

Lady of Desire
Romancing the Earl
Lord of Fortune
Captivating the Scoundrel

Contemporary Romance

Ribbon Ridge

Where the Heart Is (a prequel novella)
Only in My Dreams
Yours to Hold
When Love Happens
The Idea of You
When We Kiss
You're Still the One

Ribbon Ridge: So Hot

So Good
So Right
So Wrong

Praise for Darcy Burke's
Secrets & Scandals Series

HER WICKED WAYS

"A bad girl heroine steals both the show and a highwayman's heart in Darcy Burke's deliciously wicked debut."

—Courtney Milan, *NYT* Bestselling Author

"…fast paced, very sexy, with engaging characters."

—Smexybooks

HIS WICKED HEART

"Intense and intriguing. Cinderella meets *Fight Club* in a historical romance packed with passion, action and secrets."

—Anna Campbell, *Seven Nights in a Rogue's Bed*

"A romance…to make you smile and sigh…a wonderful read!"

—Rogues Under the Covers

TO SEDUCE A SCOUNDREL

"Darcy Burke pulls no punches with this sexy, romantic page-turner. Sevrin and Philippa's story grabs you from the first scene and doesn't let go. To Seduce a Scoundrel is simply delicious!"

—Tessa Dare, *NYT* Bestselling Author

"I was captivated on the first page and didn't let go until this glorious book was finished!"

—Romancing the Book

TO LOVE A THIEF

"With refreshing circumstances surrounding both the hero and the heroine, a nice little mystery, and a touch of heat, this novella was a perfect way to pass the day."

—The Romanceaholic

"A refreshing read with a dash of danger and a little heat. For fans of honorable heroes and fun heroines who know what they want and take it."

—The Luv NV

NEVER LOVE A SCOUNDREL

"I loved the story of these two misfits thumbing their noses at society and finding love." Five stars.

—A Lust for Reading

"A nice mix of intrigue and passion...wonderfully complex characters, with flaws and quirks that will draw you in and steal your heart."

—BookTrib

SCOUNDREL EVER AFTER

"There is something so delicious about a bad boy, no matter what era he is from, and Ethan was definitely delicious."

-A Lust for Reading

"I loved the chemistry between the two main characters...Jagger/Ethan is not what he seems at all and neither is sweet society Miss Audrey. They are believably compatible."

-Confessions of a College Angel

Legendary Rogues Series
LADY of DESIRE

"A fast-paced mixture of adventure and romance, very much in the mould of *Romancing the Stone* or *Indiana Jones*."

-All About Romance

"...gave me such a book hangover! ...addictive...one of the most entertaining stories I've read this year!"

-Adria's Romance Reviews

ROMANCING the EARL

"Once again Darcy Burke takes an interesting story and...turns it into magic. An exceptionally well-written book."

-Bodice Rippers, Femme Fatale, and Fantasy

"...A fast paced story that was exciting and interesting. This is a definite must add to your book lists!"

-Kilts and Swords

The Untouchables Series
THE FORBIDDEN DUKE

"I LOVED this story!!" 5 Stars

-Historical Romance Lover

"This is a wonderful read and I can't wait to see what comes next in this amazing series..." 5 Stars

-Teatime and Books

THE DUKE of DARING

"You will not be able to put it down once you start. Such a good read."

-Books Need TLC

"An unconventional beauty set on life as a spinster meets the one man who might change her mind, only to find his painful past makes it impossible to love. A wonderfully emotional journey from attraction, to friendship, to a love that conquers all."

-Bronwen Evans, USA Today Bestselling Author

THE DUKE of DECEPTION

"...an enjoyable, well paced story ... Ned and Aquilla are an engaging, well-matched couple – strong, caring and compassionate; and ...it's easy to believe that they will continue to be happy together long after the book is ended."

-All About Romance

"This is my favorite so far in the series! They had chemistry from the moment they met...their passion leaps off the pages."

-Sassy Book Lover

THE DUKE of DESIRE

"Masterfully written with great characterization...with a flourish toward characters, secrets, and romance... Must read addition to "The Untouchables" series!"

-My Book Addiction and More

"If you are looking for a truly endearing story about two people who take the path least travelled to find the other, with a side of 'YAH THAT'S HOT!' then this book is absolutely for you!"

-The Reading Cafe

THE DUKE of DEFIANCE

"This story was so beautifully written, and it hooked me from page one. I couldn't put the book down and just had to read it in one sitting even though it meant reading into the wee hours of the morning."

-Buried Under Romance

"I loved the Duke of Defiance! This is the kind of book you hate when it is over and I had to make myself stop reading just so I wouldn't have to leave the fun of Knighton's (aka Bran) and Joanna's story!"

-Behind Closed Doors Book Review

THE DUKE of DANGER

"The sparks fly between them right from the start... the HEA is certainly very hard-won, and well-deserved."

-All About Romance

"Another book hangover by Darcy! Every time I pick a favorite in this series, she tops it. The ending was perfect and made me want more."

-Sassy Book Lover

THE DUKE of ICE

"Each book gets better and better, and this novel was no exception. I think this one may be my fave yet! 5 out 5 for this reader!"

-Front Porch Romance

"An incredibly emotional story...I dare anyone to stop reading once the second half gets under way because this is intense!"

-Buried Under Romance

Ribbon Ridge Series

A contemporary family saga featuring the Archer family of sextuplets who return to their small Oregon wine country town to confront tragedy and find love...

The "multilayered plot keeps readers invested in the story line, and the explicit sensuality adds to the excitement that will have readers craving the next Ribbon Ridge offering."

-Library Journal Starred Review on YOURS TO HOLD

"Darcy Burke writes a uniquely touching and heart-warming series about the love, pain, and joys of family as well as the love that feeds your soul when you meet "the one."

-The Many Faces of Romance

I can't tell you how much I love this series. Each book gets better and better.
-Romancing the Readers

"Darcy Burke's Ribbon Ridge series is one of my all-time favorites. Fall in love with the Archer family, I know I did."

-Forever Book Lover

Ribbon Ridge: So Hot
SO GOOD

" ...worth the read with its well-written words, beautiful descriptions, and likeable characters...they are flirty, sexy and a match made in wine heaven."

-Harlequin Junkie Top Pick

"I absolutely love the characters in this book and the families. I honestly could not put it down and finished it in a day."

-Chin Up Mom

SO RIGHT

"This is another great story by Darcy Burke. Painting pictures with her words that make you want to sit and stare at them for hours. I love the banter between the characters and the general sense of fun and friendliness."

-The Ardent Reader

" ...the romance is emotional; the characters are spirited and passionate... "

-The Reading Café

SO WRONG

"As usual, Ms. Burke brings you fun characters and witty banter in this sweet hometown series. I loved the dance between Crystal and Jamie as they fought their attraction."

-The Many Faces of Romance

"I really love both this series and the Ribbon Ridge series from Darcy Burke. She has this way of taking your heart and ripping it right out of your chest one second and then the next you are laughing at something the characters are doing."

-Romancing the Readers

About the Author
⊸⦃•3⊷

Darcy Burke is the USA Today Bestselling Author of hot, action-packed historical and sexy, emotional contemporary romance. Darcy wrote her first book at age 11, a happily ever after about a swan addicted to magic and the female swan who loved him, with exceedingly poor illustrations.

A native Oregonian, Darcy lives on the edge of wine country with her guitar-strumming husband, their two hilarious kids who seem to have inherited the writing gene, two Bengal cats and a third cat named after a fruit. In her "spare" time Darcy is a serial volunteer enrolled in a 12-step program where one learns to say "no," but she keeps having to start over. Her happy places are Disneyland and Labor Day weekend at the Gorge. Visit Darcy online at http://www.darcyburke.com and sign up for her newsletter, follow her on Twitter at http://twitter.com/darcyburke, or like her Facebook page, http://www.facebook.com/darcyburkefans.

.

CPSIA information can be obtained
at www.ICGtesting.com
Printed in the USA
LVOW12s2255230518
578337LV00001B/20/P